A Romantic Thriller

by

Jo Robertson

Acknowledgements

Thanks to the many women who've enriched my life and supported me on my writing journey: my daughters Shannon, Kennan, and Megan; to the extraordinary women at Romance Bandits. Thanks also to the writers who've helped me along the independent publishing trail.

And gratitude to the men in my life. They balance out my overwhelming estrogen moments: Boyd, my husband, and my sons, Lance, Robb, Tyler, and Rand.

Dedication

This book is dedicated to the lovely boy, the chuckling baby who entered our lives and left five months later. Baby Tyler, I knew you for forty minutes, but I'll miss you forever.

Chapter One

Gabriel Santos was not a man to cross.

His name among the Mexicans was *El Diablo,* and although his given name reminded José of a holy angel, the street runners had forewarned him. Indeed, the persistent rumors of the man's ferocity and the myth that he had made a pact with Satan seemed true.

Stepping from behind the industrial waste bin, Santos emerged from the shadows and caught José off guard. *El Diablo's* enormous bulk morphed from among the gray shades of the alley into one dark silhouette as he stood like a legendary titan at the narrow end.

José trembled like a leaf in the wind even though the drug runners had also told him to show no fear around Santos. With his long black hair tied at the neck, his lean hard form, and his dark scowl, he looked like *un angel caído, a fallen angel.*

But José knew the man was no angel.

"A good *soldado* does not keep his *jefe* waiting," Santos said, lips barely moving, a puppet whose strings were pulled by an unseen force. "Nor does he flinch to show his fear."

The warning was clear, and José worked to control the shaking of his body. *Sí, El Diablo.* And did he only imagine the smell of sulfur? He crossed himself and scurried to close the distance between them.

When Santos motioned toward the opposite side of the alley, José stationed himself at the brick corner of the building. Then he followed Santos' lead and crouched down to wait in the shadows. In this way as their target approached them, he would be flanked on both sides of the alley's narrow end.

There would be no escape.

Long minutes crawled by and the muscles of José's thighs began to cramp. He longed for a cigarette, but did not dare risk lighting one. He wondered, not for the first time, why Santos had chosen him for the job tonight.

José did not mind smacking the whores around. He was very good at controlling *putas*. But to take the life of a man, that was serious business.

He shifted position, dislodging minute chunks of debris under his feet. The small plink of gravel sounded like thunder to his taut nerves. Seconds later, the scratch of a match being struck preceded a tiny flare of light, and the rich, smoky odor of a cigarillo wafted across the alley.

El jefe enjoyed smoking these so-called seven-minute cigars, unconcerned about alerting his victim with the pungent odor. The boss once claimed if he could not dispatch a target in the seven minutes it took to finish his cigarillo, he himself should face a firing squad for being such an inept assassin.

José had no doubt the man they now prepared to kill would be dead long before his nostrils detected the scent of the cigarillo.

In the brief moment of the lighted match, José glimpsed *el jefe's* battled face, the vicious scar that carved its length from brow to chin, the thick black hair, the hollow eyes. Not for the first time, he wondered how such a stone-hearted man had won the trust of Diego Vargas.

And the greater mystery – how he had won the affection of the beautiful Magdalena Vargas. Wife of Diego, *el jefe de jefes,* the big boss. The one they called *El Vaquero* because he was descended from a long line of cowboys who roamed the plains of Mexico.

Ay, what a dangerous life Santos lived!

The clink of steel-toed boots striking gravel at the street end of the alley attracted José's attention. He saw Santos rise, reach for his weapon at the small of his back, and draw the silencer from his jacket pocket. Unhurriedly, he fitted

6

silencer to gun barrel, his gloved hands steady, his damaged face impassive.

Un qué corizón frío! A cold-blooded man.

Preferring the deadly quiet slice of the knife, José had his long blade in hand by the time the man reached ten feet of where they lurked in the shadows.

Santos waited until the man passed between the two of them. "Hombre." Santos' voice a deadly whisper in the night air.

The man seemed unsurprised. Without turning, he lifted his arms out from his sides, parallel to the ground as if to show that he was unarmed. At a nod from Santos, José stepped forward, knife swinging loosely from his left hand. Carefully, he patted the man down the legs and around the chest.

"He is not armed," he said.

"Ah, *amigo, mi buen amigo.*" Santos addressed the man's back. "How foolish of you to walk alone so late at night." The man turned around slowly to face them. "Especially in such a part of town. *Es muy peligroso. Very dangerous.*"

"I have important information for Diego Vargas," the man said, arms still extended. "Information concerning *el árabe.*"

José knew by the look on *el jefe's* face that Santos was surprised at this news, and it was no small thing to take a man like Santos unawares.

"The Arab, *el terrorista?*" Santos asked.

"Sí." The man smiled, revealing yellowed and broken teeth. "Ashraf Hashemi, the agent who works for the federal government."

José knew that the man he spoke of, this Hashemi, was not really a terrorist. It was the name the Norteños had given the Arab-American DEA agent who trailed them so doggedly.

Un dolor en al asno. A pain in the ass, Diego Vargas had claimed many times, one whose relentless pursuit of the Norteños and the location of their latest drug routes had caused his organization a great deal of trouble.

"What information?" Santos prodded.

"I have learned the name of Hashemi's informant."

"Tell me," Santos commanded, lowering his weapon, "and I will pass the information along to Diego."

The man let out a whoop of laughter. "Ah, I think not, my friend. I will take the information to *El Vacquero* myself. I am not so eager to die this night."

Santos smiled, but not with the black holes of his eyes. "Perhaps you will die, nonetheless."

There was a fraction of a second between the realization of the deed and the deed itself during which José knew the man about to meet his death clearly saw the foolishness of challenging one like *El Diablo*. Santos was a cold-blooded killer, but he was a practical man, which was why his next move startled José.

El jefe slowly removed the silencer from his gun and placed it in the pocket of his pants. Then he lifted his jacket and stuffed the gun into the waistband of his pants.

Finally, with a motion so quick José could not follow and the target surely never anticipated, Santos slipped a blade from his jacket sleeve, palmed it, and in one swift slash, slit the man's throat. The mark clutched both hands to his neck. Blood spurting from between his fingers, his eyes wide and vacant, he fell to his knees and toppled face down on the asphalt.

Santos squatted beside the body and slowly wiped his knife on the man's jacket. He removed the cigarillo from the corner of his mouth, glanced at the tip, and ground the butt out. He placed the remains in his jacket pocket. *"Sé el nombre." I know the name.*

Seven minutes, José confirmed, glancing at his watch.

"A good soldier knows when to keep counsel," Santos said, grinning up at José with perfectly even, white teeth that flashed with startling beauty in the scarred face. "And when to speak."

Dios. Now they would both answer to Diego Vargas for what happened here. There was no doubt at all in José's mind.

El Diablo had not only made a pact with the devil, but *él está loco!*

Chapter Two

"You're such a coward!"

Isabella sneaked another peek around her sister's shoulder in the dim lighting of Stuckey's Bar. "No, I just don't like taking risks."

"Same thing," taunted Anita, flashing her wide, sexy eyes heavily rimmed in blue shadow. Her tarty-eyes look, Consuelo claimed.

"Chaquitas, silencio," Consuelo commanded. "Stop bickering." She reached across the circular table to cover her younger sister's pale, slender hands with her own blunt-fingered one. "Bella." She spoke slowly as if to a child or a dimwit. "We went over this already. Tonight you are a fully grown and very desirable woman."

"Sí, and not an automaton," Nita piped up.

The girl fell silent as Consuelo glowered at her and turned back to Isabella. "You are going to flirt and dance, and maybe meet a delicious and very sexy man."

Isabella clapped her hand over her mouth and giggled between her fingers. The Margaritas and Piña Coladas had begun to affect her. "I think I'm a little tipsy."

"Good," Connie replied. "You need to loosen up. You are fearless in that courtroom where you work way too many hours, but *Madre del Dios,* Anita is right. When it comes to men, you are *un cobarde.*"

"A big, fat coward," Nita repeated.

Isabella eyed her evening attire. Dress neckline practically down to her belly button, thanks to Nita's wardrobe. Dangling from her ear lobes, the red and gold earrings borrowed from Mama. Hair a tumble of thick curls that hung around her bare shoulders rather than the usual tight knot she forced them into. She didn't look like an overworked and uptight lawyer tonight.

10

Bella caught the misty look in Connie's eyes. No, she looked exactly like the pictures scattered around their mother's house of their beautiful dead sister Maria.

A pain shot right through Bella's ribs, deep into her bones, and throbbed like a migraine. She knew when Connie thought of Maria, gone these many years, she wanted to stick herself away in a nunnery and spend her days on her knees bargaining with God to take her instead of their innocent sister. But God didn't want Connie's lighted candles and Hail Mary's.

"Connie," Bella interrupted softly, knowing where her sister's thoughts had wandered.

"You should march right over there." Connie wagged her forefinger under Bella's nose. "And sit down in the empty side of that booth where that man has been hanging out for over an hour and ask him to buy you a drink."

"Yeah," Nita added. "He's been checking you out, girl, for the last ten minutes. I see those snappy green eyes whipping around the room and landing right on you."

Isabella frowned.

"I'm telling you, the man can't take his eyes off of you." Anita brushed thick straight bangs off her forehead, swiping at the beads of sweat that glistened on her round, pretty face. "Trust me, *chica*. The man wants you."

Isabella sneaked another look at the man across the room. "He's looking at the door. He's waiting for someone," she protested.

"You have a chance to get out of that stuffy district attorney's office and meet someone for a change," Connie insisted, glancing casually at the stranger in the corner booth and meeting his direct gaze. *"Muy hermoso!"*

Bella followed her gaze. At first glance, she'd thought the man was Latino, but now she saw he was a strange mix of something else, maybe middle eastern, maybe Hispanic, but definitely darkly exotic and very easy on the eyes. "He could be a serial killer," she mumbled.

11

"He's too clean," Anita said. "It's just talk, Bella, and a little dancing."

"You're the clever one, Bella, the law school graduate with top honors, already an assistant district attorney." Connie gave her sister a gentle shove. "Now it's time to get a life outside that job."

"Just go over and say hello on your way to the little girls' room or something," Anita urged.

"And on the way back," Consuelo added, "see if he wants to dance." She grinned and watched Isabella make her way towards the bathroom, her hips swaying gently.

Isabella looked back at the two of them perched on their chairs where they wiggled their fingers and smiled. She dipped her lashes down once and tossed her head like a proud mare. She could do this.

#

Because Guadalupe Juan Diego Rodriquez had been born on December 12, the feast day of the Virgin Guadalupe, his mama had named him for *La Virgen de Guadalupe* and also for Juan Diego, the Mexican to whom the virgin appeared in 1594.

Lupe didn't care about the origin of his names, but he did feel unreasonably blessed. He had been a happy baby and became a cheerful man, and at this moment he delighted in the prospect of passing along information to a man he considered his friend as well as his employer.

The paper he'd tucked into his pants pocket and which he would, within the next hour, deliver to his connection, was *muy importante,* significant enough to bring down the man who'd been responsible for the deaths of many young Latinos. Thus, Lupe admitted to himself that he did this work gladly, and not solely for the money.

But, of course, the money was welcome.

At the moment, however, he glanced nervously around the dark streets. Having no car, he had walked the twenty blocks or so from the apartment of his girlfriend to the club. Twenty

12

very edgy blocks because at first he was certain someone followed him.

He zigzagged back and forth, left turn, right turn, making the twenty blocks closer to forty, in order to shake off the phantom shadow that tailed him. Crossing himself and kissing the Virgin of Guadalupe medal that hung around his neck, he made the final turn and ended up at the rear parking lot of Stuckey's Bar.

He lit a cigarette and leaned against a car parked at the darkest corner of the lot. From there he observed the movements of patrons and workers who regularly moved in and out of the popular singles bar.

Five, ten, twenty minutes passed while he smoked yet another cigarette, grinding out the butts on the asphalt beneath his feet. Nothing suspicious. *Absurdo,* he chastised himself. He was acting foolish. The only danger was in his stupid imagination. No one had followed him.

Since Francisca had become *embarazada* – with a strapping baby boy he hoped – Lupe had been increasingly edgy and nervous, like *una vieja mujer, an old woman.* Now that he was to be a father, perhaps it was time to put this dangerous business behind him.

#

Rafe took another long pull on his beer and let his eyes glide one more time around the softly lighted room. Stuckey's Bar was a classy place with high-end clientele from the looks of them. Agents, lawyers, all kinds of L.A. power brokers. He wondered briefly why his informant had chosen a fancy-priced bar like this for their meet.

Beneath the booth he stretched his legs, glanced at his wristwatch for the tenth time in as many minutes, and swore under his breath. Damn Lupe! Even though notoriously late, he'd never failed to show up altogether. Now the man was nearly an hour overdue.

The dumb bastard probably got himself made. Or worse, the somber thought intruded, killed by some very bad

13

hombres. The possibility of losing his informant disturbed him, not only because Lupe Rodriquez was an excellent source, but because he genuinely liked the man.

Nah, he finally concluded, Lupe Rodriquez was far too wily to be caught.

Chapter Three

Rafe slouched against the plush bench of his corner booth, idly running his finger around the wet circle rings on the table. He'd give Lupe fifteen minutes more. He checked his watch again as if sheer will power could urge the lethargic minute hand forward. He suppressed a yawn, loosened the knot of his tie, and finally reached for his wallet.

That's when he noticed the three women.

They surrounded a small round table across the room, flimsy, high-heeled shoes on their feet, their bare legs swinging above the floor as they sat on backless stools. A healthy row of Margaritas and Piña Coladas lined up on sturdy paper coasters in front of them, and the empty glasses showed they'd been at it a while.

He shook his head. Been too long, old man, when a bevy of pretty girls don't catch your attention right away. Even as he pulled some bills from his wallet, he observed from the corner of his eye that one of the women rose from her chair and wended her way toward him.

Deliberately and very provocatively, her legs stretched, thighs flashing beneath the deep blood red of her skirt. Her hips swayed gently and the hem of her dress swished like satin on silk as she moved straight toward his booth.

As she got closer, he saw that her skin was flawless, pale and creamy as pearls. Her eyes never wavered from his, deep coals set in a smooth face, cheekbones that spoke of the ancestry of some long-ago Spanish conquistador.

Holy Mother of God. Had it been that long?

Her tangle of dark brown curls fell messily to her shoulders, bare except for two ridiculous tiny straps that rose from the mounds of her breasts. And very lovely breasts they were, displayed from the deep vee of her neckline.

Rafe tilted his head to look around her. Behind her, the remaining two women stared at the girl's back, their hands shielding mouths that held back laughter. Their eyes sparkled and twin dimples flashed in their cheeks.

Sisters, he thought instantly. Older than the sultry vixen making her way toward him, but definitely sisters. Macbeth's three witches, concocting some seductive brew for their unsuspecting thane.

He flashed his most congenial grin and watched the woman approach.

Bella hesitated and then ploughed on, undaunted by the grin on the stranger's face. Damn her sisters! *Come on, Bella, don't be so serious, Bella. Let down your hair, Bella.* And here she was. Over an hour and too many drinks later, she rose to the challenge of her meddling sisters.

After all, what did it matter? Except for her family, she knew no one in Los Angeles. As soon as she delivered the papers on Diego Vargas to the DEA field office tomorrow morning, she was heading straight back to Sacramento. She'd never see this man again.

And that was a good thing because she was dressed to the nines in a borrowed garment that surely made her look like a hooker, neckline plunging clear down to the Promised Land. Her hair pulled from its usual tidy knot, curled and then ruffled so it looked like a tempest had swept around her. Her sisters had pinched her cheeks until she looked like someone who'd just tumbled out of bed after a very satisfying romp.

And now this very lean, dark stranger with crisp black hair and an attractive five-o'clock shadow looked like he wanted to do things to her that she'd only read about in magazines.

Faltering at the last moment, she stumbled in the four-inch heels Anita had pushed on her, toeless shoes with thin red straps. A startled look crossed the man's face as he rose to catch her. Perfect, she thought, but the idea was foiled when another man, a short Hispanic dressed shabbily in Levis and tee-shirt brushed past her.

That gentle bump was all it took.

As graceless as a top spinning down, she wavered, wobbled, and crashed to the floor. Her dress front dipped dangerously close to her nipples and her hands reached backward to cushion her fall. She felt the jolt from wrists to elbows and wondered briefly if the tiny crack she heard was the breaking of some small bone. Or her stupid pride.

Worse than anything, the hem of her dress bunched around her waist and Bella remembered the devilishly skimpy panties she'd purchased last Christmas and wore for the first time tonight. She opened her eyes to the amused look and extended hand of the stranger.

Up close, she recognized the swarthy complexion of a desert tribe descendant, the black slash of brow across his face, the kink of curl in the cropped dark hair. He skimmed oddly flecked green eyes down her body, reminding her again of her underwear.

While she lay there in a stupor, he grabbed her hand, a knowing smile carving a beautifully sculpted mouth as he pulled her to her feet. "Are you all right?"

Good God, he was lovely, Bella thought, imagining his eyes sparkled with more inane questions. *Are you single? Are you available? Are you really wearing underwear because I wasn't sure what I saw while you sprawled in front of me?*

Bella shook her head mutely, heat creeping into her face and chest, and glanced over her shoulder. Her sisters sat twirling thin straws in colorful drinks. They smiled calmly and waved. They knew she'd hurt little more than her pride.

The stranger's hand, large and warm, enclosed hers in a strong grip. "Why don't you have a seat?" *So polite, so suave.*

She wrenched a modicum of dignity from within and tugged her hand from his gentle grip. "I believe a trip to the ladies room might restore a little of my decorum."

Rafe swept his arm to the right where the restrooms lay and executed a courtly bow. She laughed. Classy woman, he thought. She'd need a moment to recover her pride, and he needed to deal with his very tardy informant.

When Rafe turned back to the booth again, Lupe had already settled into the opposite corner, a toothpick protruding from between his teeth, a whiskey in front of him.

"You're late," Rafe growled. "Again." He slid into the booth across from his informant.

Lupe Rodriquez tilted his head to observe the retreating figure of the woman Rafe had just pulled off the floor. "Hey, man, seems like you was passin' your time real nice."

Rafe glowered and leaned across the space between them. "Don't screw around, Lupe. What have you got for me?"

Rodriquez withdrew a crumpled envelope from his jeans pocket, smoothed out the crinkled edges, and handed it across the table. Rafe scanned the contents quickly. Dates, docking times, and pier numbers, but no ship names or ports of entry.

"What the hell, Lupe? I need more information than this." He slipped the paper into his inside jacket pocket and crumpled up the envelope.

Lupe glanced around and lowered his voice. "Don't worry. I'm seeing a guy tonight. He has the rest of the info."

Rafe nodded. "Were you followed?"

"Possibly." Lupe spread his hands and grinned. "But, *hermano,* I am as slick as the oil on my mama's tortilla pan. No one sees me if I do not want them to."

"Some day that cocky attitude is going to get you killed," Rafe warned, wondering again why he trusted this exasperating, over-confident man. He opened his wallet, extracted a large bill and pushed it across the table. Lupe swiped them up faster than a street huckster.

"See you around*, amigo,"* the little man said, sliding across the bench.

18

At that precise moment, the woman in the red dress glided past the table on her way back from the restroom.

"Chica," Lupe hailed her retreating back, *"mi amigo está aquí."* *My friend is here.*

When she turned at the sound of his voice, he added. *"Por favor. Mi amigo piensa que usted es muy bonita."*

My friend thinks you are very pretty. Christ, no one was more of an ass than Lupe with a few whiskeys in him.

Rafe stood belatedly and indicated the seat opposite him. The woman hesitated a moment, then inclined her head as regally as a queen and occupied the place Lupe had just vacated.

"Buenos noches," Lupe tossed over his shoulder as he sauntered across the room and exited through the large wide doors of Stuckey's entrance.

Now what?

What did this bold, dark-eyed beauty want? If Rafe hadn't glimpsed the underlying vulnerability in her eyes, he'd have thought she was a high-priced call girl. If he hadn't observed how the sisters watched like hawks from their position nearby, ready to swoop down at the first sign of danger, he'd have thought she wanted something quick and elemental.

At her smile a swirl of desire quickened his groin. A few hours with a woman like her would do wonders for his mood.

He stretched his hand across the table. "Hello," he said, giving her the slow smile his mother always said could melt the icebergs of Greenland. "I'm Ashraf."

Chapter Four

Lupe almost reached Francisca's apartment.

He had delivered the information to Rafe. Tomorrow he would meet with the young Norteño gang member who could supply him with the last pieces of information to pass along to Rafe. Life was good. The night was still young, and the thrill of his love for his girlfriend overshadowed his natural caution.

Lupe was only half a block away, deep in the thought of snuggling up close to his *esposita*, when a warning raised the hackles on his neck. The limousine appeared out of nowhere, its windows tinted so dark Lupe could not see inside. He did not need to.

He had no doubt who drove the black sedan. Who sat in the backseat. Though he had no reason to believe his cover had been blown, he felt irrational fear as he fingered the Guadalupe Virgin's medallion.

The driver's door swung open. Gabriel Santos climbed out and rested his giant's hands covered in expensive leather gloves on top of the car. *"Hola."* The single-word greeting sounded ominous to Lupe's guilty ears.

"El Jefe," Lupe said, *"Porqué está usted aquí?"* But he was very much afraid that he knew why Santos was here, so close to the home of the woman he loved.

"Consiga en el coche." Get in the car.

Lupe did not dare to disobey Santos' command, so he quickly slid into the back seat.

At first he thought there were two passengers in the back. He smelled the distinctive cologne and knew one of the occupants was Diego Vargas, *El Vaquero.* The other person sat in the middle, but his head slumped forward and his limp hands dangled between his legs. Lupe dared not look at either of the men and kept his eyes drilled to the back of Santos' head as he pulled the car onto the street.

They drove in silence for thirty, forty minutes. Lupe lost track of the time. His only thoughts were of Francisca. He pictured her waiting for him, a bowl of salsa and chips on the coffee table, the television tuned to her favorite show. Waiting. But he was not sure he would return to her this night.

He desperately wanted to ask the name of the third man.

Abruptly the car stopped and Santos reached up to turn on the dome light. Lupe glanced involuntarily toward the person beside him like a man drawn to a fatal car crash. Jesús Novato, the young Norteño.

His face was a bloody pulp, but Lupe recognized the tattoo on the left side of his neck, a red X4, fourteen. Home-grown, a prison tat. He glanced at the hands between Novato's knees and saw the missing fingers and the dark stain that covered the groin of his jeans.

Madre del Dios! Lo castraron. Lupe would never see Francisca again. Nor his beautiful baby boy. They would castrate him too.

#

Fueled by the unaccustomed liquor, Bella had babbled about her family's immigration from Zihuatanejo, Mexico, before she was born, of her three older brothers and sisters and the family's difficult adjustment to life in North America.

After two hours of conversation and coffee – no dancing – her loose-tongued chatter revealed that she had three older sisters, one who'd died at a young age. Died, she'd told Rafe, although in her heart of hearts she believed Maria was still alive somewhere.

Frivolous chatter between strangers. Neither had revealed a last name.

All the while, she'd escaped in the swirling emeralds of his eyes slashed through with tiny black flecks like angry cuts.

21

Sharp and probing, the eyes were a strange contrast to his coppery skin and short thick lashes. A wide scar bisected his left eyebrow and gave him the roguish look of a pirate. A rush of pheromones flooded her as his gaze wandered to her mouth and lingered there, then dipped to the cleavage that spilled from the juncture of her breasts.

By contrast to her, she realized, he'd revealed almost nothing about himself. Which was fine because all she wanted was a few hours of casual flirtation.

Breaking off from his steady gaze, she glanced around the bar. Consuelo and Anita gave her the sign it was time to go home. For all their urging, they had no intention of letting their baby sister leave with a stranger. Not that she would, even though she quite liked Ashraf. Call him Rafe, long A.

Isabella, she'd said in turn, call her Bella. No last names.

Which was exactly how she wanted it.

She liked his wry sense of humor and gentlemanly manners. And there was the assurance of his badge which he'd flashed early on. They were practically comrades in arms, she thought, but of course, she didn't tell *him* that.

A part of her almost wished he hadn't revealed that he worked for the government. Although, in truth, she'd hardly glanced at the badge.

Was he FBI, CIA or ... ? Some triple-letter acronym. And Bella didn't want to know which one.

What she really wanted to know was if he were as sinewy and muscled as he appeared beneath the fine white shirt and the expensive gray suit. If his skin were as cool and smooth as it looked. His fingers lay on the table top, long and dark, strong and capable looking.

She imagined all kinds of clever things those hands, those fingers, could do. Involuntarily, she ran her tongue over suddenly dry lips. A delicious chill ran up her spine.

"Are you cold?" Without waiting for an answer, he scooted around the booth, removed his jacket, and draped it around her shoulders. He lingered there, his arm draped around her body while her fingers caressed the expensive wool. She wanted to savor every moment of the evening with this exciting man.

She stared at the cup of coffee in front of her as the caffeine hit her brain. Her eyes lowered, she pulled the jacket closer around the deep red of her dress.

What now? How would they end this delightful seduction? She wished she'd paid better attention to Romance 101 in law school. But, no, discovery motions and appellate court cases had always been more interesting to her than socializing. But now, in spite of knowing next to nothing about Ashraf, call me Rafe, long A, she wasn't eager to leave.

He placed a warm hand over hers and smiled a flash of brilliant white. Her eyes flickered toward the bartender, a rotund, heavily-bearded man who used a gigantic bar mop to wipe down the backsplash. With swift, efficient movements, he stacked clean glasses beneath the counter and restocked the liquor section.

Rafe's eyes followed Isabella's. "Looks like we've closed down the bar." He smiled, noting the dwindling number of customers. "And your sisters are waiting for you."

He hesitated, naturally cautious. "Unless you want to get the hell out of here," he added. He ought to put her into a cab and send her on her way, safe and sound, toward the secure arms of her witchy sisters. "My apartment's a few miles from here."

She laughed her silver bell sound. "Is this the part where you offer to show me your etchings?" She sidled closer to him, her lips hovering inches from his mouth, her thick straight lashes shadowing her pale skin.

He opened his mouth to speak, but impulsively brushed his lips across her cheek, inhaling her clean scent. Beneath his mouth he felt the jump of the vein at her temple and the steady thrumming of her pulse beneath his hand. Any thought of putting her in a cab flew out of his mind.

"There are many things I'd like to show you," he whispered in her ear, "but not one of them is an etching."

He slid from the booth and took Isabella's hand, leading her past the bar where the bartender hardly acknowledged their leaving. That casual lack of interest should've sent a warning jiggle to the back of Rafe's mind, but they arrived at the sisters' table and introductions were made while the gentle scent of Isabella's perfume banished all thoughts of the bartender and his shifty eyes.

"I'll walk you to your car," Rafe insisted.

The sisters left first while he and Isabella followed at a discreet distance. Outside, in the balmy air, typical southern California weather, he removed the jacket from her shoulders and slung it over his arm.

The dark alley stretched to the right side of Stuckey's, flanked on one side by an over-sized blue industrial bin and by a large flat of crates on the other. The alley was strangely clean, with only the slight odor of ocean some miles to the west.

Rafe glimpsed the light winking through the faint mist at the other end where the sisters had already disappeared. He felt the cool, smooth grip of Isabella's fingers inside his hand and the gentle knocking of her hip against his thigh. Just the swish of her dress against his pant leg aroused him, and the next moment, the mere touch of his hand to her bare back sent a rush of blood to his groin.

Halfway down the alley, he swung her around, trapping her against the cool brick of the building. He hesitated, hoping he hadn't misread the cues he'd gotten all night. The rough texture of the wall grazed his palms as they pressed the wall on either side of her head.

Without a word of protest, she wrapped her arms around his shoulders and ran her fingers through the hair at his neck. Her body quivered against him as he brushed his lips across her warm mouth, tentatively, then with greater urgency.

Another electric jolt of desire ran through him as their tongues met and danced in an urgent mating rhythm.

His jacket dropped unheeded to the ground as he ran his hand down the side of her dress, reached the short hemline, and explored upward along the smooth curves of her thighs. The sound of her groan fueled his desire. He pinned her to the wall, feeling himself grow harder as he ground his body into her, trying to relieve the tension in his groin.

The improbable thought crossed his mind that if he threw her to the ground on the hard cement beneath their feet, she'd open herself to him with the same fever that gripped him.

Brain addled with passion, he suddenly remembered himself. Who he was, and why he was here. He halted his rigorous assault on Bella's mouth and cursed himself for being so caught up in the taste and smell of her that his mind ignored everything around him.

Every other sensory image.

That final unlikely thought clanged a warning in his brain.

Chapter Five

Even as Isabella clutched at him, Rafe's rational mind warned him to pull back from the heady distraction. She dipped her tongue into his mouth in sensuous simulation, and logic clanged another alarm in his head. The allure of her mouth tamped it down. *Good God.*

His right hand worked up to grip her bare bottom beneath the panties while his left tangled in her dark curls, roughly tugging her head backward to expose the vulnerable flesh of her neck. He tasted the tang of cologne and sweat mingling on her neck as he broke away from her lips again to run his tongue along the smooth skin.

A third tiny ping registered at the same time he remembered the sly look on the bartender's face. Rafe snapped back to reality with a rush of adrenaline that screeched danger. By then it was too late. He barely had time to swing around, shield Isabella's body with his own, and reach futilely for the handgun at his ankle. A split second to acknowledge the burly body of the attacker who'd crept up on them. *Shit!*

The sharp blow to his temple might've felled him except that the woman's body braced him at the back. A trickle of blood ran from his forehead into his eye, blurring his vision as he sank against her and they both toppled to the ground. A soft groan escaped her as she collapsed under the full force of his hundred and eighty pounds.

Swiping the blood from his eye and shaking his head to clear the dizziness, he unholstered his weapon and braced himself on one knee. By the time he'd swung around and gripped the pistol in a two-handed stance, the attacker had fled down the alley and darted around the corner toward the rear parking lot.

Rafe chased him to the end of the alley, ran past the waste disposal bin, and leading with his gun, eased around the corner. The lot was empty except for his green Hummer, a battered white truck and Isabella's sisters huddling beside a blue sedan.

He put his finger to his lips and cautiously moved along the exit doors that lined the back lot, twisting each knob as he reached it. All locked. Crouching low, he approached the truck and peered through the windows, then checked in the bed and beneath the carriage. Nothing. The attacker had vanished.

"Which way?" Rafe barked at the older sister. Consuelo, he thought her name was.

With wide eyes both women shook their heads and pointed tremulous hands toward the street and the dark night beyond. "Where's Bella?" Consuelo asked sharply. "What have you done with her?"

As the three turned back to the dark mouth of the alley, Isabella limped slowly toward them. Belatedly, he remembered the thud of her body hitting the pavement. *Ah, shit!*

"You always leave a woman sprawled out like that?" Bella quipped.

Her hip felt as if it had been ripped from its socket, her left knee burned from a bloody scrape, and her right arm tingled from wrist to elbow. But, damn it all, she would keep her sense of humor even if it killed her. Twice now she'd tumbled in front of Rafe, sprawling as gracelessly as a toddler. She was not going to revert to the shakiness that threatened her limbs.

"Bella," Nita wailed. "Are you hurt? Is anything broken?"

Connie ran practiced, assured hands over Bella and glared at Rafe. "What kind of a thug are you?"

Isabella felt her face flush. "He's okay, Connie. I'm not hurt."

"Looks like you're well enough to wrangle with them," Rafe joked, edging Connie aside. He took Bella's hands and turned them over, observing the knuckles and then the palms, "so I guess you'll live." He glanced down at her knee. "My place is close. We'd better get some antiseptic on those abrasions."

"Gringo," Connie spat, although Rafe clearly was darker than she was. "She's not going anywhere with you. *Tonto torpe!" Clumsy idiot.* Connie didn't mince words.

Rafe daubed at his temple with a snowy white handkerchief, but made no reference to his own bleeding wound, Bella noticed. Without another word he trotted back down the alley, retrieved his jacket from the ground, and gazed carefully around.

A few feet from where he'd dropped his jacket, he crouched down and touched his fingers to what looked from a distance like an oil stain on the asphalt close to the brick wall of the building. He dipped his fingers into the stain, lifted them to his nose, and sniffed. What had he found?

Bella shivered and Connie clutched her harder around the waist. What if their assailant came back while Rafe dawdled and poked around in the dark alley?

Suddenly she remembered the gun. Rafe's weapon. She had felt it jab into her leg when he slammed against her, but she hadn't realized what it was until he pulled it out after they tumbled to the ground.

Her analytical district attorney's mind clicked into gear. What kind of government agent was Rafe that he carried a weapon? Definitely not a paper pusher. Not the local police either. She would've immediately recognized one of their badges.

After several long minutes of examining the alley, leaving her and her sisters in the murky parking lot, Rafe returned. "Let's go." He touched her arm and started to guide her toward a giant Hummer parked directly beneath a street lamp, its dark green color shiny and fluid in the night air.

Connie shoved his hand away. "No!" she commanded, fierce as a momma bear with her cub. "She will go home with us."

Bella started to agree, but curiosity overtook caution. What was the elusive Ashraf, call me Rafe, long A, up to? He wore a gun to a fancy bar and met with a guy who clearly didn't belong there.

He engaged in a pickup, but got mugged in an alley. In her mind his badge was protection enough for her to go along until she discovered what he was up to. Some kind of undercover, she decided. Anyway, she didn't want to go back to her mother's small house in Pico Rivera, and apart from the cursory flash of his badge hours earlier, she knew innately she was safe with him.

"Consuelo, I'll be fine," she insisted. "Rafe ... uh ... works in ... uh ... law enforcement."

He grinned wickedly and flashed his badge again, aiming it Connie's way. "I'm close by," he said, "and I'll bring her home. No worry."

Connie reluctantly agreed to leave with Nita after they'd exchanged phone numbers, addresses and car license plates. Rafe got a grilling stricter than screening for the CIA.

His apartment was indeed a short distance from the district that housed Stuckey's Bar. His neighborhood was one of those gentrification projects that sprang up from time to time in crowded cities. Abutting a more worn, seedier area to the west and upper-middle class property to the east, it accommodated young professionals with incomes on the rise.

Up a flight of well-worn stairs and down a poorly lighted corridor, a door at the end of the hall opened into a surprisingly spacious and homey apartment. Bella took in the sparse furnishings and understated décor. A man's place, arranged for convenience and comfort with minimal distraction.

Rafe pushed her into a deep, oversized arm chair that faced a giant plasma television screen, propped her feet on the hassock in front of the chair, and left the living area through a white shuttered swinging door. Bella glanced at the small end table to her left, littered with half-opened mail, yesterday's newspaper, and the latest television guide.

He returned moments later bearing a small first-aid kit containing bandages, antibiotics, and hydrogen peroxide, along with a clean white towel. He pushed the end-table contents onto the floor, set down the items, and knelt to inspect her knees. As he hunched over her wounds, she noted the flecks of gray woven through the thick jet curls.

"This might sting," he warned, dabbing at her knee with a peroxide-soaked cotton ball.

"Ouch!"

"Don't be such a baby," he chastised, blowing on her knee and sounding exactly like Consuelo. But the slight roughness of his callused fingertips as he held her calf wasn't anything at all like her sister's touch.

"That's fine," she said impatiently, attempting to rise from the chair.

"Whoa, there, you're not going anywhere until I bandage that knee."

He shoved her back down and quickly smoothed ointment onto the abrasion, then fitted on a large bandage. Without a word he took her hands in his and examined the scrapes on the heels. Dabbing them with more peroxide, he then placed them in her lap, his own large hands covering hers.

Now his face hovered inches from hers as he examined her eyes. She hated the strong betrayers of her emotions, the flush that crept into her normally pale cheeks and the pattering of her heart.

"Is it that hard for you to let someone help you, Isabella?" Rafe's breath fanned her cheek and the tangy scent of liquor filled her nostrils. He seemed sincerely curious and rather gentle.

She blinked furiously and protested, "I let people help me." Her voice sounded thick in her own ears.

"Like hell you do," he said softly, tucking an errant curl behind her ear. An eternity passed as he alternated between staring at her lips and examining her eyes. And then he said what she'd been thinking all along. "Do you want to kiss me, Isabella?" Her name rolled off his tongue with the intoxicating accent of one schooled in her native tongue. Ees – sah – BEL - la.

She expected it, but even so, she felt a thrill of shock when what they'd begun in the bar and continued in the alley looked like it might finish right here in Rafe's apartment. The danger that'd happened in the alley fled her mind like trees stripped bare on a windy day.

"Do you, Isabella?" he murmured again, just as if he'd read her mind, and the answer to the question was a simple, unqualified yes.

"What about my knee?" she whispered staring at his mouth. "What about the scrapes on my hands?" She held them up for his inspection as if they were proof of required kissing.

He took her hands in both of his, smoothing rough fingertips over the tender palms, and then in turn, lifting each one to his mouth and placing gentle kisses on them. Then he leaned in slowly to kiss her mouth. Not like the kiss in the alley, not the heated passion of mating, but a gentle melding of two people in tentative like with each other.

Tremors started in her thighs and injured knee and traveled upward to her shoulders while tears prickled her eyes. Clearly noting her case of the shakes, Rafe pulled her into his arms. He brushed back the damp hair from her forehead and wrapped his large, hard body around her.

"It's just a delayed reaction." He spoke into her temple, his lips warm against her skin. "Don't worry."

31

Swiping at her tears, Bella gave him a little shove, her arm braced against his chest. "What kind of an idiot reacts to an event hours after the fact?"

He smiled. "A normal kind of idiot." He picked up another bandage and affixed it to her shin where a smaller abrasion had begun to redden. Then he sat back to admire his handiwork. "There, I think you're put back together again, Humpty."

Chapter Six

Diego Vargas stepped back from the dead body and wiped his feet on the short grassy patch at the water's edge. "Fuck!" He leaned over to peer at his shoes. "These loafers just came last week from Italy. You want to know how much they cost me?"

Gabriel Santos glanced up in carefully controlled irritation from where he crouched over the man's body. The question was rhetorical, he knew, but still a ridiculous comment when compared to the more serious problem he knelt over – the bluish body lying on a black tarp.

He eyed his boss's scowl and erased all emotion from his own face. Santos had been an actor in the old days. Well, a stunt man at any rate. But perhaps that was not the same thing. Perhaps he was no actor at all, but had only the credentials to take and give a serious beating.

The dead man lying naked before them had been an actor too, an up-and-coming young star full of bright promise. At least, according to the tabloids. He lay on his back, his lips a darker blue than the pale tinge of his flesh, his muscled body glowing in the light from Santos' flashlight. Fresh needle tracks marred his right arm, and his open eyes showed wide dilations of black that nearly eclipsed the blue of the irises.

Santos knew if the actor's so-called friends had called 911 at the onset of overdose, the naloxone cocktail the EMTs administered might have saved his life. But paramedics and emergency room doctors asked too many questions whose answers could not safely be scrutinized. So the young actor had died with fatally low blood pressure, rattling respirations, and convulsion.

It was an ugly death to behold.

Apparently the dead actor was too *estúpido* to realize the smack he'd just purchased at the Blue Mango Cocktail

Lounge in Bakersfield should be used sparingly. The China White was much purer than the black tar heroin the gang-bangers schlepped over the border from México. A fraction of the drug was enough to kill someone.

As evidenced by the body before them.

"Idiota de mierda. Such pure smack is wasted on someone like this! *Fucking idiot."* Diego shook his head and spat toward the body.

Santos sighed inwardly and shuttered his eyes. "DNA," he reminded, referring to the spit, although of course, the warning was too late. *Ay,* sometimes he believed that Diego was the fucking idiot. Spitting near a dead body? Now Santos would have to dump the young actor's body somewhere else to avoid any chance of *El Vaquero's* DNA being connected to the overdose victim.

Santos sighed again as he reached for the edges of the tarp he'd used to transport the body. He wrapped it around the stiffening corpse, hefted the slight weight onto his shoulders, and trudged toward the black sedan parked in the breakdown lane at the top of the promontory. Diego strolled ahead of him, fishing in the breast pocket of his jacket for a cigarette and whistling a tuneless melody.

Santos wondered yet again why he worked for such a man.

On the drive to another dump site, Santos thought of the beautiful face of Magdalena Vargas and knew exactly why he put up with such a pig of a man as Diego Vargas. He smiled to himself. It was true that *El Vaquero* paid very well for the kind of services only Santos could deliver.

But it was also true that the wife of Señor Vargas was worth more than gold. What was it the Bible said? Her price was far above rubies.

"Why do you grin like a jackass?" Diego complained from the back seat. "A man's death is a funny event?"

"El Vaquero, I deal in death every day." Santos shrugged philosophically. "If I did not find humor at such a time, when would I laugh?"

"Verdad." Vargas barked out a harsh laugh. "And the loss of such a man is not so significant."

He leaned over the seat to tap his bodyguard on the shoulder. "There must be no more of these foolish deaths, Gabriel. No more." He punctuated each word with a sharp jab to Santos' shoulder and then blew cigarette smoke into the side of his face. "Our distributors must let their customers know how pure the China White heroin is."

"Yes."

Vargas sat back and gazed at the glowing tip of his cigarette. Through the rearview mirror, Santos watched him. *Ay*, did *El Vaquero* expect the distributors to hold a seminar in safe drug usage of illegal substances?

Santos smiled again, but this time discreetly.

#

Humptey dumptey, indeed, Bella thought, pushing away. Rafe, no-last-name, was trouble with a large dose of sex appeal, and while she'd thought that was what she wanted, she now realized, with the Vargas case on her plate, a distraction was the last thing she needed. "I should call a cab," she decided.

"Nuh uh," he insisted, "You've had a shock and you're not going anywhere until you rest."

"But my clothes ... my sisters ... " She stared at her sister's dress smudged with dirt, oil, and God knew what else. The ruined clothes against her skin made her feel vulnerable. She heard the rising panic in her voice, the shakes taking over again. "I don't want to wear these anymore."

"Okay, I'll find something for you to put on." He headed down a short hallway off the main room, and she heard the opening and closing of drawers and closets. Returning a few moments later, he handed her a stack of clothing. "Try these. You might have to roll up the sleeves and legs." He examined her face. "Maybe you should get washed up first. You'll feel better when you've showered."

She opened her mouth to protest, but clamped down on her jaw, then snatched the clothes from his hands and marched down the hall to the door he'd just exited. At the entry, she paused, eyeing him suspiciously. "Don't think I don't know what you're doing," she said as she reached the door. Did he think she was a complete fool?

She glanced around the luxurious bedroom suite. To the left rose a bank of four narrow windows that stretched from floor to ceiling with white wooden shutters opened wide so she could see the clear, dark sky through the slats. All three doors to the right of the bed were closed. Maybe she *was* an idiot. She didn't know which was the bathroom.

Amused, Rafe listened to the slamming of the bedroom door. He'd let her keep her pride. The first tremors of panic after an assault were all too familiar to him, the vulnerability that hung on long after the attack was over.

He hadn't felt these emotions in years, but he remembered them vividly. Right now, showing her claws was healthier than giving way to hysteria. When he heard the sound of running water minutes later, he figured she'd found her way around his bathroom. He used the time to make a call about the suspicious evidence he'd examined in the alley.

Max Jensen, a local homicide detective, was catching tonight. "Blood, huh?" Max said after listening to Rafe's account of their attack in the alley. "Why'd you call me, Rafe? Why not your field office?"

"Just reporting an assault."

"But you didn't go to the hospital, right? No one sustained injuries?"

Rafe ran his fingers over his temple. "The lump over my eye might argue with you, but no, neither of us got seriously hurt."

Max laughed. "Damn, I figure your head's too hard."

"Check that alley, Max. I'm pretty sure that was blood I found. Recent."

"I'll send a crime scene unit out."

"And, check out the bartender, would you? I have a feeling about him. Hold him overnight if you can."

Max snorted. "Sure, old buddy. LAPD lives to serve the DEA's needs."

By the time Isabella walked back into the living room, Rafe had tended to his own wounds, showered in the guest bathroom, and dressed in sweats and a long-sleeved police academy tee-shirt.

"Feeling better?" he asked when she curled up in the wide armchair across from where he sat nursing a brandy.

She nodded. "Thanks for the clothes."

The oversized tee-shirt was a remnant from his college days at Stanford. The hardened peaks of her breasts told him she wore nothing underneath it. She'd turned up the sweatpants several times so that her red painted toes stuck out beneath the rolled hem.

The unexpected image of a pair of red panties popped into his maverick brain. Tonight was stacking up to be a long night, and his self-control was ebbing fast. Maybe calling that cab wasn't such a bad idea.

But instead, he strode toward the bedroom, calling over his shoulder. "I've got fresh sheets for the bed. You should get some sleep."

She followed him into the bedroom and stood in the door frame. "Where will you sleep?"

"Couch," he said shortly, ripping off the used sheets and replacing them with fresh ones from the linen closet.

She watched him silently. He wondered what was going on in that pretty little head of hers. Was she thinking about their earlier flirtation? Their interrupted passion in the alleyway? His fingers had touched her and found her wet right before the attack. Had she even been aware that he'd felt the moist heat of her ... *there?*

"There," he said aloud. He pulled an extra blanket from the closet and laid it at the bottom of the bed. From the bathroom, he retrieved his toothbrush and shaving gear, and a clean change of underwear from the dresser.

He paused at the door to the hall and looked back at her as she sat on the edge of the bed. "There's an extra toothbrush in the medicine cabinet." He waited for her to respond. "Well then, goodnight." He shifted awkwardly before adding, "Are you going to be all right?"

She stared at the black maw of the windows. "He won't come here, will he?" Her voice sounded small.

He knew instantly what she meant. "Of course not. He doesn't know where I live."

She nodded slowly as if contemplating how valid his claim was. "But he knew who you were when he attacked us in the alley."

He hesitated. "Don't worry. I have a friend in LAPD. He's taking care of everything."

"I'll call my sister," she answered by way of consent to remaining for the night.

After she'd made the phone call, she sat down on the edge of the bed and eyed him tentatively. "Rafe?"

"Yes?"

"I don't want to be alone." She flushed and he thought the admission embarrassed her.

He stood beside the bed while Bella crept beneath the sheets and pulled the covers up to her neck. Then he lay down on the top of the bedspread beside her.

Shit, if he'd known she'd end up wanting him to comfort her, but not ... well, sleep with her, he'd never have made that first invitation for her to sit down in the booth opposite him. A chaste night in bed with a gorgeous woman was not what he imagined when he'd first noticed her across the room at Stuckey's Bar.

Chapter Seven

Diego Vargas' white, powdered gold played a significant role in the import-export business along the northern California coastline.

An inland deep water port, the Port of Wintuan lay thirty-two nautical miles northeast of the Port of Stockton. It rested on the rich delta of the Cache River and emptied into the San Francisco Bay. The channel itself was a mere thirty-odd miles long and over thirty feet deep, but sufficient for the ships to make their way into port.

Always less popular than either the Stockton Port or the Port of Sacramento, the Wintuan Port had been an important route for importation and navigation from San Francisco during the mid nineteenth century. After the gold rush fever dwindled, however, the decrease in commodities shipments to miners gave way to an increase in agricultural transportation.

But the other two ports garnered the lion's share of this business, and most cargo ships no longer followed the Cache River inland to Wintuan Port. Although it had fallen into less and less usage, construction materials like lumber and concrete, as well as bulk and bagged rice still made up a major portion of the port's cargo volume.

Therefore, the port was ideal for the kind of shipping a businessman like Diego Vargas engaged in.

Vargas' cargo of white gold was easy to slip among the packages of legitimate products. This expensive, powdered cargo was small in volume, but very profitable for a man intent on creating new drug trade routes. Diego intended to carve out a hefty share of the profits from the prolific trafficking of a drug seldom seen on the west coast – China White heroin.

The seclusion and erratic use of the Wantuan Port appealed to a man of Vargas' enterprise. The irregularity of these cargo deliveries up the Cache River was his best protection against government detection and interference.

Standing now on the dock, staring out at the murky blackness of the Cache River, Vargas awaited his next shipment from the green hills of Afghanistan. The cargo made its way weeks ago from the Golden Crescent, the world's largest illicit opium production, to end up here on the shores of northern California.

Grinding out his cigarette under the heel of his Bruno Magli Calvos, Vargas jammed his hands in his overcoat. The winds blowing through the delta penetrated his woolen full-length coat. Mexican-born, he complained often about the early coastal chills of northern California.

"Santos," he barked at his bodyguard, *"Qué va mal? What's the delay?"* He could see nothing through the pitch of the night and his eagerness to receive the new shipment stamped out all patience.

"Nothing's wrong. Está bien," Santos responded, waiting until the ship made anchor and the workers began to unload the cargo before turning back to Vargas. "She's here now. No problem, *El Jefe."*

Forty-five minutes later the crates were unloaded and stacked five deep on the dock. Buried among the packaged rice were the one-kilo plastic bundles which half a dozen Mexican workers then recovered and stacked inside canvas bags. Several vans stood at the ready and the workers rapidly stowed the canvas bags in them. The entire process was completed in less than ninety minutes.

"Wait," Vargas commanded before the workers could close the back doors of the last van.

He extracted a kilo from the van, slit a one-inch opening in it, and dipped his knife into the white, powdery substance. A very tiny amount, for the smack was so pure it took his breath away, and Diego did not wish to become euphoric.

40

Only a foolish businessman used his own product, especially in this particular business.

He sighed with satisfaction. *"Ésta es droga muy buena."*

At one hundred thousand American dollars a kilo, Santos thought, the supply should be very excellent dope indeed. He slammed down the back of the van and slapped the palm of his hand firmly on the side. Immediately, the van pulled out, followed by a second, and then a third vehicle.

Santos and Vargas watched until the red taillights could no longer be seen, and then Santos opened the door of the black sedan while Diego eased his sturdy bulk into the back seat. *"Buen trabajo, a good night's work,"* Diego said.

"Do we head north, then?" Santos asked. *El Jefe* would have a strong need for a woman tonight and the whorehouse in Storey County was a mere three-hour drive.

"Si, necesito a puta esta noche," his boss laughed, a harsh guttural sound that spoke more of pain than pleasure. *"I need a whore tonight.* We will go south. No nice college girls tonight."

And no Magdalena, Santos added mentally. Tonight *El Jefe* would not force himself on his wife. Northeast through California and over the border into Nevada would take them to *La Casa de Mujeres,* one of two legal brothels Vargas owned in the only state in the country that allowed legalized prostitution.

Going south meant something entirely different. Crossing the border into Mexico would take eight hours or so and meant that Vargas wished to procure more girls for his other brothel in Nevada. The one which was both legal and not-so-legal.

Santos clamped down hard on his jaw. He preferred to take his boss north to *La Casa de Mujeres,* the House of the Women, to slack his lusts. Santos did not like El *Vaquero's* second whore house, the one which housed young girls like his sister Esperanza.

41

"Wake me when we arrive," Diego ordered and slid down on the leather seat.

#

Bella opened her eyes to the alien green glow of a clock on an unfamiliar bedroom nightstand. Four-thirty-five. Morning still. She'd slept over an hour. A firm band of flesh supported her shoulder and another draped casually over her hip. Her rear nestled against a hard body.

The moment she moved, she sensed a change in the rhythm of Rafe's breathing. He remained silent, but the subtle pressure against the juncture of her legs gave him away. She knew by the quiet rigidity of his body and the controlled breathing against the back of her neck that he wanted her.

She felt a sudden giddiness and the urge to have his body tighter around her, on top of her, inside of her. Alive with anticipation, she thrust the dark moments of the alley to the back of her mind. Turning eagerly, she wrapped her arms around his middle, buried her face in his chest, and worked her fingers up under the tee-shirt to the smooth flesh of his back, hot against her cool hands. The pressure against her thighs increased. She snuggled against him and inhaled the scent of citrus and warm flesh.

She trailed her lips along the side of his jaw and then followed with her tongue. "You taste good." She liked the huskiness of her voice, making her feel strong and bold and sexy. She edged her way to the corner of his mouth.

Rafe groaned and flipped her onto her back, nudging his knee between her legs, grinding his mouth into hers and plunging his tongue inside. The insistent thrusting of his tongue urged her on, his weight on her body a heavy welcome. A warm gush of arousal dampened the flesh between her legs and she thrust her hips upward to meet him.

"I want more of you," she breathed rapidly, tearing at his shirt.

"Ah, Bella, wait, slow down," he groaned against her temple. He lay unmoving on top of her a moment, his weight

42

supported by his arms. His heart raced against her breasts, and she held her body still, knowing he was trying to control himself, even as she fought every screaming instinct to undulate against him.

Finally, he lifted himself off her and jerked her tee-shirt over her head. Hooking his fingers in the waistband of the sweats, he pulled them smoothly down her legs. They landed on the floor with a soft thud, followed quickly by his own shirt. She reached for him, trying to loosen the thick shaft of him from his sweat pants.

"No, God, no. I'll be too fast. You first," he panted and trailed his fingers lightly between her breasts and down her slick thighs before cupping her buttocks with both hands and lifting her to his mouth.

As he planted firm, moist kisses low across her belly, her muscles spasmed in anticipation. His lips, those beautifully carved lips she'd watched all night, continued a sensuous journey to the crevice of her leg and trailed along her inner thigh. He lifted her hips higher and, like a man well used to satisfying a woman, circled his thumb with exquisite pressure around the perfect spot.

All thought vanished with the next ragged wave of pleasure. Bella bit down hard on her lower lip and hung on for the sweet, tortuous ride. She dug her fingers into the wiry crispness of his hair and let the first throbbing waves of release wash over her.

"Oh, oh," she gasped and then gnawed at her bottom lip again to keep from moaning aloud. When she came, his fingers joined his tongue and she felt filled and stretched, pulsating in hard, rolling spasms of pleasure that crested again and again like foaming breakers on the shore.

"Oh god," she whispered on a groan, unable to hold back any longer. "Oh my god."

He slid up her moist body to kiss her mouth, continuing to kiss her, fondle her, and nuzzle her neck, his fingers deep inside her, until her throbbing climax ebbed and crested again and finally gave way to a tender fullness between her legs.

At last, he rolled to his side and pulled her naked body close to him, covering them both with the sheet. She felt the still-hard thrust of his erection against the back of her thigh. His heart thrummed an urgent bass rhythm beneath her ear until it gradually gave way to a sure, steady drum beat.

She drifted off, incredibly relaxed, the concerns of her current case on hold, her meeting later today with the stubborn DEA agent forgotten for the moment. She thought smugly that she owed Rafe. And in a few hours, she'd let him collect on the debt.

Chapter Eight

The vibration of his cell lying on the bed stand roused Rafe from a light sleep. He struggled to remember why his head pounded as the naked ass tucked against him and the warm body attached to it tortured his hard-on. He swung his gritty eyes toward the alarm clock sitting beside his cell phone and watch on the bed stand.

Eight-sixteen! He should've been in the office already. In the fraction of a second before he saw the black strands of hair draped over Isabella's face and remembered the events of last night, he reached for the phone and swung out of the bed.

In the bathroom, he sat on the closed toilet seat and flipped open the cell. "Hashemi."

"Agent Hashemi, you'd better get down to the office right away." The normally unflappable voice of his assistant quavered through the receiver.

"What's wrong, Mrs. Roberts?"

"Detective Jensen is waiting for you." She paused and lowered her voice, heavy with disapproval. "Waiting. In your office. You know I don't like anyone going in there when you're not here."

Marilyn Roberts had been with Rafe nearly seven years, his first secretary – assistant she insisted on being called – in his Los Angeles office. She organized his life and ran his office with military efficiency. She protected him with the ferocity of a pit bull and made the best damn coffee he'd ever tasted. But she was a little obsessive about the sanctity of his office.

It was in his best interests to keep her happy. "I'll be there right away," he promised, closing the phone.

He relieved himself, flushed the toilet, and stared at his scruffy reflection in the bathroom mirror. He splashed cold water on his face, washed his hands, and brushed his teeth.

45

The rest of his grooming he left for later. By now he was sure the bathroom noises had woken Isabella up, and he was already regretting his lapse of judgment last night.

When he opened the door, she was sitting upright, her legs crossed yoga-style, her hair in wild tangles around her naked shoulders. The bed sheet covered what he vividly remembered as very full and beautiful breasts.

She smiled. "Hi."

He smiled back and sat on the edge of the bed smoothing a black strand from her cheek. "That was my office," he said tilting his head toward the open bathroom door where the cell phone lay. "I'm sorry, but I have to leave."

"Oh." Her face deflated like a disappointed child, and after a moment she scrambled off the bed and retrieved the tee-shirt from the floor. She pulled it over her head and tugged downward, but the shirt barely covered the tops of her thighs.

"Hey, you don't have to go, though. I have to put in a few hours following up on that incident at Stuckey's. I'll be back by noon." He glanced at the bedside clock. "One at the latest. I promise."

"You know, really, I should just go. This ..." She waved her hand vaguely at the jumble of bedclothes. "This isn't ... I don't usually ... "

"Look, stay, relax, have some coffee." He walked to the closet and pulled out his blue striped dress shirt. "I'd like to see you again. Honestly. So, if you feel the same, stay until I get back."

Isabella lifted one dark eyebrow and he knew he'd tossed out too casual an offer.

"Or leave a phone number, okay?" he said hurriedly.

She gave a tiny nod and appropriated the bathroom. Moments later he heard the water running. As he dressed in fresh underwear and socks, his mind raced with a dozen questions about what the investigators had discovered last night. Nothing definite or Max would've paged him. Still, he needed to get there as soon as possible.

He glanced toward the closet where last night's jacket hung, Lupe's information folded carefully in the inside pocket. Christ! Last night he'd let his senses get so addled that he'd risked blowing his informant's cover. Let his guard down so that he hadn't even seen the attack in the alley coming. Gotten entangled so deep with a woman that he'd taken her back to his apartment when the smart thing to do would've been to put her in a cab and send her on her way.

Now his white-knight fucking conscience was intervening. He sighed heavily. God knew, he was no saint, but something innocent and almost virginal about Isabella made him believe her. She'd told the truth. Last night wasn't typical behavior for her.

He opened the closet and grabbed his tan suit and silk tie off the clothes dowel and finished dressing. Gathered his briefcase and holstered his weapon. When he heard the water shut off, he listened at the bathroom door. He rapped softly.

No answer.

"I'm sorry, Isabella," he said through the door. "I really am. But I've got to get to work."

The door eased open and Isabella stepped through the archway. Desire shot through his loins like a flame-thrower's sword. Steady, he warned himself, but his heart thundered in his ears like a herd of mustangs and his forehead felt suddenly clammy.

He shoved aside the shards of lust that ran through him. At least he could keep his hands off her now and not complicate an already awkward situation.

They hadn't really had sex, not the real kind, the kind that could get her pregnant or ... Jesus Christ, what had he been thinking of? Taking a strange woman to his apartment, to his bed? Doing those intimate things to her body?

He wouldn't go there again. Wouldn't compound the problem.

47

Decision made, he reached for his suit jacket. "Look, it's late and I've got to get to work ... " He shrugged helplessly. "Uh, why don't you grab some coffee and, uh, maybe you can let yourself out. Last night was great, but ... look, we hardly know each other and ... maybe last night was a mistake," he ended in a rush.

"A mistake," she echoed, her eyes wide with an emotion he couldn't read.

He watched the heightened color edge upward toward her face and clenched his jaw. "You seem like a nice girl. I'm sure you're not used to hopping into bed with strangers, so let's chalk this ... situation up to the intensity of the attack or too many drinks, and leave it at that."

As he closed the door behind him, he reminded himself again of the reasons last night should never have happened. First, agency matters ought to be at the front of his mind at this delicate stage of his investigation. Also, he had no business taking advantage of Isabella.

Both of them had been caught up in the intensity of the attack. Neither had been thinking straight.

#

"You're telling me that isn't blood in the alley?" Rafe tented his fingers, elbows resting on the arms of his desk chair, and tried to stare down the homicide detective who sat across from him in his Temple Street office.

"Oh, it's blood all right, Hashish," Max Jensen answered, throwing in the nickname because he knew it pissed Rafe off. "Crime scene says animal, not human, but they need to run forensics to be sure."

He spread his hands, palms up. "So, my good friend, you wanna tell me what this is all about?" He eyed Rafe speculatively. "And while you're at it, what about that cut on your already fucked-up ugly mug? How'd you get that?"

Max Jensen had always been too observant for his own good, starting during their Stanford undergraduate days when he'd noticed Dr. Henderson's preoccupation with his computer during class. At the mature age of nineteen, Max had sucked Rafe into breaking into the lab to screw around with Dr. Henderson's settings.

The straight-on hetero porn Henderson had been salivating over became heavy-duty gay porn. A joke, but Rafe always wondered if atonement was why Max had gone into law enforcement instead of being some computer geek mixing things up in the Silicon Valley.

"My face met the butt-end of a door," Rafe answered in such a way that should warn Max off. "Find anything else in that alley?"

"Yeah, a lot of garbage and shit." Max laughed. "What were you expecting?"

Rafe ignored the question. "What about the bartender?"

"One Joseph X. McHenry."

Rafe lifted his brow. "X?"

"What can I say?" Max shrugged. "Xander, go figure."

"Any record?"

"About as long as your arm, but nothing in the last seven years. He jumped the SHU in oh-one and has stayed below the radar since." Max pronounced the acronym "shoe."

"The Security Housing Unit at Pelican Bay State Prison?"

"Yep, that one, where we keep some of our most violent criminal offenders, lucky us."

"How'd he manage to get out?" Rafe asked.

"Everything's about DNA now. Old Joe was doing life without parole in the SHU on a rape-murder charge with special circumstances. And then bing! DNA exonerated him." Max's face tightened in anger. "Never mind that the bastard committed dozens of crimes he was never convicted of."

"But he's stayed cleaned since?"

"Yeah, the lucky son-of-a-bitch."

"Known associates? Dirty pee test? Carrying?" Rafe knew most parolees got violated on one of these charges.

"Wouldn't matter," Max said.

"Right, exoneration, not parole."

The state retained a hold on a released offender who waived his Fourth Amendment search and seizure rights to get parole. He could be stopped and searched, any time, any place, all without a warrant because of his parole status.

Most parolees reverted right back to the life. Joseph X. wasn't on parole, but Rafe still wondered how a guy with his record had managed to avoid getting busted on one charge or another.

"There was something in the blood, though," Max added. "Mostly animal blood contaminated by a bunch of gunk." Rafe raised his brows at the unscientific term, but the detective continued. "Crime scene techs speculated about trace amounts of human blood along with the animal blood."

"You think someone tried to cover up the human blood?"

"Could be, *amigo,* could be." Max pushed his long, lanky form out of the chair and adjusted his shoulder pistol before turning to the office door. "I'll give you an update as soon as the lab report's complete."

His hand on the doorknob, Max turned around and eyed Rafe speculatively. "So, if you're not going to tell me how you got that goose egg on your head or what put that shit-eating look on your face ..."

Remembering last night, Rafe suppressed a smile.

"A broad? Jesus, Rafe, you finally got laid?" Max smacked his palm against the door and laughed. "When were you going to tell me about her?"

"There's no 'her' to talk about. Someone I met at Stuckey's." He leaned back on two legs of his chair, tossed the pencil on his desk, and tried to speak casually. "Ended up taking her back to my apartment. Had to, as a matter of fact."

Max moved back into the room, sat down, and leaned forward eagerly, a salacious look on his face. "Had to?"

Rafe waved a hand. "Long story."

"Hubba-hubba, old man. So, did she spend the night?" Max pretended to pant like a dog. "What's her name? Goddamn! You old devil."

"Don't get so excited. It was just a casual thing, you know? Besides, nothing happened." Not much, anyway, he amended silently.

"No, I don't know." Max waved his ring hand in the air. "Hello, married ten years. Leg shackles and all. The only way I get lucky I get is through hearing your escapades. At least tell me her name. Give me a bone, here, Hash."

Rafe chuckled, the sound of her name sexy as it rolled off his tongue. "Isabella. No last name. Bella," he said, the taste of it on his lips still feeling great. "Maybe she'll leave her phone number."

"You dick, you didn't get it last night?"

"What I got, Maxwell, was a frantic phone call from Mrs. Roberts about you in my office early this morning."

Max grinned liked an idiot while Mrs. Roberts appeared from nowhere and stood beside him, her eagle eye piercing him. Max jumped up, snapping his jaw shut.

Giving him a scathing look, she spoke to Rafe. "Agent Hashemi, excuse me, but your eleven o'clock appointment has been waiting quite a while. Assistant District Attorney Torres," she added, clearly believing he'd forgotten.

A short, middle-aged woman with a no-nonsense attitude, Marilyn Roberts put everyone from the governor to the custodian in his place. She always called Rafe by his title, expected him to address her as Mrs. Roberts, and reminded him of his sixth grade teacher who'd scared the hell out of him. Privately, he called her The Little General.

Rafe looked at Max and shrugged. "Sorry, this guy's been deflecting my emails for over a week. He has case files he doesn't want to hand over."

"Oh?" Max peeked his head out the door at the lone figure fidgeting in the waiting room.

"Send him in, Mrs. Roberts." Rafe moved behind his desk and pulled out a folder that contained ADA Torres' emails. If not the smirk on Max's face, then at least the puzzled expression of Marilyn Roberts should've warned Rafe.

She never lost her composure, never missed a beat even in the worst situations, and absolutely never seemed confounded. "Him?" she questioned, raising both penciled brows until they seemed to disappear into her very black hairline. "I don't think so, Agent Hashemi."

Chapter Nine

Seven *muchachas jóvenes* lined up along the corridor of the tavern, youngest girl to oldest, although most of them looked to be the same age, around eleven or twelve. Perhaps the one in the middle was thirteen, but none older than that. He could tell by their flat chests and straight hips as well as the baby-soft skin on their cheeks.

Santos crossed his arms over his chest and stared at the dirty faces and ragged clothes.

"Una cosecha fina de muchachas, a very fine crop this time. You agree?" The proprietor of La *Taberna Afortunada* – The Lucky Tavern – smiled broadly at Diego Vargas and chucked the first girl under the chin.

A fine crop, as if he were speaking of corn or coffee bean harvest, Santos thought.

"Dé vuelta alrededor," the tavern owner ordered the girl, making a circular motion with his hand. Thin and brown, barefoot and dressed in a dirty white chemise, she turned slowly around at the command.

Santos peered into the girl's eyes, listless and dilated, like a cat's in the dark. She'd most certainly been drugged. Probably one of the benzodiazepines, but he couldn't be certain.

El Vaquero wanted the girls mildly sedated for transport, but not completely wasted. It was much safer that way to make the nearly fifteen-hour van drive north through California until they crossed the California-Nevada border.

"See, I told you," the fat proprietor said. *"Muchachas finas, eh?* And I can get you plenty more."

"Shut up, old man," Santos growled.

He watched lust play across the face of Diego Vargas. Santos knew his boss was calculating the price of having his way with one or two of the girls first and thereby lowering their value.

Lust and greed always battled inside Diego. Usually, his love for money won out, but sometimes the power of his lust overcame him and he succumbed. Often with tragic consequences. Although *El Vaquero* usually preferred his women large and lusty, he occasionally liked to sample the wares he purchased before he turned them over to the women in charge of his two legal, and one not-so-legal brothels.

Yes, Santos thought for the thousandth time, Diego Vargas was a fucking pig, *un cerdo de mierdo.* However, he allowed none of these thoughts or emotions to register on his face or in his stance. After all, he was *El Vaquero's* lawyer, as well as his bodyguard, and he was wise enough not to make his personal opinions available for perusal.

He was not afraid of Diego Vargas. In truth, he feared nothing and no man. His strength had been forged in pain and his reputation in fire. There were few enterprises Santos refused to engage in, few men or women he would not kill when necessary, few appetites he would not satisfy.

But some lines should not be crossed.

Santos did not remember his father. Miguel Gabriel Santos had been killed in the village square when Santos was a small boy. He well remembered the square, the burnt adobe stones of the surrounding buildings, the deep stone well that stood at the end of the street. But he did not remember his father's actual death.

To this day in the village where he was born, stories of that event were widely repeated. Of how Miguel stood up to the *oficiales federales.* Of how he died slowly in the village square after hours in the baking sun. Of how he choked on his own *tesículos.*

The small boy Gabriel Santos did not recall the event of his father's death.

But he did remember his mother, however, and this trafficking with the girls – Santos knew his *madre* would not approve of a man who made his life's work out of the flesh of innocents. Santos did not fear the *fuego del infierno* or death's end, and he did not believe many true innocents walked the face of this earth. But the few there were should not be sacrificed.

Drugs, fine, *una opción.* The users made their own choices. Killing, *una necesidad.* Often very necessary.

But the girls, *absolutamente no.*

Santos knew the day would arrive when he would draw his boot across the sand and tell *El Vaquero* that he could not cross that line. That would be a very bad time for all of them, and Santos was not eager for that day to arrive. But, nonetheless, it would come.

The tavern owner pinched the scrawny backside of the last girl as she climbed into the back of the battered van.

Sí, the day would come.

#

Bella didn't leave the bathroom until she heard the door shut firmly when Rafe left the apartment. Even then she waited what she guessed was five minutes more before entering the bedroom. After searching, she found her dress hanging from the shower curtain rod in the second bathroom. He'd apparently tried to clean it for wet spots dampened the bodice and hem.

That hadn't worked. The dry cleaners might be able to get the stains out, but Bella guessed she'd owe Anita the price of an expensive new dress. The panties and bra were soaking in the kitchen sink and her shoes rested on the counter on a piece of newspaper. The evidence of her wild night brought fierce color to her cheeks.

She felt like snarling. Rafe must've been sure she'd stay. And who would've guessed he'd be so ... tidy. She imagined him touching her underclothing, but more embarrassing was him thinking she'd be here waiting for him when he returned, like a favored lapdog. At the back of her mind she knew she was more furious with herself than him, but she enjoyed her moment of pique a little longer.

She washed out her panties and blotted them on a towel. As uncomfortable as it was, she dressed in the damp clothing and slipped her shoes on. Her wisp of a purse lay where she'd dropped it in the armchair.

Finally, she searched about for paper and pen. In one corner of the bedroom a desk rucked up against the tall windows. Rummaging through the drawers, she found what she needed and sat down on the walnut chair to write a note.

"Rafe," she wrote, "I had a great time. Call me, Bella, 916-781-3043." She crumpled up the note and tossed it in the waste basket. "Bella, 916-781-3043." No, she should give him her cell number. She tore that paper up and grabbed another from the middle desk drawer. "Bella" ... She stared out the window and tapped the pen against her teeth.

This wouldn't work. So she'd had a one-night stand. She wasn't going to let her Catholic guilt rule her. Why make more out of it than it was? Because, she answered herself, because she liked Rafe. He was probably one of the good guys. And because they hadn't really ... well, hadn't really had sex, *per se. Per se,* lawyer talk. She shook her head. She was an idiot.

Somehow their encounter seemed unfinished, but in the end she left no note at all. She left Rafe's apartment, pushing the button to latch the front door. She scarcely had time to make it home to change for her eleven o'clock meeting with the bull-headed DEA agent.

The cabbie dropped Bella in front of her mother's modest three-bedroom house in Riverside. If the gods were really on Bella's side, Mama wouldn't even hear her sneak in. Sometimes her mother stayed up so late at night watching her Spanish soaps that she slept until ten or later the next morning. No such luck today.

Orotea Torres sat upright on the floral-covered sofa that faced the entryway of the small house. Her arms gripped each other tightly across her ample bosom, and Bella knew without seeing the grim look on Mama's face that she was mad. Great! Her sisters had wheedled her into going out and then abandoned her to face their mother's strict Catholic questioning.

"What? Have I worked so hard to raise a daughter only to see her sneak into the house like a thief after being out all night?" Mama's lips were a thin, hard line and her eyebrows were a jagged carving across her forehead. Her spine was as straight as a rod, her feet barely touched the carpet, and her plain cotton housedress smoothed modestly over her knees.

"Mama," Bella began before she was interrupted by the simultaneous opening and closing of both the front and back doors to the house.

Consuelo entered on a rush of words from the front entry. "Bella, why did you leave without telling me this morning?" she chided. "I wanted to prepare your breakfast."

Anita scurried from the kitchen, throwing off her coat and tossing it over the back of the sofa. "Hey, I thought we were meeting at the coffee shop for breakfast." She paused and looked from Connie to Bella and back, her eyes like saucers at the sight of her damp red dress.

"Nita, if your brain had any more holes in it, I could use it as a sieve," Connie said. "At my place. We were supposed to have breakfast at my apartment, not the coffee shop. How could you forget?"

"Sorry," Anita muttered, for once not putting her foot in her big mouth.

Mama eyed the three of them suspiciously. "Humph. And you don't have decent clothes to lend your baby sister so she has to dress like this in the light of day?" She paused and shook her head. "Well, I will prepare breakfast for all of you then." She rose heavily from the sofa and gestured toward the kitchen, herding them like little chicks. "Come, come.

You can tell me all about your big night over *jámon y huevos."*

Thank you, Bella mouthed to Consuelo when her mother turned toward the kitchen sink. She eyed her mother's back as she washed her hands and dried them on a colorful hand towel. Bella couldn't face Mama's censure. The facts were awful enough. She'd gone home with a virtual stranger and spent the night with him. She was too busy kicking herself to take on Mama's disapproval, too.

Consuelo lifted her palms in a what's-up gesture as she reached for the plates to set the table. The look on her sister's face clearly said, come clean or else, *muchacha del bebé.* Still a little baby girl! Bella had no intention of telling her sisters about last night. She'd give them a sanitized version while she packed to catch her flight back to Sacramento. Otherwise, they'd hover around her like well-paid bodyguards.

For now Bella ignored her sisters and checked the clock as she set out the silverware. Still time to eat, pack, and make her eleven o'clock appointment. She wrinkled her nose. After a week of back and forth emails, this Hashemi character had simply flat-out refused to turn over jurisdiction to her in the Diego Vargas case. Then he'd gone over her head to her boss, Bigler County D.A. Charles Barrington who had caved in to the superior power of the feds.

No surprise there. Charles had the spinal column of a flatworm, so Bella found herself on a flight to L.A. with instructions to turn over her notes to this Hashemi guy. *Enseguida. Right away.*

Already she detested the federal agent and she hadn't even met him. She hated being ridden roughshod over and despised even more someone going over her head.

And even though she was duty bound to turn over her files, she didn't intend to make it easy for this ... Hash – shem – whatever. She relished the idea of getting into a good

58

scrabble with the feds. She folded the paper napkins and slapped them on top of the plates.

But right now her mama's ham and eggs sounded really good.

Chapter Ten

Bella pulled her rental car into the parking space near the Roybal Federal Building. Her luggage was stowed in the trunk, and she'd already said her goodbyes to her mama and sisters.

The lobby information kiosk indicated that Agent A. Hashemi occupied space on the third floor and listed an office number. She took the stairs and entered an opaque glass-windowed door at the far end of the corridor.

A large, empty waiting room lay behind the door. An older woman with the face of a saint and the roar of a dragon asked her to state her business and afterward indicated she should take a seat in the row of plastic chairs against the wall. Bella eyed the closed office door to her left and sat down.

After waiting twenty-two minutes, she began tapping her foot and shuffled in her seat. She looked at the military-issue wall clock over the receptionist's desk and frowned. The older woman caught her glance and plastered a reproving smile on her face. "Agent Hashemi is a very busy man, Ms. Torres. He'll be with you momentarily."

Bella was sure the illusive Agent Hashemi – and what the hell kind of name was that anyway – was a busy man, apparently far busier than she was as a mere assistant district attorney in a much smaller county than Los Angeles. She drummed her fingers on the hard edge of the briefcase lying on her lap and debated leaving just for spite. Her already foul mood grew fouler.

Hashemi kept her waiting over a half hour. If he didn't see her soon, she would miss her flight. And the mountain of work piled on her desk. She could schedule a later flight, but she had no intention of leaving behind any of her Vargas files without getting an explicit working agreement with Hashemi for continued access to their information.

She knew the agent would fight her on this, but she came prepared for opposition.

The door to the office swung open and the receptionist – Mrs. Roberts, the name sign indicated – rose from behind her desk in time to greet the person leaving. A lanky, fair-skinned man with an open, laughing face – too open to be the DEA agent, Bella surmised – eased past the dragon lady and caught Bella's eye. He wiggled his brows in a passable Groucho Marx imitation and swept piercing blue eyes over Bella as she rose from the waiting chair.

"Sorry you had to wait," he said, a grin splitting his pleasant face. He shook his head and smiled knowingly as if he were in on a huge joke. "Hashish will be very surprised."

"Hashish?"

The man tossed the words over his shoulder as he exited through the reception area door. "Agent Hashemi," he explained with a wider grin. "What I wouldn't give to see the look on his face."

The door clicked shut behind him as Bella heard Mrs. Roberts say something about an eleven o'clock appointment. Humph – more like eleven-thirty.

And then distinctly, her voice amused and motherly at the same time, the assistant said, "I don't think so, Agent Hashemi." The older woman turned to Bella and gestured toward the open door. "Don't keep him waiting, Ms. Torres."

Bella smoothed her suit skirt, adjusted her cuffs, and clutched the briefcase firmly in her left hand. She spared Mrs. Roberts a brief look of challenge before she stepped through the office door, her chin tilted and her eyes snapping.

Not a girl from the barrio for nothing, she prepared to do battle – and immediately froze in shock. Damn her silly sisters and their stupid tricks! Double damn her own reckless sense of adventure. She took a fraction of a second to recover, quicker she was satisfied to note, than Agent Hashemi – Ashraf call me Rafe, long A – Hashemi, the son of a bitch.

She extended her hand in greeting and put on her court voice as he stood behind his desk, mouth still gaping. "Agent Hashemi, I'm Assistant District Attorney Isabella Torres from Bigler County."

#

And I am seriously fucked, Rafe thought, the moment Mrs. Roberts ushered ADA I. Torres into his office. He stumbled to his feet, at a loss for words for the first time in longer than he could remember. Dressed in a professionally-cut gray suit with a white blouse buttoned at the neck, Isabella looked like a school teacher or a minister's wife. But neither her long hair pulled into a severe knot at her nape, nor her minimal makeup, could hide her natural beauty or the memory of the siren from last night.

Christ, who could've imagined the sexy woman he'd spent the night with was the ADA from up north? The one whose repetitive emails contained a single annoying refrain: *Their office would not turn over their case files on Diego Vargas.*

The hand she extended was far firmer than the one which had trailed fingers across his body twelve hours ago. With a voice far more strident than sexy, her first question was like a thrown-down gauntlet. "So, tell me, Ashraf, did you know last night who I was?"

Before speaking, Rafe nodded to dismiss Mrs. Roberts, eyeing the composed and modestly dressed Isabella Torres until his assistant left. This Isabella was a sharp contrast to last night's woman who'd moaned beneath his ... *Shit!*

Why had he ever thought those dark eyes were warm and inviting? Right now they snapped at him as sharply as a whip in a lion tamer's grip. He pulled himself together and met her coolness with a glare. "Of course I didn't know who you were. Whatever you think of me personally, I'm a professional."

Rafe had known all along that Bigler County had no option but to turn over their Vargas case files to him. He'd just never expected the man – woman – to turn up *in person* to do it. He gestured toward the padded chair in front of his desk. "Please sit down, Ms. Torres. Let's straighten out this misunderstanding."

Torres took the chair opposite his desk and perched on the edge, setting her briefcase on the floor. Her slender hands clasped in her lap. She looked pale. And severe, with her long black hair pulled tightly back from her face.

Silence. Her dark, clear eyes remained unfriendly.

Unnerved in the face of her quiet militarism, Rafe sat down, folded his hands, and pasted what he hoped was a pleasant smile on his face. "When D.A. Barrington called a few days ago to say the files were on their way," he began, "I assumed they'd arrive by courier or special delivery."

"You probably never dreamed the – what did you call me, oh that's right – ballsy ADA would deliver them herself." She referred to a momentary lapse in judgment when he'd used the term in an email to Charles Barrington.

"Actually, I thought 'himself,'" Rafe replied with a calm smile that belied his turmoil.

Merde! Scheisse! Shit! The ability to swear – and speak – half a dozen languages made him quite good at his job, but right now his mind scrambled for a way to handle the current situation. Should he ignore it, pretend last night never happened? Blow it off like a bad joke? *Jesus!*

After a moment, he said, "Look, maybe we should meet the uh, issue head on and agree to put it behind us." Bella from last night would've gladly agreed, but he wasn't sure about today's Isabella of the fiery eyes. He paused and waited for a reply that didn't come. "Would that work for you?" he asked a long moment later, curbing his impatience.

Torres contemplated the scene out the small window and then swept those bottomless eyes up to meet his through thick lashes. She inclined her head gracefully as if she was doing him a big favor. "Of course. What happened between us last night was very ... unfortunate, but hardly the end of the world."

Unfortunate?

He scowled before catching himself and continued in as smooth a voice as he could manage. "Okay, then, we're in agreement. We go on as if it never happened."

Since Rafe never had any intention of cooperating with Bigler County in the Vargas investigation, the idea of putting it behind them was the best resolution. Get the uncomfortable moment over with, obtain the damn files, and move on, never to see ADA I. Torres again.

Isabella, call me Bella, Torres.

They would treat last night as a casual encounter between consenting adults.

Right?

Why had he assumed only a man could be so ferocious in refusing a request from a federal agent? And what a cosmic joke that he, who rarely had time to date, would hook up at a bar with the very person he'd been wrangling with over the Vargas case files! What the hell were the odds of that?

Suddenly he recalled that his email address had also contained simply his initial and last name. A. Hashemi. And he'd only mentioned his full given name Ashraf last night. Call me Rafe, he had insisted.

And then he wondered. "Did you know who I was?" he countered belatedly.

"Don't be ridiculous." She seemed restless as she jumped up from the chair and examined the enlarged photo of Parker Center on the east wall. "I had no idea who you were."

For some odd reason, relief flooded through him and on the heels of that, genuine remorse. "Look, Bella, I'm sorry."

Her back to him, her voice small-sounding, she whispered, "Yeah." Then she squared her shoulders and turned to face him. "You're right. Let's put this thing behind us."

A wave of regret washed over him for the what-might-have-been. He'd heard that remembered passion was sweeter than the real thing. If so, he was in a helluva lot of trouble. Last night the warm, willing proffer of Isabella's body had clouded every sensible restraint he usually put on himself.

Instead, he'd thrown himself into the intensity of giving her pleasure. And there was no doubt that Isabella had been thoroughly pleasured. He felt himself grow hard behind the desk that shielded his lower body. He'd almost given her what she begged for.

Now what?

Would Torres use their brief relationship as leverage to stay involved in the Vargas case? Looking at her grim face, her minimal makeup, and her set jaw, he couldn't believe she would risk her career by going against her D.A.

She couldn't be more than twenty-eight. Twenty-nine? Young for an ADA, and that meant she was ambitious. No, he didn't think she'd want last night's events splattered all over the small world of law enforcement any more than he did.

He stood and bought himself time by adjusting the blinds behind his desk and looking out over Temple Street. When he resumed his seat, he felt calmer, ready to proceed. "After all," he smiled, "the stakes are the same. The Bigler County District Attorney's Office has information on Diego Vargas that is germane to my federal case."

She nodded, throwing a glance at her briefcase still resting on the floor by her chair.

"There's never been any question that your office would turn over the files," he reminded her.

"We have no choice?" He knew her asking closed the door to any secret hope she might've harbored.

"Exactly." And, he thought, last night didn't alter that fact.

Rafe took in the appearance of the woman standing under the picture. Isabella Torres looked as different from the bright, sexy Bella who'd spent the night entwined in his arms

65

as oranges were from lemons. Even her mouth, drawn in tight puckers, hid the other woman.

He recognized both her conservative suit and prim hair style as attempts to detract from her looks. Torres wanted badly to be dealt with on her abilities, not her beauty. Well, she failed miserably.

In just a few moments of observation, Rafe had learned a great deal about Isabella Torres. Whatever that said about him, he intended to use this knowledge to his advantage.

Chapter Eleven

"So, Ms. Torres." Agent Hashemi leaned back in his chair and let the words hang as she moved back to stand behind the straight-backed guest chair. She glanced around the office, noting the relative plush of his compared with her own meager, cramped one.

Clearly Hashemi expected her to fill in the unspoken blanks. She shifted her position, gripped the back of the chair, and put on her best prosecuting attorney's look. "Agent Hashemi," she countered.

Except for his initial reaction, the federal agent was a cool one. He now sat in front of her as relaxed and unruffled as if they'd never met, as if nothing had ever happened between them. She'd give him points for his professionalism. The opposite of her, where every cell in her body worked double time to control her emotions.

The sense of betrayal that sucker punched her the moment Mrs. Roberts had announced her hit again like a mortal blow. Trying not to betray her agitation, she gripped the chair back more tightly to keep him from noticing her trembling hands. And to keep him from looking down at her.

Over the years, when interrogating suspects, she'd learned to stand over them to indicate her superiority. Right now she needed to feel she had more power than Agent Hashemi, even if it were an illusion. She'd get down to brass tacks, but she'd make him work for every scrap of information.

Rafe cracked first. She had hoped he would. She was very, very good at the power play game. However, his voice was all reason and rationale when he spoke. "Should we continue now that the awkward part is out of the way?"

Rafe. She had to stop thinking of him as Ashraf, call me Rafe. The shortened name reminded her of how she'd groaned his name aloud. She shook her head abruptly and prayed the color in her cheeks didn't betray her thoughts. "That's probably a good idea."

She reached for the briefcase she'd left by the chair, propped it open on the edge of his desk, and extracted a thin file. She pushed it across the desk to Agent Hashemi. Watched him frown and heft it in his hand, noting the weight of it.

He stood and sat on the edge of his desk, their eyes nearly on the same level. He looked first at the folder then at her and back again to the file. "The Diego Vargas report?"

She nodded.

After a long moment, he opened the manila folder and quickly perused the contents. It didn't take long. "What kind of shit is this?" he grated out, slapping the file down on his desk.

Bella forced sarcasm into her voice. "Isn't it obvious?"

His face burned under the burnished color of his skin and he drummed his fingers on the desktop. "Where's the rest?"

"It's all there," she answered pointing to the meager file, "all the official stuff. Any other material on Vargas is work product. My *personal* work product." She watched the truth dawn on him.

She didn't really need to add the rest, but she did anyway. "I'm not required to turn over work product to anyone." She paused and smiled sweetly. "Not even to the federal government."

Hashemi eyed her with irritation and reached for his phone. "We're not on opposite sides concerning Vargas, you know."

She raised her eyebrows, and he shook his head as if dealing with a recalcitrant child.

"You know it'll take less than a minute to get what I want," he threatened, his voice mild but his jaw clenched.

"Maybe, maybe not," Bella replied. "Charles Barrington may eventually coerce me into giving you the rest, but do you really want your investigation to stall that long?"

Rafe didn't like the smug look on her face. If she wanted to play hardball, she would learn he'd invented the game. "What makes you think your information's that important. You sound pretty sure of yourself."

"I am. I have to be. A woman in a man's world and all that." She shrugged slender shoulders.

He let his right hand relax on the phone and tapped the skimpy file with his left. "Are you trying to tell me that you have no other official notes except what's in here?"

She nodded, as if satisfied with the strength of her position, and sat down, crossing her legs at the knees and tucking her skirt around them like a prissy school teacher.

Rafe didn't like the game she was playing, but he'd bet he was better at it than her. He was curious about only one thing. Why would she lead an investigation in such an impractical way? Wouldn't it be easier for her to copy her notes and pass on the originals to him? Run a quiet parallel investigation of Vargas?

Why make such a big fuss over jurisdiction when she had to know she'd lose in the end. What was her hidden agenda?

He eyed her speculatively. "What about the rest of your investigative team? The cops' reports, witness interviews?"

While Isabella stared at her lap, Rafe's intuition told him she was wondering how much to tell him. And that fact informed him she was holding back much more information than he'd initially supposed. She flat out didn't trust him.

He didn't trust her either, but her hesitation pissed him off. "Look, sooner or later I'll get everything. Why not cooperate with me?"

"What's in it for me?"

He knew what she meant and it sounded like blackmail. She wanted to continue on the investigation. He considered what it would cost him and how much she could compromise the direction he was taking the case if he didn't cooperate with her. On the other hand, did he really want to work with her? See her every day? That could be a recipe for disaster.

He almost decided to tell her she could go to hell, but thought about how he needed to switch his headquarters anyway. Diego Vargas lived in Sacramento and Rafe would have to fly up to Bigler County, which bordered on Sacramento County, right away. He suspected Vargas' drug dealings had their origins up north, not here this close to the Mexican border.

At least, that was part of his latest strategy – he didn't think Vargas was getting his drugs from Mexico.

"I won't promise anything, but maybe we can work something out," he finally answered, sliding back from his desk. At the surprised look on her face, he repeated. "No promises. Understood?"

"Absolutely." She smiled like a child who'd gotten away with something on Daddy's watch.

He had the distinct feeling she'd just played him. What the hell had he gotten himself into? Isabella Torres was much craftier than he'd thought. "Now what about the rest of those documents?"

She grinned. "They'll be waiting for you when you arrive in Sacramento."

"Our Mr. Vargas has his fingers in a hell of a lot of enterprises," he said, pulling out his own thick book on Vargas and watching her eyes grow larger. "What particular part of his criminal activities are you looking at?"

Before she could respond, the noisy buzz of a cell phone sounded inside Rafe's pocket. He reached inside his jacket and removed it, held up a forefinger to forestall her answer, and flipped it open. A feeling of relief surged through him. *Lupe Rodriquez. Thank God.* Rafe wondered if Torres noticed the relief that must show in his expression.

He'd already beaten himself up over ignoring his intuition in the alley and getting the two of them assaulted. Since then, an irrational idea had begun to worry him, the thought that the blood in the alley belonged to Lupe Rodriquez and Rafe was guilty of not protecting his informant better.

"Sorry, I need to take this." He swiveled his chair toward the window, his back to Torres. "Lupe, what the hell ... " he barked into the phone before being interrupted.

It was Lupe's phone but not Lupe's voice.

"Lupe's not here anymore." A deep voice with a slight accent.

"Who the fuck is this? Where's Lupe?"

The voice ignored the question. "Lupe's not anywhere anymore. And you should be very careful, *amigo,* or you might be next."

The cell phone went dead in his hand.

"What's wrong?" Isabella asked, her finely arched brows drawing together at the sharp sound of his response. "Lupe – that's the man who was with you in the bar last night, isn't it?"

He couldn't answer her, couldn't even look at her. If anything had happened to Lupe because Rafe had been ... God, he didn't want to think about the possibility.

"Is this about what happened last night?" Her voice sharpened to a razor's edge of frustration and curiosity.

Rafe lifted an eyebrow and made his face as hard and glacial as the spot in the middle of his chest felt. "How can you ask about something like that now?"

Her face flushed prettily and somehow that made him angrier. Lupe might be dead and she was thinking of their tryst? Irrational to blame her, he knew, and so he clenched his jaw to keep from making a complete jackass out of himself.

Recognition dawned on her and her words stumbled over themselves. "Oh God, no. I didn't mean that. I meant the attack in the alley."

"Sorry," he said shortly, annoyed with himself for having thought the worst of her. Irritated that his own mind had gone to the bedroom first.

"What's wrong," she asked again, her voice more insistent this time.

But he ignored the question, grabbed his cell phone, and speed-dialed Detective Max Jensen. He turned his back on her for the second time in as many minutes.

"Yeah?" Max's voice seemed distracted.

"Can you hurry up the forensics on that blood?" Rafe looked over his shoulder to see Isabella leaning across the desk, her brow furrowed in concentration.

Eavesdropper.

"Fuck you, Hashish," Max returned good naturedly. "No greeting, no hello? And here I thought your eleven o'clock appointment was about getting laid."

"Why would you think that?"

"Duh. Maybe because the woman I saw when I left your office was exactly your type? Porcelain skin, hair like a Hershey's chocolate bar. Oh, and the legs, don't forget the legs, man."

Damn Max's powers of observation. "Cut the poetic crap." Rafe lowered his voice. "The blood in the alley might belong to Lupe."

"Aw, fuck me!" Max was the only person who knew Lupe was a C.I. for the feds, and he knew that only because he and Rafe had been friends since college and were still tight. Lupe's safety depended on complete anonymity. Rafe's too.

"Sure, buddy, right away. I'll get on it immediately." Max hesitated, his voice strained. "But Rafe?"

"Yeah?"

"Don't worry about it, okay? It's probably just the animal blood anyway. Lupe's smart."

"Yeah, sure. You're right. But, Max, just in case ... "

"I'll get right back to you."

Max hung up with a click, and Rafe sat staring at the phone in his hand.

When he turned around to face Isabella, he worked hard to keep the emotion from his face. Lupe had been his C.I. for

72

almost three years, infiltrating Vargas' gang and passing the information on to the DEA.

He swiped his hand across his face. He needed a shave, he thought irrelevantly. He looked at Isabella, momentarily forgetting why she sat opposite him and what she wanted. She lifted her brows expectantly.

And then he recalled that Lupe had a pregnant girlfriend and ... *Jesus Christ!* But there was nothing he could do about Lupe or his girlfriend right now.

The low rumbling of his stomach reminded him that he'd missed breakfast this morning. "I'm leaving," he said abruptly, replacing his cell phone in his jacket and striding toward the office door.

When he looked back, Isabella still sat there, turning to stare at him. "Well, come on," he snapped. "If you want to work this case with me, you'll have to move faster than that."

Max would check out the blood and call him back as soon as he knew anything. Rafe couldn't worry about Lupe now.

Chapter Twelve

Bella waited until the outer office door slammed behind Rafe with a resounding thwack. Who did he think he was, issuing orders like that? Usually she was the one telling people what to do.

She didn't want him to get the lead in the Diego Vargas case, but she'd do anything to stay involved. She'd won the first round. Better to put her pride aside for the moment. She jumped up and scrambled after him, leaving her briefcase unlocked on the floor.

For Maria's sake, she told herself.

The sudden image of her dead sister and the last time she'd ever seen her popped into her head. Seven-year-old Bella was hugging her sister's neck with pudgy hands. Maria was laughing and kissing her sticky fingers and mouth. "Hey, baby-girl, it's only a week," Maria had said. "And I'll be back before you know it."

"Don't go, Casa," Bella begged, using her pet name for her older sister. "I'll miss you so much."

Maria pulled her sister away and knelt beside her, hands on her shoulders. "I'm all grown up and graduated high school now, Button. I worked hard to get this celebration trip. You don't want me to miss it, do you?"

Bella's lower lip trembled and tears spilled down her baby cheeks. "N – no," she muttered.

"I'm coming back, Button. I promise you."

But Maria hadn't come back and she'd never kept her promise to her baby sister.

Bella caught up with Rafe at the elevator banks just as the doors were closing. "Whoa, there, buster," she said, sticking her handbag through the opening and alerting the sensor. The elevator doors bounced open again and she stepped inside. "You can't get rid of me that easily."

74

Rafe slanted a look at her from the corner of his eye. A look that said he'd not only like to see the last of her for good, but he'd also take pleasure in strangling her. Then he turned his attention to the closed elevator doors, a worried frown between his dark brows.

The two of them descended in silence to the lower level where he stepped out into the spaciousness of a vast underground parking garage. He strode to the left where parked cars waited in designated spaces. His assigned space read, "Director DEA," on a big, blue sign attached to a pole, like a handicapped space.

As Rafe bleeped off the car alarm, Bella couldn't help quipping, "Director, huh? The whole damn Drug Enforcement Agency. That's pretty impressive."

"Don't be a smart-ass. Get in."

"Where are we going?"

Rafe glared at her over the top of the car. "It's lunchtime. Don't know about you, but I'm hungry." He got in the car, started the ignition, and pulled out sharply just as Bella shut her car door. Not big on fastening seat belts apparently.

Bella felt a momentary pang of regret at resorting to trickery and snide comments to get what she wanted from him. She wished the A. Hashemi she'd planned to barrage with all kinds of rudeness when she was back in her Bigler County office wasn't this Rafe, long A guy, the man whose company she'd enjoyed so much last night. But if A. Hashemi wanted to get tough, she figured she could do that, too.

They pulled onto the Santa Monica Freeway and fifteen minutes later exited and turned into the parking area of a sleek, low restaurant that sat back off the road some distance and had the authenticity of a real Mexican hacienda.

"You like Mexican food?" Rafe asked.

Had he not noticed she was Latina? She gave him an exaggerated duh look, but when he didn't respond she said, *"Absolutamente."*

Inside the restaurant, a matronly woman of indeterminate age greeted Rafe with familiarity and eyed Bella frankly. "Hola, Rafe. Your usual booth?"

"*Cómo estás, Carmen?*" he asked, hugging her in greeting and kissing her soundly on both cheeks. "Yes, the booth, *por favor. Estás tu familia en buena salud? Comó es su nieto?*"

The woman beamed and patted Rafe's arm affectionately. *"Ay,* my family is very well and *mi nieto,* my grandson, is so beautiful he breaks my heart."

A minute later, seated at the booth, Bella appraised Rafe over the top of her menu, pretending to scan the lunch choices. The charm he could whip out so easily and put away again just as quickly annoyed the hell out of her. Was that what he'd done last night, deluged her with charm so he could get laid?

And how come he was downright sweet to others but uncivil to her? And why the hell was she bothered that he could put their ... their brief encounter behind him so easily? "You come here often, Agent Hashemi?"

He glanced up, a blank look on his face, almost as if he'd forgotten she was sitting there, and she knew his mind was far away. "Often enough."

"Sounds like you know that woman pretty well." She nodded toward the hostess, who smiled from her station behind the entry podium.

"I do," he answered shortly.

"Your Spanish is excellent."

"It is."

"Almost as good as mine," she said fiddling with the condiment holder as a young Hispanic teenager laid salsa and tortillas chips on the table and then retreated.

Rafe finished studying the menu and laid it aside. "Look, Torres, let's get something straight." He leaned his elbows on the plastic tablecloth and steepled his fingers. "You don't have to make nice with me. You don't have to like me. You don't even have to turn over those ... what did you call them? Ah, yes, work product files," he said, an edge to his voice.

She opened her mouth to form a half-hearted protest.

"But," he interrupted with a steely gaze, pointing a finger at her like a pistol, "you do have to be honest with me. I won't put up with any bullshit tricks if I'm going to let you work this case with me."

She began sputtering. "Wh – what, you're *letting* me work the case? Diego Vargas has committed crimes in Bigler County. He's been under our scrutiny there, in my county, for over a year. You have no more right than I to nab him for the depraved and accumulated atrocities – "

"Shut up, Torres," he said pleasantly, which effectively took the wind out of her sails.

She stared at him with her mouth a round oh of surprise while their server returned and Rafe gave the woman both their orders.

"The federal government has jurisdiction over anything interstate," he reminded her after the server left. "You know that and I know that. Vargas' atrocities include intra-state and international drug trafficking which comes under federal drug enforcement."

He continued in a neutral, even-tenored voice as if his logic were reasonable and indisputable. "Now, in exchange for your personal files, I'll continue to *allow* you to work the case rather than call your boss and have you jerked off it and sent back to Hicksville.

Bella felt the hot sting of outrage creep up her neck to stain her cheeks. Not only had he steamrolled her case, but he had the affront to order her lunch for her! She blinked furiously while trying to formulate a sharp enough response for both insults.

Rafe reached for a chip and dipped it in the thick salsa. "Actually, it's a pretty good deal. You ought to take it." The chomping of his tortilla chip and the calm look on his face made her want to smack him, but she snapped her teeth

77

together, nearly biting the inside of her lip. She resisted because she recognized the pragmatism in his words.

He was right. He had the power to call in a hell of a lot of favors. And D.A. Charles Barrington never took on anything controversial. Or difficult. He'd pull her off the case in a heartbeat, sloth that he was, forcing her to turn over every single file she had.

Except those she'd hidden at home in a thin, plastic box under her bed, she thought smugly. The ones Charles knew nothing about. The ones she wasn't about to tell Hashemi about.

"What gives you the right to offer a deal?" she grumbled, feeling herself capitulate. Other than that you're a big bully.

He confirmed her thought by leaning across the table and answering, "Because I'm a whole lot bigger than you are, I'm infinitely more influential, and" – his eyes dropped to her mouth, "I'm more experienced."

She didn't miss the double entendre. Bella shut up just as Rafe had suggested.

The middle-aged server plunked their lunches down on the table and beamed cheerfully at the two of them before placing the check under the basket of warm tortillas. With relish Rafe tackled his plate of beef enchiladas. He dipped a home-made tortilla into the rich, reddish-brown sauce and looked up at Isabella. "Good, huh?" he asked, his mouth stuffed.

Bella positioned a small bite of chicken and sauce on a tortilla chip. "Hmmm." Her mouth opened wide around the concoction as she popped it into her mouth. "Delicious," she agreed around the mouthful of food. *"Absolutamente perfecto!* I gotta tell you, Hashemi, this is the best Mexican food I ever ate." She swallowed a large gulp of Pepsi and frowned. "But don't ever tell my mom that."

Amused by her hefty appetite, Rafe smiled. "Scout's honor." He quickly sobered up, the grin slipping. He shouldn't be enjoying anything, much less lunch with an attractive woman, until he learned what'd happened to Lupe. He cleared his throat. "Let's talk about your notes on Vargas," he said. "When can I get hold of them?"

"We're really going to put this whole personal thing behind us?" she asked quietly.

He almost flinched under her clear, direct gaze. Wasn't that already a dead issue? Why did she want to take it on again? God, women were so unpredictable.

"Yes." He paused before continuing. "Unless you can think of a better idea."

She wiped her mouth. "It was just a casual thing anyway."

"Right, nothing serious."

"Just a lot of talk at the bar."

"And then we got attacked."

"Sure, and those kinds of high-tension moments cause people to lower their guards, do things they wouldn't otherwise do." She looked up at Rafe through her lashes. "You said so yourself."

"So I did."

"And we were two consenting adults who got caught up in the moment of ... Besides, nothing really happened. Right?"

Rafe stared at her wide, dark eyes, at her full lips and porcelain skin, at the high color of her cheeks.

Nothing really happened?

Chapter Thirteen

Shirley Winston had been in the business a long time. More years than she admitted to the few johns who still asked for her when they visited *La Casa de Mujeres.*

Heaving a sigh, she hauled her body off the chaise and plopped down on the delicate stool in front of the small vanity she used for putting on her makeup. The brassy blonde that looked back at her as she applied a thick layer of cosmetics looked old, she thought. Shit, she was forty-one, but looked sixty, no matter how much makeup she smeared on. She lit a cigarette and blew the smoke out of the side of her mouth.

Shirley liked to say she was in the management portion of the business. She was very good at her job and ran the house with an iron hand, mainly 'cause nothing bothered her no more. Live and let live, that was her motto.

She started working for Diego Vargas when she was a natural blonde and barely eighteen years old. A looker in those days, even if she said so herself. Diego didn't ask for her no more like he did in the old days, which was hunky-dory by her.

She'd had enough of ugly bruises and broken bones.

A loud pounding on the downstairs door brought her to the top of the staircase. Little Audrey sat behind the reception desk and Buck guarded the door as it swung open. Damn! Too early for regular customers, she thought as Gabriel Santos walked into the entry and stared up at her with those damned flat eyes of his, silent as the grave, like usual.

Diego Vargas followed right behind him. "Shirley, *bebé!*" Diego beamed up at her. "How is my favorite madam?"

It cost Shirley a lot to smile at him. Last time he visited, the girl he asked for bled to death before he finished with her. Business was business, but still, Diego liked mixin' his business with too much pleasure for her taste. "Hey, there, Councilman. What can I get for you? Wine, whiskey?" Not my girls, she thought silently.

"No, no, I have brought the girls with me."

"Yourself?" Shirley couldn't hide her surprise. Diego almost never delivered the girls himself. Transporting them across the border was a tricky business.

"This was *muy especial,* a very special trip for a particular cargo." Vargas beckoned her down the stairs. "Come, I will show you."

Shirley wrapped the silk gown around her plump belly and started down the curved staircase.

"Bring the girls into the sitting room," Vargas ordered Santos.

Five minutes later, the big giant brought the girls in and lined them up in front of where Shirley and Diego sat on a soft paisley print sofa. God, what a string of dirty kids, she thought. Children. What the hell kinda thing was Diego gettin' her mixed up in now? "I don't wanna deal in no kids," she whined.

"Don't be *estúpida,* Shirley. How many times do you have customers who ask for *peticiones especiales?"* Five of Vargas' *special requests* stood there, all of them with blown pupils, leaning weakly on each other. Drugs, prolly. He woulda drugged 'em for the trip to keep them quiet.

"Take their clothes off," Diego ordered. "I want to see my merchandise."

The girls were dressed skimpy and it wuddn't long before they were all naked, looking around the fancy sitting room with bruised eyes. Just babies, she thought. Flat-chested babies. Jesus on a crutch, but what the hell could she do? She was just a old worn-out hooker, way past her prime. No one was gonna pay to screw her any more.

She turned away as Diego reached for the smallest girl.

#

81

Rafe stared at Isabella across the restaurant table and wondered how she could say nothing had happened between then, even though a few hours ago he'd tried to convince himself of the same thing. He'd kissed her, hell, fondled her in a pretty damned intimate way. How could he think *nothing* had happened? How could *she* think it?

Under other circumstances, it might've been everything. What they'd done last night seemed sexier than if he'd been inside her, pounding his urgent lusts into her more than willing body.

He coughed and got his head together. Water under the bridge. No point to that kind of thinking. Right now, he needed to find out whose blood was in that alley. Determine if his confidential informant was safe or ...

"You're right," he said, reaching for the check and standing. "Let's put this behind us. And get the hell out of here."

Torres didn't hide the flash of surprise that crossed her face. "Sure," she said slowly. "Right now the important thing is to focus on the human trafficking case against Vargas."

Rafe sat back down, raised his eyebrows, and thought surely she was joking. "Human trafficking? How about a very big drug trafficking ring? One that puts the Colombian cartels to shame."

"Drugs?" Her voice pitched higher and he heard the strain under her words. "What are you talking about?"

"Diego Vargas and his use of the Norteños to create brand new drug routes into the country through California." He shrugged. "What else?"

"Illegal drugs have been around for decades. What we need to get Vargas on is the human trafficking." Her face was a study in astonishment. "Surely, you can't think the drug deals are more serious than the slavery of human beings?"

"I know we have completely different agendas, Torres," he said, slamming out of the booth, "but I thought you could be flexible."

She grabbed her purse and tried to stand face to face with him; her nose barely reached his chest. "If you think I'm going to let you grab Vargas on some half-assed drug deal, Hashemi, you're *loco.*"

"Half-ass – listen, little miss know-it-all, I'm going to see that Vargas and his sidekick Gabriel Santos go down for one of the biggest drug schemes since the beginning of the twentieth century."

Bella clutched her purse to her body and sputtered, "What did you call me?"

If she could've killed him with a look, he'd be dead. "Oh, right, how about Isabella, then?" He drew her name out as his voice dripped with sarcasm and he shoved past her, heading toward the cashier.

"Es todo aceptable, Sr. Hashemi?" the woman asked.

"Si, Angelina ... "

"El alimento era muy delicioso," Bella interrupted. *"Es usted el dueño de este restaurante?"*

Before the surprised Angelina could respond, Rafe glared and grabbed Bella's arm, ushering her out of the restaurant. "Yes, the food is delicious, and Angelina's family owns the place. Are you trying to show off?"

"No," Bella, muttered, although she had been trying to regain some sort of control. Why should he assume she couldn't speak Spanish when she was obviously Latina. "Never mind that."

Rafe opened the car door and held it while she swung her legs inside. "I won't." He snarled and leaned close to her face. "Don't screw around with me on this case, Torres. It's too important." He slammed the car door before she could answer.

Bella decided to delay the argument until they got back to the DEA field office. After a serious discussion of the human trafficking issue, she would convince him it was the more serious charge to bring against Vargas. If she could.

But when they arrived at the Roybal Building, Rafe simply reached across her lap and opened the car door – ever the gentleman, the jerk – pointed to the curb. "This is it, then," he said. The brief spark of his touch made her tingle. "I'll see you in Sacramento."

She turned toward the concrete steps leading up to the entrance, but realizing his intent, she turned back to the window. "Wait a minute. What's going on here? I thought we were going to exchange information."

"We are," he grinned, "but obviously your information is tucked away somewhere up north. So I'll meet you there."

"But when? How are you getting there?"

His look clearly said those were stupid questions, and they were, she thought, but she'd been surprised at what seemed to be his hundred and eighty degree turnaround.

"Uh, I'd thought about swimming up the Pacific coast, but decided to drive instead," he mocked.

She ignored his tone. "Why not fly? It's quicker."

"I like the idea of having my own car in case I need to scout around somewhere."

She didn't like the sound of that. Was he planning on going off on his own and snooping into her case? Her doubt must've registered on her face because he said, "Don't worry, Torres. I'm not going to screw up what you've been working on. Besides, I have to make a stop in Stockton first."

"Stockton? Why?"

"We'll talk about it later."

"When are you coming?"

"In a few days," he answered while a car's horn blatted behind him.

"Will you bring your files?" she shouted as he drove off.

"Absolutamente." He laughed in what she took as a peace offering.

She had to admire his chutzpah. She walked through the building's entry doors, remembering that she'd left her briefcase in his office. *Damn.*

Less than an hour southwest of Sacramento, Rafe pulled off Highway 5 and took West Fremont Avenue to the dirt road at the edge of the river. He stood beside his car and gazed across the body of water to the docks of the Port of Stockton. He counted three freighter ships docked across the San Joaquin River and eleven docking bays.

Damn, this was way too busy a port. Vargas wouldn't be using Stockton Port for his drug running. If the cargo the drug traffickers brought in was unloaded in the northern part of the state, as his intel had suggested, Rafe figured there were four major possibilities – Stockton, Richmond, Oakland, and San Francisco.

The last three ports were large, the tonnage of their ports huge. They were subjected to thorough cargo inspections. Examinations too close to suit the drug businessman. Rafe needed to look at ports that weren't even ranked by tonnage, like Stockton and Redwood City.

If he intended to check out every port on his list, he'd be longer in getting to Bigler County than he'd anticipated. Short on manpower, he couldn't afford surveillance on more than two or three ports at a time and had to narrow the list down. Damn, maybe he was wasting his time.

Lupe would have gotten the rest of the information by now. If his C.I. were alive. Max hadn't called since yesterday, meaning the blood work wasn't back from the lab. Rafe knew his informant wasn't safe at home with his pregnant girlfriend because he'd called her last night. Francisca was frantic with worry because she hadn't seen Lupe since he left her apartment on the night he met Rafe at Stuckey's Bar. She'd called frantically around to his friends and family.

No one had seen or heard from him.

Rafe cursed silently and dug his toes into the grainy dirt at the edge of the water. Then he jumped back in his car and merged onto Santa Monica Boulevard, taking Highway 5 north to Richmond. He'd check at least one more port before he swung east from the coast toward Sacramento.

He checked his voicemail again. Still no message from Lupe. Nothing from Max. A feeling of dread came over Rafe that any news he got would be bad.

Very bad.

Chapter Fourteen

Isabella Torres placed her hands on her slender hips and glared at the Bigler County District Attorney. "I can't believe you were sneaky enough to go around me on this one, Charles."

Benjamin Slater, Sheriff of B.C., suppressed a smile as the three of them crowded into his small office in the historic old Placer Hills Courthouse. He watched Bella's brown eyes flash and her jaw jut out pugnaciously as she towered over Charles Barrington, a diminutive man an inch shorter than her, three inches with the spiky shoes she wore.

"Come on, Izzie," Barrington cajoled. "You know that I don't have to get your permission for decisions I make as district attorney."

Uh oh, Barrington was in trouble now. Slater had known Bella to practically decapitate a junior deputy sheriff who made the mistake of using that nickname on her. But this time, Bella merely continued her silent glaring.

Barrington shuffled from one foot to another, and Slater knew the man was dying to sit down. He didn't look so short that way. What with Slater at several inches over six feet and Bella a foot shorter than that, Charles was the designated Lilliputian in the room.

"I have to make decisions that are best for this office," Barrington continued, still fidgeting, "and if you can't see that, then there's nothing more to discuss."

Slater tried not to roll his eyes at Charles' spineless excuse for an officer of the court. Isabella Torres was experienced in a way Charles had never been and never would be. She knew how to use her body, her facial expressions, and her voice to good advantage. If the D.A. weren't such a putz, he'd have figured out how to use her strengths by now. Instead, he constantly threw roadblocks at her.

Bella was the one who should be district attorney. But the position was an elected one, and Charles was a local, born and bred in Placer Hills, and Bella was a newcomer, a woman, and a Latina.

"I've been working the Vargas case for nearly seven months, Charles." Bella's voice held an undertone of quiet desperation. "I'm this close." She held her thumb and forefinger nearly together and then looked to Slater for help, but he remained silent.

He knew she hated anything that smacked of pleading, but he was pretty sure Barrington was oblivious to her tone. Anyway, although Slater tried to avoid taking sides, on this particular case he happened to agree with the ruling to turn everything over to the feds. For the first time Barrington made sense. Slater just didn't like the sneaky, underhanded methods the D.A. used.

Charles turned his back on Bella and reached for the door knob. "This Hashemi guy comes highly recommended. He'll get the job done."

"Wait a minute." Bella's voice caused Barrington to pause, but he didn't turn around.

Slater leaned against the corner of his desk and waited. What ploy did she have up her sleeve? He knew her too well to think she'd give up without a bigger fight than she'd shown so far.

She coughed and cleared her throat as if it cost her something important to dicker with the D.A. "What if we worked the case together? The feds and our office?"

Charles looked back over his shoulder at this suggestion, a little smirk on his face. "Oh, I don't think that would work, Izzie."

Bella bit her lip and Slater watched her struggle for control of the temper that flared so easily around Barrington. "Maybe not, but why not give it a try?" Charles was already shaking his head with fake sorrow, and she rushed on,

"We've put a lot of work into this case. If we help them out, the DEA has to give us at least part of the credit."

A gamble, Slater thought, and a good one. The only thing Charles was better at than laying around on his lazy ass instead of prosecuting cases, was taking credit for work he didn't do. Slater watched the play of speculation cross the D.A.'s crafty face. The little wienie was already thinking how he could spin the case to snatch the glory away from Bella.

Bella's face, on the other hand, was flushed and full of bright hope. Slater swore to God that if Barrington let her remain on the case, he'd do everything he could as her friend and in his position as sheriff to see she got the credit she deserved. On the heels of that thought, he wondered if she'd planned it just this way. A ploy to bring Barrington around and get Slater firmly entrenched on her side. He'd even bet she had already made a deal with the DEA agent. Atta girl, he thought affectionately.

Bella waited for the weasel's answer and held her breath, thinking she really hated this puny excuse for a man and an officer of the court she loved so much.

"All right," Charles relented, drawing out the words so it sounded as if he were doing her a big, fat favor. "But the minute the DEA complains, you're off the case. Understand?"

Bella nodded vigorously, pleased with the outcome. She despised toadying to Charles, but for the moment it didn't matter. She glanced at Slater with a smug grin, which he returned with a quick wink. Fortunately Charles missed both. He wouldn't like being played.

This was perfect. They could use the federal agency's budget and still get the result she wanted. Mainly, putting Diego Vargas behind bars for the rest of his life. Maybe even putting a needle in his arm if she could prove the allegations she'd uncovered in the last few months.

Thank God California still had capital punishment. She was sure she could prove special circumstances and this man deserved nothing less than the death penalty.

"Hey there, Izzie," Slater needled her after Charles had banged the office door loudly behind him. "Not a bad job of manipulation."

Bella put on a mock frown. "If you call me that again, Slater, I'll have to kill you." Then she smiled. "Wow, can you believe that nincompoop gave in?"

"You were pretty persuasive." Slater eyed her speculatively, suspicion etched in every line in his face. "What do you know that Charlie Nincompoop doesn't?"

Bella wrinkled her nose and waved her hand as if Charles had left a stench in the room. Which, as far as she was concerned, he had – the stench of incompetence. "I might have already arranged a little cooperation with the feds. Maybe."

"Really? What'd you have to give up for that agreement? Doesn't sound like any federal agent I've heard of."

Bella looked quickly at Slater. She felt her face grow warm. He had sharp eyes and excellent instincts, but he couldn't possibly know what had happened to her in the last several days.

"Quid pro quo, I imagine," he continued, "and that makes me wonder what you gave him."

Slater was too damned good at detecting.

"Don't be silly. Agent Hashemi and I are just going to swap notes, share our toys, and play nice in the sandbox."

Slater laughed aloud, a hearty robust sound that rose from his chest like an engine roaring. "Ah, Bella, you're one of a kind, that's for sure." He returned to his desk and sank down in a large leather chair that matched his impressive size. "Off with you now, missy. I've got work to do." He waved several sheaves of paper in the air as proof.

Bella grabbed her purse and opened the door. "Thanks, Slater. We'll talk later."

As she reached the door, he called her back. "Isabella?"

Uh oh, he only used her real name when he got serious and went all friendly-protector on her. "Yes, Benjamin," she countered.

"Watch your back, okay? Barrington's a little nuts and a complete idiot, but he's crazy like a fox in the hen house."

She nodded in agreement. Somehow Charles Barrington had convinced the primarily conservative residents of Bigler County that he was tough on crime, so they'd re-elected him. But, in fact, he made outrageous plea bargain agreements every day. The man had no moral center, no sense of fairness, and no idea that he turned hardened criminals out on the streets with his inappropriate deals.

"You too, Slater," she said, blowing him a kiss. "Charles watches you like a hawk. He'll take you down if he can."

"Nah." Slater smiled. "He'd have to grow some balls first."

#

The phone call came while Rafe drove northeast on Interstate 80, fifteen minutes south of Placer Hills, the Bigler County seat. He glanced at the readout. Max. Icy fingers ran up his spine in spite of the sun's heat through the windows warming the car's interior. God, he hoped the detective had good news. He pressed the receive button. "Max, what have you got for me?"

The pause at the other end of the phone told Rafe all he needed to know. Lupe Rodriquez was dead. He lowered the phone to his chest, but he could still hear Max's voice. He closed his eyes against the pain and bitterness.

When he put the phone up to his ear again, he heard Max's voice continue, " ... so I guess the good news is it's not Lupe's blood in the alley."

Relief washed over Rafe. "What? I thought ... Whose blood was it?"

"An ex-con named Morris Sullivan, thirty-six year old white dude, did a dime at Chino for assault, released six months ago."

"Is he dead?"

"Dunno, Hashish, no body. We don't know what happened to him, if anything, or why his blood was in that alley."

"You're checking it out?"

"Got several guys tracking him, but if he's alive, he probably went to ground."

"Connection to Lupe?"

"None, but Rafe – " Max paused. "Didn't you hear what I said about Lupe?"

"Yeah?" And that's when Rafe realized he hadn't heard the first part of Max's sentence because he'd pulled the phone away from his ear. Max had said, "I've got good news and bad news."

A mixture of sorrow and anger funneled through him like a dark, reckless tornado, but he kept his voice flat and unemotional. "What's the bad news about Lupe, Max?"

"We found his body a few minutes ago in East L.A., Obegon Park." Another pregnant pause. "I'm sorry, buddy."

"Jesus Christ," Rafe whispered.

"I think you should come back right away."

Rafe paused while he shook off grief. "Why? I'm almost to Placer Hills."

"Check into a motel, park your car, and take a flight back," Max advised, his voice low as though he thought someone might overhear his side of the conversation. "If you can be here in an hour or so, I can hold off the coroner."

"Why?" Rafe repeated. "Can't you handle it?"

"There's something you need to see for yourself."

Chapter Fifteen

Rafe hadn't been more precise than to say he would arrive in Bigler County in "a couple of days," so his call caught Bella completely off guard when she answered the telephone the next morning.

"Isabella Torres," she snapped into the phone cradled under her right shoulder, both hands busy, one negotiating the lid on a huge latte, compliments of Ben Slater, and the other riffling through a stack of current-case file folders

"Whoa there, Sparky." The intimate sound of his laughter jerked her into the past where it wasn't safe to go. "Who's this?" She kept her voice aloof, even though she knew damned well who was on the other end of the line.

"Ah, come on, Isabella." An amused chuckle as if he'd read her mind. "Take a guess."

No sense pretending, just get it over with. "Agent Hashemi, how nice," she said with a false sweetness belied by her next words. "I'm busy. What do you want?"

"Make nice if you want to run with the big dogs, Torres."

"Sure, Hashemi." Pause. "What can I do for you after you tell me what you want?"

He chuckled again, and she put down both the latte and the papers, feeling ridiculously light-headed at the sound. "Cut right to the chase, huh?"

"Tell me what you want, Hashemi," she said on a weary sigh, suddenly tired. She'd been at the office since six this morning after working late last night, catching up on paperwork that'd grown like mold while she was gone. Her patience was threadbare.

"I won't get there until day after tomorrow, and I'd like you to pick me up at the airport."

Did he think she ran a cab service? "I thought you wanted your own car up here."

"Oh, my car is up there, Torres, just not my body."

"What?" She felt a massive headache coming on and reached for the bottle of Excedrin in her top drawer. "Do I need to ask how that happened?"

"Better if you don't. Here's the airport info. Got a pen?" Without waiting for an answer, he rattled off an airline flight number and time for tomorrow evening.

"Wait, slow down," she muttered, writing furiously. "Why the delay? What happened?"

After a lengthy pause, she heard the quiet hiss of expelled breath like a groan of pain over the line. "Lupe's dead."

She scanned her memory without success for a clue. She didn't know the name, but she recognized the mixture of grief and anger in his voice. She'd heard it often enough in her mother's voice after Maria disappeared. "Lupe ... ?"

Rafe answered the unspoken part of her question. "Lupe Rodriquez, my confidential informant on the Vargas case."

A shudder rippled through her. A storm was gathering, and Mama would've said someone was walking over her grave. Whatever was brewing in her insides, Bella sensed trouble and put a hand over her stomach.

"Lupe was the guy who knocked you down at Stuckey's." The softness in his voice was gone now, replaced by sharp angles. "Remember him, Isabella?" The words burned her ears with their intensity. "Well, he's dead now."

Bella easily recognized the displacement of anger and the shifting of blame. In her family, there'd been plenty of that, too. "I'm so sorry," she whispered.

"Me too. Just be there tomorrow," he ordered and hung up.

#

The corpse lay under a small clump of trees in Obegon Park, where North Mariana intersected with East First Street in East Los Angeles. The public display of the body, coupled with the viciousness of the attack, told Rafe that Lupe Rodriquez's death had two purposes: the murder of a suspected informant and the sending of a message.

94

The area had been cordoned off, and yellow and black crime scene tape dangled like last year's party streamers. Max had used his department connections and the medical examiner had just now arrived at the crime scene. With the assistance of several officers a second perimeter, approximately fifteen yards from the inner perimeter, held an increasingly large group of onlookers at bay.

Rafe lifted the tape, moved inside the first area, and stared down at the body. He hardly recognized the mass of bloody contusions and swollen flesh as the carefree face of his informant. Lupe had been severely beaten, his neck slit open, and his tongue pulled out through the neck opening.

"Colombian necktie," Max stated unnecessarily.

Dr. Horace Gaitán looked up from where he crouched over the body. "Actually, the Colombian necktie, although attributed to Pablo Escobar and his drug cartel, has been around much longer than the Colombians as a method of punishment and warning." He glanced at Rafe. "But you probably know this, right, Agent Hashemi?"

Rafe shook his head. "No, sir."

"Humph, you'd think a high-ranking DEA agent would know something about the history and origin of drugs and their associated terms."

Max rolled his eyes behind the M.E.'s back.

Dr. Gaitán was something of a medical history buff and liked to be treated with old-fashioned courtesy, so Rafe always approached him with respect. "I take it that Escobar didn't invent the Colombian necktie."

"Right you are, Agent Hashemi."

Rafe squatted down beside the doctor. "Lupe Rodriquez was a friend of mine, sir. I appreciate anything you can tell me about his death."

The doctor snapped on latex gloves. "How are you so sure this is your friend? Not from his face, I imagine."

"No sir. I recognize the tattoo." He indicated the black and red design of kissing angels on the right thigh, with the name

Francisca in a banner below the design. "His girlfriend's name." Three lives destroyed he thought and sighed heavily, imagining the pregnant Francisca.

"Well, we'll confirm with fingerprints. He's in the system?" Gaitán lifted the hands one at a time, inspecting them carefully, and Rafe saw what he hadn't noticed before. Every finger on both hands had been broken or smashed at the joints, and most of the fingernails were missing.

"Perhaps not fingerprints then," the doctor corrected. "Dental records maybe. Or DNA."

"Cause of death?" Max asked.

"Judas priest, any number of possibilities for COD." Gaitán indicated the man's crotch where a dark stain pooled in the genital area. "When you look around, maybe you'll find the rest of him. He was alive when they removed it." He pointed to the slit throat. "Obviously this wound. But until I get him on the table, I won't know if he died from that or from the beating." He touched the spot where a white shard of bone poked through the blue-tinged flesh.

He looked at Rafe solemnly, his large rheumy eyes droopy with sad knowledge. "I'll get to your friend as soon as possible. I'll back-burner my other cases."

Rafe nodded and then watched as the emergency techs loaded the body into the van for transport to the morgue. After they'd left, he and Max scoured the area surrounding the body with a member of the forensic team, but the persons who killed Lupe Rodriquez had left little evidence.

One of the new crime scene technicians, a woman, shouted, "Over here!" and they rushed to the area farthest from the street on the Marianna Avenue side.

At first, it looked like a shriveled hot dog, liberally smothered with catsup. But upon closer inspection, Rafe saw that the lump of mangled flesh lying in the grass was the missing appendage that had belonged to Lupe.

The female tech looked queasy. "They castrated him."

To Rafe the message was loud and clear. Back off or you're next. And the earlier phone call made it clear who the next person was. Gutsy son of a bitch, to threaten a federal officer. And how had the killers gotten wise to Lupe?

"Come on, man." Max tugged at Rafe's arm. "Let the techs do their job."

Fifteen minutes later, they sat in a local bar near the Federal Building. The place, normally frequented by cops and other law enforcement officers, was almost empty today. Max ordered two beers on tap and when they came, led the way towards a corner booth.

Music from the juke box wailed about flying too close to the ground, which Rafe found remarkably apt, considering his current situation. For the last five months, he'd felt like he was a bird of prey swooping down to capture another, larger bird of prey – Diego Vargas. Now he wondered if he'd been flying dangerously close to a fast-moving terrain he hadn't realized was so treacherous. "Goddamn it," he ground out after taking a deep swig of the beer. "Lupe deserved better than to die like that."

Max looked hard at him. "You're not gonna go all loose cannon on me, are you?"

Rafe raked a hand through his hair. "God knows, I'd like to ... but, no, I'm cool." He glanced at his watch. "How long, you think, before Gaitán calls?"

"We could observe the autopsy," Max offered.

"No ... no." He took another pull and emptied his drink, then spun the bottle around on the table. "I don't want to see him like that again. I trust Gaitán. He won't miss anything."

Max looked around, caught the bartender's eye, and held up two fingers.

Rafe thought of Lupe's pregnant girlfriend again. "Jesus, Francisca. We have to talk to her."

"Why? You think she knows something?" Max shifted in his seat. "Why would she?"

97

Rafe tightened his grip on the bottle. "She was pregnant. Lupe kept saying what a lucky man he was." He slanted a sidelong glance at Max. "Besides, wasn't she the last person to see Lupe alive?"

"Hell, no, Hashish, the killer was the last person to see him alive," Max quipped. "And before that ... you."

Rafe stared at his friend and realized something was wrong. Max was edgy, nervous, not his usual easy-going self. "Lupe was on his way home. Either he made it to Francisca's apartment and went out again, or he never got there." He paused, waiting for a response that didn't come. "Is there something you're not telling me?"

A dark flush crept over Max's face before he answered. "Nah, man, I'm just worried about you, that's all."

"I've been taking the hard hits for a long time, Max. What is it? Something about Lupe that I don't know? Francisca?"

"I don't know, Hashish." Max met his eyes for the first time in a few moments and leaned across the table. He glanced around and then lowered his voice. "Word is Vargas has someone on the inside."

"What? My department? Yours?"

Max shrugged. "God, I don't see how. But now you're wanting to see Francisca, maybe ask her questions about him. Who saw him last? Who talked to him? What do they know?"

Rafe tightened his jaw. "Tread carefully, Max," he warned. After a moment he asked, "What are you suggesting? That Lupe was working both sides?"

Max sat back abruptly, silently shaking his head.

Finally, Rafe pushed out of the booth. "Let's talk to Francisca."

Chapter Sixteen

Bella was prosecuting a routine DUI when she glimpsed Slater as he entered the side door of Judge Carson's courtroom. A film of sweat glinted off his upper lip, and he looked like he'd run three steps at a time up to the third floor of the Bigler County Courthouse. He caught her eye and flashed a meaningful look before he sat in the gallery section.

She knew Slater wouldn't interrupt a court proceeding unless it was important, but other than the enigmatic glance, his face remained inscrutable. She nodded acknowledgment and glanced down at her yellow legal pad of notes. "Officer Richardson," she addressed the young man on the stand, "when you conducted the field sobriety test of the defendant on the night of March 29, what evidence of intoxication did you find?"

"First I noticed horizontal gaze nystagmus when I tracked the movement of his eyes." As the young officer explained the procedure, Bella's mind wandered, silently fuming at Charles Barrington for assigning her this driving-under-the-influence case instead of giving it to one of the junior assistants. No doubt, punishment for her stance on the Vargas case. Aware of an expectant pause in Officer Richardson's testimony, she continued, "What else did you observe?"

"Mr. Jackson's pupils were dilated beyond the normal range, and also there was non-convergence of the eyes."

"And what is that?"

"The person is unable to cross their eyes and can't track a stimulus that's brought to their nose, in this case my finger."

"And what can cause this non-convergence?"

"A number of drugs, including marijuana and alcohol."

As Bella sat down, the defense attorney, an older woman whose office was in Sacramento, asked her first question. "Officer Richardson, what other factors can cause horizontal gaze nystagmus besides intoxication?"

"Beg your pardon, ma'am? I don't understand the question."

"Let me rephrase. Are there conditions other than intoxication that can cause horizontal gaze nystagmus? Diseases, for example."

"Yes, ma'am, epilepsy can cause it."

"Thank you."

The defense attorney returned to her seat. Bella asked one question on redirect. "Officer Richardson, was there any indication that the defendant was an epileptic?"

"No, ma'am. He wasn't wearing a medical alert bracelet and didn't say he had a condition."

Bella glanced at the wall clock, waiting for Judge Carsons to declare a lunch break. "Thank you, Officer Richardson."

Right on time Judge Carsons banged his gavel. "We'll adjourn for lunch now and reconvene at 1:30. Let me remind the jurors not to discuss the case among yourselves."

Bella flashed a look at Slater, who was bouncing his knees in a gesture she recognized as impatience. He met Bella at the table where she gathered up her papers and stuffed them into her briefcase. His face was solemn as he took her arm and led her from courtroom number three. "Let's walk," he suggested, guiding her to the ancient elevator and pressing the button for the basement floor.

When they reached the lower level, Slater led the way past the records and evidence department into the underground tunnel of the heating and ventilating system, and up the back cement stairway to the rear of the courthouse. His battered, late-model truck was parked under a clump of trees, but he bypassed the vehicle and walked to a shaded area on the sloping lawn where several picnic tables were scattered along the asphalted walk path. He sat down heavily on one of the tables, his feet planted squarely on the bench, hands dangling between his knees.

Bella sat beside him on the rough surface of the picnic table. "What's this about, Slater?"

"Waylon Harris found a dead body out by Beale's Lake early this morning." Harris, one of Slater's deputies, was his protégé. If he'd alerted Ben, this wasn't a routine death.

"Homicide?"

"Could be. Doc McKenzie's doing the autopsy. Looks like a drug overdose, but the victim didn't get out there by himself."

"What do you mean?"

Slater stared toward the eastern horizon where the slope of the Sierra Nevada Mountain Range showed brilliant against the crisp blue of the sky. He turned westward toward the gentle, rolling foothills and their verdant farming land. "God, this is beautiful country this time of year."

Bella followed his gaze. "Yes," she said simply.

Slater sighed and finally continued, "Male victim, nude. No evidence of clothing discarded in the area, body wrapped in a tarp. Somebody dumped him out there." He scratched his blackish beard, more heavily flecked with specks of gray than when she'd worked with him a few years ago on another murder case that involved an old childhood friend of Slater.

"Accidental drug overdose and subsequent cover up?" Bella stared at the side of Slater's face, not sure yet why he felt the case merited pulling her out of court. She paused, her instinct pushing into overdrive, and then ventured a guess. "Does this have something to do with Diego Vargas?"

"Maybe. I think so. Hell, I don't know. But the preliminary toxicology screen showed high-grade heroin, almost ninety-eight percent pure."

"That's ridiculous!"

Most of the heroin in California was a low-grade quality called black tar heroin that came up through Mexico from Central and South American. Bella stared at Slater's profile.

"We never get that high-quality smack up here. You think the lab made a mistake?"

"That's what worries me, Bella. I have a feeling pure shit like this came straight from the Triangle."

"Afghanistan?"

"Yeah." Slater stopped, stared at the horizon, and swiveled on the table to bump knees with her. "If it's China White that killed the guy at Beale's Lake, that's sophisticated drug trafficking. We've got to get the DEA involved."

Damn it! Why did everything come back to Rafe Hashemi and his federal drug task force? If he found out about the recent death, he would definitely appropriate everything she had on Diego Vargas and likely cut her out of the loop. He wouldn't have to worry about playing nice. He probably wouldn't let her play in the sandbox at all.

"Bella?" Slater took her hands in both of his, swallowing them with his giant paws, and looked her straight in the eye like her father had when she was younger and got into trouble. "This drug case against Vargas might be bigger than we can handle here in our little county."

"But what about ... about the other thing?" Slater knew all about Maria, understood that Bella referred to the human trafficking charges she wanted to bring against Vargas.

"The feds aren't so bad at prosecuting that kind of thing either," he said gently.

She jerked her hands out of his grasp and jumped off the picnic table. "I'm due back in court."

"Bella – " Slater's voice held a warning.

"I know, I know. I won't go off the deep end. I promise."

She hurried toward the walkway that ran from the parking lot to the cement steps of the courthouse. Damn it! If the body lying in Dr. McKenzie's morgue were a result of a high-grade heroin overdose, Hashemi would have even more reason to usurp the Vargas case. He'd rip it out of her control faster than she could bat her lashes.

102

Not that she had any intention of doing that to Rafe Hashemi ever again.

Almost as if she'd been expecting Rafe and Max, Francisca Munoz answered the door at the first knock. Her bare brown feet peeked from below the hem of a modest dress that clung to her swollen belly. Her face was blotchy and her red-tipped nose glistened.

Even though Rafe had never met Francisca, a jolt of empathy hit his gut like someone had sucker-punched him. Lupe always chattered in his amiable, optimistic way about the woman who stood in front of them. Rafe saw by the lines etched in her face that she knew something about sorrow and now understood more was headed her way.

"You are the one he reports to, *si?* Her tongue trilled the R's softly in accented English. "You are Rafe? You are his *amigo?* Tell me this is not true, that Lupe is not dead," she pleaded, twisting her dress in frantic hands.

Rafe had no business telling her anything until the autopsy was complete, until forensics proved the bloody mass of flesh in the morgue was really Lupe Rodriquez. What had he hoped to gain by coming here and adding to her grief? He glanced down at her belly, large and hard beneath the purple and blue print of her dress. The child would grow up without a father, and life would be hard for both of them.

Rafe felt his anger mounting furiously. He wanted to hunt down whoever did this and smash him into an unrecognizable pulp. Until he resembled the scarlet heap of decaying tissue that was Lupe.

He jerked himself back from the precipice. "Can we come in, Francisca?"

Silently, she opened the door wider and ushered them inside. A small but tidy living area held an old sofa covered with a colorful throw. As he sat, Rafe felt the sharp jab of broken springs beneath his hips. No one spoke for long minutes as if the quiet were a requiem for Lupe, a mass of three.

At last Max broke the silence. "Excuse me. Where's the bathroom?"

Francisca gestured to the hall on her right, and Rafe watched Max's retreating back. Had courtesy prompted him to leave them alone? Or was Max uncomfortable around the dead Lupe's pregnant girlfriend?

Francisca laid her hand on his. "Are the police sure it is Lupe?"

Rafe nodded slowly. *"Lo siento mucho."*

Sorrow settled on her face and tears trickled down her round cheeks. *"Me siento mucho también."* She held her hand over her belly in a protective gesture. "Who killed Lupe? *Quién mató al padre de mi bebé?" Who killed the father of my baby?*

He shook his head. "I don't know, but I hoped you could help me. Can you answer a few questions?"

Francisca nodded.

"After Lupe left for our meeting, did he come back here?"

"He called me around eleven o'clock. He said he had something to do, but he would be home within an hour."

"Did he call after that?"

"No." Fresh tears squeezed from the edges of her brown eyes. "No, and he never came home." She fingered a tiny gold cross hanging from her neck. "When I woke up this morning and he was not beside me in our bed, I knew something terrible had happened to him."

"Francisca, did Lupe ever talk about anyone else he did business with?"

"I do not think so." She frowned. "But something was on his mind the last few days."

Rafe heard the toilet flush and a moment later Max reappeared at the end of the hall. "Do you have any idea what was worrying him?"

"No, I'm very sorry." She paused and looked down at her hands, but a moment later leaned close and whispered in his ear. "But he began to carry a gun with him when he left the apartment."

"He hadn't done that before?" Rafe hadn't noticed Lupe carrying when they met in the bar.

"No, no, I made him promise when we learned about the baby. *No más de armas.*"

No more guns.

A few minutes later, Max and Rafe climbed into an unmarked police car and merged into traffic. Lupe Rodriquez wasn't a violent man, and he wouldn't have carried unless he had a good reason. What was Lupe worried about that he hadn't told Rafe?

Was that what got him killed?

Chapter Seventeen

Slater drove his convertible from Placer Hills to the airport instead of the work truck he usually preferred. Bella loved northern California in April. The hot sunny days of summer hadn't descended yet to turn the hills to brown wastelands. The apricot and plum trees were in blossom, their delicate pink and white petals littering lawns and sidewalks.

With the top down, air whiffled through her loose knot of hair, strands escaping the band. Finally she gave up and removed it along with the tight clips that held it in place.

She'd be a mess when they met Rafe's flight, but what did it matter? She wasn't trying to impress him anyway. That ship had already sailed. The only thing about Bella that intrigued Hashemi was the files she had on Diego Vargas.

When Slater had learned about Bella's arrangement with Rafe, he insisted on accompanying her to the airport. As sheriff of Bigler County, he argued, he had a vested interest in where the federal agent intended to poke his nose. And the dead body at Beale's Lake was county business.

Bella didn't protest. She felt better having Slater along.

Hashemi's flight was late. Because of enhanced security since September 11, Sacramento International Airport denied access to the upper level to all but ticketed passengers. Slater and Bella waited by the baggage claim for the DEA agent to arrive.

She drummed her nails on her purse and checked her watch again, stood up to check the flights display, and then walked back to the row of plastic chairs where Slater sat. He glanced up from his magazine over the tops of his sunglasses. "Sit, Bella. You can't hurry the plane by pacing."

He was right. Checking her watch every few minutes only added to her edginess. She sat down, blew a strand of hair out of her eyes, and then attempted to tuck the straggly pieces back with the hair clips. When she began tapping her foot, Slater reached over and placed one large hand on her knee. His slow smile made her laugh.

And it was at that moment, out of the corner of her eye, that she saw Rafe Hashemi descend on the escalator, an overnight bag in hand, what looked like a laptop case over one shoulder, and a garment bag over the other. Bella absorbed the hard look of him while he was as yet unaware of her. The moment he spied her, he pulled sunglasses on and headed straight her way.

Rafe saw at once that Torres wasn't alone. He hesitated a few feet away to observe her and the man she was with. Broad-shouldered and an inch or two shorter than Rafe, he stood up with Torres, his hand cupped around her elbow. Good looking, in an outdoorsy sort of way. Sunglasses hid the man's eyes, but Rafe detected the hardened assurance of law enforcement in his bearing. A cop, then.

"Agent Hashemi, this is Ben Slater, Bigler County Sheriff."

They exchanged handshakes, warily summing each other up.

"Good flight, Agent Hashemi?" Slater asked.

"A slight delay," he smiled. "Security didn't like me bringing my weapon."

Torres gaped at him. "You brought a gun on an airplane?"

Slater and Rafe exchanged glances, and a moment of camaraderie passed between them.

Slater laughed. "It's a guy thing, Bella."

A puzzled look crossed her face, which the two men ignored as they turned toward the automatic double doors and walked out into the pleasant California sunshine. They were silent as they crossed the street to the space where the sheriff had left his car, a classic convertible in a shade of baby blue that seemed out of character for the hardened officer.

He tossed the keys to Isabella and she grinned widely. "You trust me with the baby?"

"Don't let me think about it too hard," Slater warned.

She laughed and slipped into the driver's seat, while Slater and Rafe stored the luggage in the trunk. As soon as she'd negotiated the parking lot exit and pulled onto Interstate 80 heading northeast toward Reno, Slater got down to business and explained the discovery of the dead body and the heroin overdose.

"You think the heroin was China White?" Rafe asked.

"It was too pure and we haven't seen that grade around here before. Never." Slater scratched his head and turned in the passenger seat to look at Rafe seated in the back.

From his position Rafe could see Isabella's eyes in the rear-view mirror. She tracked him during the entire conversation, her large, brown eyes luminous. Their gazes met for a moment and she looked quickly away. Why the wariness? What did this cop mean to her?

"Hard to imagine where that quality dope could've come from," Slater continued. "We get a lot of the black tar heroin, but nothing as pure as this stuff."

"Any I.D. on the body?" Rafe asked.

"Nope. Waiting for DMV records and fingerprint hits through AFIS."

Rafe leaned his head back on the seat and closed his eyes. God, he was tired. Nearly forty-eight hours straight and he'd hardly slept.

He barely dozed off when the wailing musical tones of what sounded remarkably like a Willie Nelson tune startled him awake. Sheriff Slater reached into his pocket for his cell phone and flipped it open. He listened for a few minutes with no response other than a few grunts.

"What's happening?" Isabella asked Slater in a familiar tone that made Rafe think she and the sheriff were longtime friends.

"DMV records on the dead body."

Rafe leaned forward, his interest piqued.

"A Hollywood actor, twenty-five," Slater said, "name of Jacob Foster. Ever heard of him?"

"Nope," Rafe said, looking at Isabella. "Are we supposed to know him?"

"He's a new star on that daytime soap," Isabella supplied, "called The Heart and the Heartless."

The look Slater gave her was comical. "You're kidding us, right?"

Isabella laughed. "You've never heard of the show?"

Slater reached over and tosseled her hair. "Why the hell would I have heard of it, Bella?"

"I've never heard of it either," Rafe added.

"What a pair of Neanderthals. Jake Foster is the newest hottie on the 'tween scene."

"Humph, that explains it," Slater grumbled.

"The important question," Rafe interjected, "is why a well-known Hollywood star is lying naked and dead in your county?"

The words had a sobering effect, and Slater and Isabella exchanged a meaningful glance. Slater unloosened his seat belt and turned fully around so he could look Rafe straight in the eye.

"And you're gonna help us find the answer to that question, right Agent Hashemi?"

Rafe had a feeling he wouldn't like to go toe to toe with Sheriff Slater. Should it come to that, the sheriff would be a formidable opponent.

#

Slater, Rafe, and Bella joined Dr. McKenzie, the coroner, in the basement of the Sutter Memorial Hospital which housed the Bigler County Morgue. The medical examiner pulled out the metal drawer which held the body of Jacob Foster and pulled the sheet down to his waist.

In death Jacob Foster, budding movie star, wasn't as pretty as on daytime television. Bella stared at the putty-like, sallow flesh of his face and neck. The Y-shape of the

109

autopsy incision slashed crudely through his torso. The pathetic body of this young man contrasted sharply with the ebullient, lively actor Bella remembered from the small screen.

"The toxicology report is on your desk, Sheriff," McKenzie said. "But the lab confirmed a lethal dosage of a 97% pure quality of heroin in the bloodstream."

"Addicts think they're taking a lower quality and unintentionally overdose," Rafe speculated.

"But where'd he get it?" Slater asked. "You can't find high-grade heroin around here. Our local addicts prefer meth. It's cheaper and easy to make." Slater rubbed his five-o'clock shadow. "There's been no word on the street about this stuff."

Bella shifted her feet restlessly. She knew the drug connection was important and Slater had to follow up on it, but she didn't want to lose focus on what she considered the human trafficking problem. "Let's go back to my office and talk," she suggested, turning away from the empty body. "We need to tie Foster's death to Diego Vargas."

Both Slater and Rafe stared at her like she was crazy, but she spun on her heel and walked to the elevator leading up to the hospital lobby. They hastened after her, catching the elevator doors as they were closing.

Slater spoke first. "Let's take Agent Hashemi to his motel room, and then we can get together and talk about the case."

Bella looked to Rafe for his opinion, and when he nodded, her fervor died down. They were right. She had a bad habit of rushing into situations without first thinking through the consequences. She slanted a glance at Rafe as the elevator rose to the first level. When would she learn?

Slater dropped Rafe off at the Wiltshire Extended Motel just off Interstate 80 and gave him directions to the courthouse. They agreed to meet at 4:00 in Bella's office on the second floor. They wouldn't be interrupted because Charles Barrington would have left by then.

110

The district attorney never stayed past four. He pretended he was out and about on county court business, but Bella knew he was just cutting his workday short.

Slater and Bella decided to have a late lunch in the interim, and after leaving Hashemi at the Wiltshire, they drove to a local Chinese restaurant in Placer Hills near the courthouse where she often ate with Slater and his girlfriend Dr. Kate Myers. This week Kate was in D.C. at a forensic science conference where she was the guest speaker.

After ordering – walnut prawns for her, explosion beef for Slater – Bella sipped on her fully-loaded Pepsi and eyed him speculatively. "So what do you think?"

"About what?"

"Ashraf Hashemi, of course."

Slater always had the knack of sizing her up immediately. She could never hide anything from him, much like her older brothers, who'd always kept close tabs on her in high school. Now he looked at her as if he knew that she wasn't talking about Hashemi's government credentials.

"Seems pretty competent to me," Slater drawled, "if a little intense."

"He's aggressive," she said flatly and then leaned in and lowered her voice. In a small town like Placer Hills, you always assumed your conversations could be overheard and repeated back to you a few days later with a gossipy-skewed slant. "He really wants the Vargas case."

"I know that, Bella. I was there when Barrington laid down the law."

"I can't let him take over my case, Slater."

Slater lifted one shaggy brow. "Can't or won't?"

She tossed her head. "Same difference."

He touched her shoulder in a reassuring pat. "You sure you're not letting pride get in the way? Now, hear me out," he continued when she would've protested. "This Rafe fellow seems like a stand-up kind of guy right?"

She nodded grudgingly.

"And, even though he's a federal lackey," he joked, "I don't think he's going to cheat you out of your fair share of the glory."

"It's not the credit I want, Slater," she corrected. "You know that."

"Right." He smiled gently. "But one day you'll have to let go of that." He lifted her chin and made her look at him. "If you don't, it'll eat you alive."

She batted his hand away. "Sure, sure, you always think you know everything." She smiled to let him know she'd take his advice into consideration, and then turned serious. "I just want to get this bastard, Ben. Vargas is pure evil and I want him so bad I can almost taste it."

Chapter Eighteen

"Eliminating Rodriquez was a big mistake." The man leaned against the car's fender, a cigarette dangling from the corner of his mouth. "One we can't afford."

Gabriel Santos placed a hand on the car's trunk and hovered close to the man's ear. Although they were the same height, Santos outweighed the man by at least fifty pounds. *"El Vacquero* does not think so," he said, although he privately agreed.

"Fuck *El Vacquero!"* The man pushed off from the car, spat out the butt, and ground it beneath his boot. He stabbed a finger at Santos' chest, move the bodyguard found both amusing and dangerous. "Vargas wants my cooperation, he plays by my rules. Rodriquez was a mistake."

Santos contemplated the cop thoughtfully. The man had been an invaluable contact for several years and perhaps it was best to let him continue to think he was in charge for the time being. He nodded briefly. "I will pass the message on."

"Good," snarled the man, his pale eyes eerie in the dim reflection from the car's taillights. "See that you do. I put my fucking career on the line for the information I've passed on to Diego." He reached into his pocket and withdrew a set of keys. He opened the car with the alarm button and settled behind the steering wheel. "I had the situation under control. Now the DEA's gonna be crawling up my ass."

Santos remained silent. He'd learned long ago how to hold his tongue and bide his time. One day, when the cop was no longer necessary to Diego's organization, he would regret the insults that now flowed so easily from his mouth. Vargas had a long memory.

"Tell Diego I'll deal with the mess he's made," the man flung out the window as he pulled away, "but no more hits unless I give the word. *Capeesh?"*

113

Santos merely nodded and watched the dwindling taillights as the man pulled out of the docking area, wondering what made the man think he was in charge. *Poli del idiota!* Speaking bad Italian to *un mexicano.* If Santos ran Diego's organization the way the the police ran theirs, they would have been out of business long ago. Unfortunately, having a man like the cop on the inside made Santos' life easier. He was necessary. For the time being.

Santos walked the few blocks to where he'd parked the black Chrysler. Good, the wheels and rims were intact. He could never be certain here at the docks near the Gerritson Housing Project where the local gangs did not recognize the automobile Vargas sometimes rode in. A young gang member might want to jump in by stealing expensive hubcaps.

The trip to his infrequently-used apartment in West Sacramento took forty minutes, and when he arrived, Santos permitted himself a single nightcap before retiring to set the alarm for his early morning ride north to pick up Diego.

Before extinguishing the light, Santos reached into the nightstand drawer and withdrew the ancient photograph. He had only a vague notion of why he kept the picture, but he'd had it so long now that its familiarity was like an old acquaintance, perhaps even a friend. Its faded colors had taken on a sepia look now and the corners curled up. Slashes cut by folds and long ago fingering of the photo made the girl's features nearly impossible to see clearly.

But he knew that she was very beautiful, a woman such as he had never before seen. That mane of rich chocolate was not easily forgotten. Santos remembered every glint of the Mexican sun that reflected off her head and captured the reddish strands running through it. In his dreams, he felt the silken touch of it as it slid through his fingers, thick softness like the rich pelt of a fine breed of animal.

He sighed. He had been a very young man then, easily captivated by a pretty girl, but he did not think it was his youth that caused him to remember this particular one. *Ella era muy hermosa – she was very beautiful* in a fragile, unearthly way. But with a strange core of strength in her, like the tensile of thin wire.

Santos turned off the light and contemplated the long journey to pick up Diego at *La Casa de Mujeres. Ay,* he despised the ugliness of this part of the business.

#

"Why is Torres so bent on making such a hard case?" Rafe asked as he and Slater waited in the sheriff's small office. "She's resisted the drug angle with Diego Vargas from the start. Doesn't she understand it'll be easier to prosecute that case than the human trafficking?"

"You'd better let her explain her reasons for that ... when she knows you a little better," Slater answered, his feet propped up on the edge of his desk.

Rafe assessed the office. Crammed with several filing cabinets, Slater's desk, and the guest chair, it offered little room to turn around. A wide window looked out into the bullpen where he watched Isabella Torres talking on one of the phone lines.

She gestured wildly with her hands, the receiver tucked under her chin. A moment later she slammed down the receiver and spat air through her lips so hard that Rafe saw the loose brown strands tangle around her mouth. Catching his eye through the window, she froze a moment, her lips still pursed, color starting to rise in her cheeks, a pretty pink color even in the harsh fluorescent lights of the bullpen.

She frowned and then gestured for them to join her in the bullpen.

"Let's go to my office," she said shortly, gathering her folders from the purloined desk of a broad man with a face like glistening coal who stood respectfully to the side.

A smile carved the man's face. "You reckon I can have my desk back now, Ms. Torres?"

"What? Oh, sure, sorry, Waylon. I'm in a mood today. Thanks." The smile that lit her features transformed them into the woman more like the one Rafe had first met in the bar.

Isabella Torres' office was more expansive than Rafe had expected for an assistant district attorney. Located at the end of the second floor of the courthouse and wedged between two courtrooms, it maintained the elegant, polished-mahogany look of the historic old building.

She'd made the place her own with a few personal effects scattered throughout – a photo of a young girl, maybe six or seven with an older girl who had Isabella's same large dark eyes and wide smile. Another picture of the two women Rafe had seen in Stuckey's Bar with Torres and an older woman, their mother he guessed.

"Have a seat." Torres indicated two large, comfortable-looking chairs in front of a highly polished but alarmingly cluttered desk.

"What's up?" Slater asked casually, crossing his foot over a knee and sinking back into one of the deep chairs.

Rafe took the other one which faced the west end of the building and a floor-to-ceiling bank of windows that overlooked the side lawn of the courthouse.

"Gabriel Santos," she answered in a clipped voice. "That's what's up." Her lips flattened in a tight line as if the name left a bitter taste in her mouth.

Rafe looked up in surprise. "Vargas' henchman?"

"And Vargas' lawyer, too." Her dark eyes were large in her pale face. "Nevada County picked him up for speeding. A friend of mine works in the sheriff's office up there." She slanted a look at Slater that might've been a token apology for stepping on his toes.

Slater shrugged and spread his hands wide as if he couldn't care less.

"Anyway, it was a bogus move. They wanted a reason to look inside the vehicle."

"Find anything?" Slater asked.

"Thirty grams of marijuana, single bag."

"Just enough to be a little bullshit, right?" Slater thought a moment. "Was Santos alone?"

Torres nodded.

"Where was he coming from?"

"South. Maybe on his way to *La Casa de Mujeres.*" Rafe noted her perfectly accented Spanish and the smug look she flashed him.

"Picking up Vargas, you think?"

"Likely."

The cryptic, short exchange irritated Rafe. "What the hell are you two talking about?"

"The house of wom – " Torres began.

"I know what the damn phrase means," he interrupted. "What's that got to do with Vargas' drugs?"

"Diego Vargas owns two whore houses in Nevada County," Slater explained, "both legit. But Torres thinks he's running at least one illegal brothel where he supplies his customers with ... special requests."

Rafe lifted his brow in question, but he already knew the answer.

"Underage girls," Torres provided flatly, "some of them as young as seven or eight."

"Jesus." He hadn't known that, but he should've.

"Right," she confirmed sarcastically, "but I don't think Jesus had that much to say about it. You still think the drug angle is more important?"

Rafe shook his head dismissively. "That's not the point – which one's more important. We could butt our heads against that wall all day. What we can actually *convict* Vargas on, what'll hold up in court, is the main thing."

"So you say." Torres tapped her foot, still standing behind her desk even though both the men were seated in front of her.

117

Rafe looked from Slater to Torres and back again. "You have any intel on an illegal house? Any idea where it's located? Evidence of ownership by Vargas or one of his subsidiaries?"

Torres shook her head and Rafe figured it cost her to admit to that weakness in her case.

He made a hand gesture as if her silence made his point. "Then let's talk about drugs. How is Nevada County holding Santos with barely more than an ounce of weed? He should've been out already."

"They're pushing it," Torres admitted.

"Tell them to spring him," Slater suggested. "You're right, Bella, it was a bad move on their part."

"He was doing sixty-nine on I-80 coming over Donner Pass," she complained. "They ran the plates when they pulled him over, saw it was registered to Santos, and used his parole from Chino to search the vehicle."

"That's legit," Rafe said.

"Yeah," Slater answered, "but dumb. Now Scarface knows he's being watched carefully."

"Scarface?" Rafe asked.

"You've seen his picture?" Slater countered.

"Actually, no. I've been looking at Vargas. He's our main concern," Rafe answered.

"Vargas already knows he's on our radar," Slater commented. "Santos, not so much. Maybe."

"You should watch out for Santos," Torres warned, the same distasteful set to her mouth.

"The power behind the throne," Slater added.

"How do you mean?" Rafe asked.

Torres finally collapsed in a heap on her chair. "Diego Vargas is a very bad man," she explained, carefully formulating her reply. "But Santos? He's not only evil, he's smart."

"Like a fox," Slater added.

Chapter Nineteen

The last time Isabella Torres had seen Gabriel Santos face to face was in Councilman Diego Vargas' office on a prior case. That meeting hadn't gone well then and she dreaded confronting the man again. Now he seemed even more of a giant as he stood for arraignment while she watched from the rear of the courtroom.

Nevada County had decided to press forward on the drug charges although they were likely to be dismissed. Possession of the small amount of marijuana, not repackaged in individual baggies for sale, was a ridiculous charge, and in any other county wouldn't have been worth the court's time. Bella could tell by the look on the magistrate's face that this judge also didn't appreciate the D.A.'s office wasting his court time.

A short, round attorney, expensively dressed in a black, light-weight suit, stood beside Santos, dwarfed by his client. Santos dipped his head to hear the lawyer whisper in his ear and then stood with military precision, looking neither left nor right, but straight toward the judge's raised podium.

"Your honor," the attorney began, "I respectfully request the charges against my client be dismissed and ask the court to sanction the aggressive actions of the sheriff's department in bringing Mr. Santos here on such ridiculous charges."

Frankly, Bella agreed with him.

Judge Schwartz frowned, his florid face a study in irritation, and after several moments of back and forth sniping between the prosecutor and the defense attorney, he finally groused, waving his hand over the podium. "Enough," he pronounced. "Time served and a thousand dollar fine."

He banged the gavel and gave the defendant a hard look. "Mr. Santos, don't let me see you in my court again. Case dismissed."

Santos shrugged inelegantly. His attorney whispered again in his ear while the bailiff removed him to the back of the courtroom to await the short return to the jail and his imminent release. Bella waited impatiently through the tedious process, alternately pacing the sidewalk and sitting in the small lobby. She didn't want to miss the opportunity to confront Santos head on.

When he finally exited through the metal detectors, Isabella stood quickly and blocked the way. "Mr. Santos, I'm Isabella Torres. I'd like a word with you."

The black, flat eyes slid over her with less concern than if she were a fly buzzing round his head. "See my attorney."

He moved around her, but she stepped in his way again. He stopped inches from her so she was forced to crane her neck to look up as he towered over her like a teacher over a recalcitrant student.

Narrowing his eyes, he raked his gaze down her body and up again, as if he were undressing her. No, she amended, nothing so sexual, more as if he were stripping her soul bare. She was grateful she'd worn four-inch heels today, although it hardly put them on an equal footing.

Bella suppressed a shudder and returned his look unflinchingly. When he examined her features more closely, for a moment she saw some emotion flicker within those obsidian eyes, a struggle for memory and then recognition. It lasted a long thirty seconds and then vanished. She shook her head, certain she'd imagined it.

Looking at a spot over her head, Santos reached into his breast jacket pocket and fingered a piece of paper. The ragged edges showed from beneath his long, dark fingers.

After a few seconds his face split into a grin, wide, white teeth shining startlingly in his scarred face. "I have heard of interesting things about the young assistant district attorney who fights so daringly in court. What does such a fierce warrior as yourself want with a humble Mexican man like me?"

They shifted aside to allow others to pass and Bella found herself pressed nearly chest to chest with Santos. His enormous size felt suffocating. "You're Diego Vargas' attorney, right?"

At his sudden scowl, she continued, "That isn't privileged information. It's a matter of public record."

"Yes, I represent Mr. Vargas," he answered at last.

"Mr. Santos," she mocked. "Are you sure a man with the vile inclinations of Diego Vargas should be called 'Mister'"? She hadn't meant to start so aggressively, but couldn't seem to help herself. She despised Vargas and, by association, this stone-faced man who guarded him.

Santos' face went hard, a granite slab transposing his dark visage. "You are speaking of my client, Assistant District Attorney Torres," he reminded her. "What do you want?"

"Like I said, I want to talk to you."

"About my client?" he scoffed.

"Yes." She watched his face carefully, both intrigued and repelled by the brutishness of his body, the intense stillness of his face. It was almost as if all emotion had been stripped from him, flayed off by a master's cruel whip.

"Un hombre sabio no traiciona secretos." Santos said softly.

Bella clearly understood the phrase. *A wise man doesn't betray secrets.*

"Are you sure?" she asked. *"Algunos secretos robarán un alma de hombre."* *Some secrets will steal a man's soul.*

Santos' eyes widened slightly before his carved lips smiled and without a further word, he walked toward the parking area. She realized she'd surprised the bodyguard, and she doubted he was often taken unawares. She called a warning after him. "I can subpoena you, Mr. Santos."

He paused, turned, and smiled grimly at her. "Perhaps you should not call *me señor,* either," he said, then strolled toward a dark gray BMW in the parking lot.

From her angle Bella could see him pull what looked like a rectangular paper the size of an index card out of his jacket. He stared at it long moments before he replaced it and eased his giant's body behind the wheel. She continued to track the car until it made the turn toward the highway.

Diego Vargas was Santos' only client. She'd known he wouldn't talk to her, but she'd tried anyway on the off chance that she could trick him into saying something damaging. Instead, she'd tipped her own hand.

The drive back to Placer Hills passed in record time, and when Bella arrived, she reported to Slater about the results of Santos' day in court, neither of them surprised by the outcome. Hours passed quickly as she worked through lunch and beyond, ensconced in her office on the second floor of the courthouse. Today was one of the few days she had no court appearances and she wanted to take advantage to catch up on paperwork and research.

A brief knock on her open office door caused her to look up to see Agent Hashemi framing the doorway. Without preliminaries, he dove right in, the accusation strong in his voice. "Why are you being so damn stubborn about the drug case?"

"Well, hello, there, Agent Hashemi. And good afternoon to you, too."

Torres made that little moue that Rafe had found endearing a few nights ago, but which now just annoyed the hell out of him. "Answer the question, Torres."

He sat down in the comfortable chair opposite her desk and shook his head at the mess cluttered in front of her. How could she work in such chaos? "Why are you digging in your heels?"

The look Isabella flashed him would've killed a lesser man, Rafe decided, but even with her color high and her lips pursed tight against her teeth, she looked pretty damn good.

"You haven't given me anything, Hashemi," she answered mildly, continuing to riffle through papers. "Not a damned thing. So tell me how I'm the one who's being stubborn."

He shrugged his shoulders and shifted in his seat. "Okay, what do you want to know?"

She thought a moment, staring through the doorway into the dimly lit hallway and the rickety elevator. He could see the wheels turning in her head and almost laughed. She wouldn't appreciate the humor in her bargaining for information he planned to give her anyway.

"I want to know what you found in that alley."

He smiled to himself. It had to be hard for her to mention the alley and conjure up images of the night they met. "Blood."

"Blood?"

"Yeah, you know, that red, viscous liquid?"

"I know blood," she snapped. "Whose?"

"Ex-con by the name of Morris Sullivan."

"Oh." That stopped her for a minute. "I don't know the name. Is he dead?"

"Don't know. We can't find a body." He looked away, thinking of Lupe's mangled body.

She pounced on his hesitation, probably thinking he was holding back. "What else aren't you telling me?"

"The human blood was covered up with animal blood."

"Someone didn't want you to know about Sullivan." It wasn't a question, and he liked how her mind wrapped around the problem so fast.

"I thought maybe your office could tie Sullivan back to Diego Vargas," he suggested, getting up and casually walking around the office, noticing how much more spacious it was than Sheriff Slater's.

She frowned, following him with her eyes. "Sullivan, that's Irish. You think a white ex-con would be mixed up with the Mexicans?"

"Strange things happen in prison."

She nodded as if she'd just come to some important understanding. "Is that why you told me about the blood in the alley? Because you wanted my help on Sullivan?"

"Yeah, probably." He grinned sheepishly. "I'm pretty much a bastard."

"That's what I figured," she said, but with a smile that made his heart skip a beat or two.

Rafe tried again, this time gentling his voice because he sensed something grievous under the surface of her smooth façade. "Why are you so hell bent on ignoring the drug case, Torres, when it's much easier to prosecute than human trafficking?"

She lowered her eyes, but not before Rafe saw a flash of pain in them.

"Okay, never mind about that," he said, unwilling to probe into whatever had caused that distress, unwilling to hurt her more. Time enough to pour salt in the wounds later, he thought. "How about another *quid pro quo?*"

She raised those dark chocolate eyes to meet his and from his higher position he noted how they were lushly surrounded by thick black lashes. Aha, a spark of interest. "What do you have in mind?"

"Tell me what happened at the Santos arraignment." The Nevada court proceeding was information he could easily obtain, but he wanted to broker a truce with her. Five minutes later, she'd given him the shortened version, but he didn't mind. He still believed any information about Gabriel Santos wasn't significant enough to pursue.

"I think Santos is the key," she said, completely upsetting Rafe's train of thought.

He perched on the edge of her desk and leaned forward. "How so?"

"Santos is the attorney of record." She held up her fingers one at a time. "He's been with Vargas a very long time. He's moved from thuggish bodyguard to closest confidant. We should be tailing Santos as closely as we follow Vargas."

Rafe considered. "If there are secrets, you think Santos will know where the bodies are buried?"

She nodded, started gathering up her papers and stuffing them into a battered briefcase. The top of her desk remained as cluttered as when he'd walked in, but Torres seemed ready to call it a day.

An impulse he'd no doubt later kick himself for took over his brain and the words tumbled out of his mouth before he had time to reconsider. "How about we get a late dinner?"

She glanced at the clock before saying, "Oh, I don't know if that works very well for us, Hashemi."

"Why's that?" he pressed.

She walked to the door where he trailed her out and watched her lock up. "Because every time we eat or drink together, we fight."

"Not every time, Torres." He grinned and watched the flush creep up her neck to paint her pretty cheeks a dusty rose beneath the dark skin.

Chapter Twenty

The leggy blonde staggered out of the downtown Sacramento bar ahead of the guy, groped in her jacket pocket for her keys, and pressed the unlock button on the brand new, silver Lexus. All riiight, he thought, this babe has green. Or else Daddy does. Slightly less drunk than the girl, the guy tried to wrestle the keys from her grip.

"Nuthin' doin,' pretty boy," she laughed and then hiccupped loudly. "Oops, sorry." She burst into a series of giggles that both of them found hilarious.

"Hey," he warned, "it's your ride."

"Damn straight. Come on, Shel," she urged the dark-haired girl just coming out of the bar. The brunette tottered on alarmingly high heels. "Thas right, girl, get going."

The second girl – Shelby, the guy thought her name was – climbed into the back of the Lexus and immediately stretched out on the seat. For some reason the blonde – what the hell was her name? – burst into another round of laughter. Come to think of it, the whole situation was pretty hilarious.

The blonde climbed into the driver's seat and fumbled with inserting the key into the ignition. "Damn key. Whas wrong?"

After a few tries she made it, and by this time, the guy had settled into the passenger seat and hooked up his seat belt. The broad wasn't sober enough to drive and he didn't want to be scraped off the asphalt. This reminded him of the drunk driving video they watched in high school – Red Asphalt – which he'd found unbelievably comical and he started laughing again.

The blonde looked so adorable trying to figure out what to do next with the car that he reached over and kissed her soundly on the mouth, sticking his tongue hard between her lips. He hoped he could get it up with all the booze in his system. Shame to miss doing this one.

The girl in the back seat started to snore softly as they peeled away from the curb on Sixteenth Street. The blonde got a dozen or so blocks from the bar without an accident and approached the onramp.

They'd left the bar before midnight, too early to call it a night. "Hey, I got an idea," the guy said. "Take the next ramp, no, not there, next one." He directed her south on Interstate 80, and they lurched onto the freeway. "I just 'membered where we can get some really good smack."

"Oh yeah, baby, I like that idea," she said, running her hand up his thigh and lingering over his crotch.

God, he really hoped he could keep a hard-on. Maybe the H would help. After turning east on Highway 50, he directed her to the Folsom turnoff and pointed the way toward a middle-class neighborhood in an older section of Folsom.

When they arrive at the blue-trimmed stucco house shrouded in shrubbery and barely visible from the street, he stumbled from the car and lurched toward the porch. No light on. These kinds of people liked to stay under the radar.

A few minutes later, he made the exchange and returned to the Lexus. "Babe, this is primo shit. You'll like it."

"Where to?" she asked, staring at the white glassine packets.

"Turn right onto Auburn-Folsom. Let's go to the lake."

"Ooh, I like that idea," she said, starting up the car. "Beale's Lake, right?"

They pulled up to the barricaded entrance gate at Beale's Lake twenty minutes later, and the girl – Joanie was her name, he suddenly remembered – parked the car in the turnaround. They left Shelby in the backseat of the car sleeping off her drunk, and hauling a blanket out of the Lexus' trunk, walked the short distance to the beach.

They spread the blanket on the sand near the water. The lake was closed at this hour and the beach deserted. He used to come here all the time when he was a teenager. The park was closed, but he knew the rangers hardly ever bothered anyone unless they built an unauthorized fire on the beach.

After settling down, the guy produced the packets and prepared the heroin for snorting. Then they both lay back on the blanket and looked at the night sky. In minutes he could feel his heart rate slow down and his blood pressure drop. Euphoria swept over him like a warm blanket, a surge of pleasure that was better than sex. He glanced at Joanie, but she'd already closed her eyes. God, this was great stuff. He thought he said the words aloud, but wasn't sure.

When he looked over at Joanie again, he saw her lips had turned blue and her body was very pale in the light from the moon. With effort he propped himself on an elbow and opened her lid, looked at the pinpoint pupils. Damn, she was probably unused to the high quality heroin. Was she going into a coma?

Fuck! he thought mildly, but couldn't bring himself to get worked up about it. Why was this his problem? He didn't know how to do CPR, so what the hell could he do? And anyway, he didn't want anything to interfere with the melting away of all his troubles. He lay back down and stared at the stars, feeling the girl's body begin to tremble next to him.

As she convulsed, he wondered why the fuck she was raining on his high.

#

"Not every time," Rafe repeated as he followed Isabella to the elevator. He remembered the night she had spent in his apartment, the excitement and thrill of all that soft fullness and warm passion against him. He knew she was thinking the same thing by the way she avoided his eyes.

He shook his head and warned himself off, thinking it was just as well she'd refused his dinner invitation. "Suit yourself," he said with as much nonchalance as he could muster when she refused a second time.

She cleared her throat and jabbed at the elevator button. They stepped into the elevator and rode down to the first floor in silence.

The antique old Otis was slow as molasses in January and Rafe couldn't wait to hit the bottom floor and head back to his motel, but after they'd gone through the metal detectors and said goodnight to the on-duty guard, her voice stopped him.

"I guess I have to eat," she muttered, sighing theatrically, "but you'd better not fight with me again."

He laughed, relief and trepidation mixing together as he wondered what the hell he was getting himself into.

They decided to take her car, but as they walked toward the parking lot, she turned to him. "You know, I'm not all that hungry." She looked up at him from beneath impossibly thick lashes. "How about I fix us something light at my house? Would that work for you?"

He hesitated. That would more than work for him, although he wasn't sure being alone with her was such a good idea. She probably wanted to worm more information out of him. Before he could think better of it, his maverick tongue overrode his brain. "Sounds good. I'll follow you in my car."

Isabella pulled her car into an attached garage to the left of a neat, bungalow-style home in Placer Hills, a few miles from the courthouse. Rafe parked his rental car on the street and walked up a long path of flagstones across a deep, beautifully tended lawn to meet her at the porch landing. Rose bushes riotous with color lined the front of the house and what looked like every space possible.

The front double-doors had impressive stained glass windows from waist high up to the top. Too easy to break into, Rafe thought, but inside the foyer, Torres coded numbers into what looked like a sophisticated alarm system.

The front entry opened into a long hall, a huge great room to the left and the kitchen to the right where she headed after hanging their jackets in the entry closet. He wandered down

129

the hall, examining the small, one-story house, two bedrooms and a bath angling off to the left and what looked like a master bedroom and bath, along with a small utility room, to the right.

The kitchen was small and cozy, a recessed window over the sink looking out over all the crazy colors of her front landscaping. She would enjoy standing there and looking out at the mass of flowers, and he briefly imagined her dressed in skimpy night clothes, her hair mussed up and drinking her morning coffee.

While Torres prepared several turkey and cheese sandwiches, Rafe leaned against the stove beside her and admired the taut stretch of her breasts beneath the filmy blouse. When she bent over to retrieve potato chips from a lower shelf, he watched the play of her ass beneath her slacks and thought of gripping the firm flesh with his hands.

A sharp image of his hands and mouth on her, his fingers deep inside her, slapped him back to reality. He shifted uncomfortably and moved to sit at the table in the small kitchen alcove while Torres brought the sandwiches on plain white plates which she set on floral placemats.

"Why don't you get the drinks?" she asked as she reached for glasses in a high cupboard.

He looked inside the refrigerator. "Beer or soda?"

"I'll take soda." She filled the glasses with ice from the ice-maker and smiled at him standing to her right. "Anything wrong?" Her voice sounded too innocent for her not to be aware of how his damn body reacted to her.

He shook his head and sat down quickly, setting the cans on the table.

They ate slowly and discussed the case for a long while at the kitchen table. Afterward they moved to the great room where several deep sofas in a natty fabric and a wide-screen television decorated the high-beamed room. "Wow, look at that puppy."

She grinned. "My single indulgence."

130

"Funny," he said as they took their seats on the sofa facing the screen, "you don't seem like much of a TV watcher."

"Oh, I'm an avid sports fan – the Forty-Niners, the Lakers." She laughed. "A gift from my dad and three older brothers."

"Who'd have thought?"

He turned to face her and placed his arm along the sofa back. She kicked off her shoes and tucked her feet underneath her. Music she had turned on earlier wafted from the stereo system on the far wall. In the dim light, she looked soft and vulnerable. They listened to the sounds of Ella and Louie on Bella's stereo. Obviously her tastes ran to jazz.

Later, they watched the late news and then Letterman. Rafe found he enjoyed just sitting quietly with her, a sharp contrast to the physicality of their initial meeting. Finally he dared bring up the sensitive issue between them. Why was her stance on the human trafficking charges so much stronger than on the drug trafficking? Hell, what did it matter what they got him on as long as they put that scum Diego Vargas away?

Her voice muted and quiet, she made the usual moral argument about the destruction of innocent young girls. The degradation of woman and the heinous reality of abuse, rape, and sodomy. But Rafe intuited that there was much more that Torres wasn't saying. "What else," he murmured, "what else drives you like this, Isabella?"

At first he was sure she wouldn't answer him, but then her voice hitched in her throat and she spoke so low he had to tilt his head forward to hear. "I had a sister once – Maria."

When she didn't go on, Rafe asked, "What about Maria?"

Long moments followed in which Bella stared across the room, tension in every line of her face and body. "She disappeared. Maria went on a trip to Mexico for her high-school graduation, and she never came back."

"And you think – "

She interrupted him, angry tears in her eyes which she tried to dash away with trembling fingers. "I don't know what I think, Hashemi! All right? I just don't know."

Fat tears rolled silently down her dusty cheeks, her beautiful mouth trembled so that the only thing he could do was cover it with his own. He swore his only intention was to comfort her, nothing more, but she groaned as his lips touched hers and answered his kiss with a responding hunger that flamed the fire. He ground his mouth into hers, ran his fingers through her thick hair, pulling out the pins that held it up, and tangled his fingers in the soft thick curls. He kissed her neck, pressing his mouth down her flesh until he got to the top of her blouse.

He undid the first two buttons to run his fingers along the swell of her breasts at the top of her brassiere. When he followed with his mouth, he felt her shudder in his arms and wondered if she'd climax from just this much. He felt the painful, hard thrust of his erection against his slacks and pulled her onto his lap, continuing his assault on her mouth and neck. God, she felt so good, tasted so delicious.

Bella squirmed in his lap and he knew she could feel the hard, hot thrust of him against her ass. He reached inside her bra and caressed one breast, lightly pinching the nipple between his thumb and forefinger. She moaned and began her own assault of his jaw and neck.

He flipped her on her back and quickly ripped off his shirt and undershirt before he stretched out on the sofa, half covering her body with his own. He framed her face with his hands, holding himself off her body with his elbows. His breathing was labored and unsteady. "What are we doing here, Torres?" he muttered.

"I don't know. I don't care," she answered, eyes closed as she kissed him hard, her tongue smooth and urgent in his mouth.

God, she was like a drug. He couldn't keep his hands off her, couldn't leave her alone. He wouldn't be satisfied until he was deep inside that sweet, soft body, until he pounded away at her like –

An annoying buzz sounded in his pants pocket.

Chapter Twenty-one

Diego Vargas' office in downtown Sacramento was a visual testament to every immigrant who'd made a better life in the land of the free and the home of the brave. The surroundings of the councilman's office showed his Mexican heritage and his powerful connections to California's movers and shakers, Latinos and gringos alike.

Gabriel Santos disliked being summoned here, especially at this ungodly hour of the morning after a long week of driving many miles up and down the state. He wondered privately why Vargas could not have conducted this business at his home instead of having Santos pick him up in the Cadillac and accompany him to his city office downtown.

After they entered the office, Santos remained standing while Diego sat in a stiff-backed chair behind the impressive dark wood desk, signing papers and ignoring his attorney's presence. Glancing around the room, the attorney noted the new addition to Vargas' desk – a family photo. The councilman never kept pictures in the office except political ones, him with the governor and various congressmen, with celebrities, even of him with César Chávez when Diego was a boy.

The new photo was of Diego and Corazón, his eleven-year-old daughter, a recent picture because Cory wore her new braces on her teeth and tried to hide her smile. Diego had his arm around her shoulder, holding her tight against his barrel chest.

And where was Vargas' wife Magdalena in this family picture?

Finally Vargas signed the last document with a flourish and looked up. "The RICO charges have been dropped?" he asked, continuing the thread of the discussion they'd begun as they drove from Vargas' mansion to downtown.

134

"Sí, we knew the feds were not going to be able to prove them." Santos crossed his arms and shifted his weight onto the balls of his feet. "But from last year, the rape charges – "

"That was bullshit!" Vargas' thick brows drew together in a scowl as he interrupted. "You told me the girl agreed to silence, and they have not pursued the allegations."

"They haven't, *El Vaquero,* but that is what bothers me."

"Why should that bother you?" Vargas shoved back impatiently from his desk, his ample gut stretched over his belt. "It is good, no?"

"The Bigler County D.A.'s office had too much evidence to drop the charges, but they did not follow the investigation. One has to wonder why that is, considering Sheriff Slater is usually like a bulldog with a bone."

"I do not fucking care why," Vargas growled as he pushed out of his chair and moved to stand belly to chest with Santos. "There are more pressing matters."

Santos willed his face into granite, a trick he had a great deal of practice with. "What matters?"

"Another overdose, some stupid fucking college kids."

"Local?"

"Granite Heights at Beale's Lake."

Santos shrugged. "They will not be able to tie the charges to us. Our protection runs too deep."

"Chingada! Maybe in L.A., but not here!" As Vargas shouted, spittle dotted Santos' tie and shirt front. Diego raised his meaty fist as if he would strike. "Take care of it. Get rid of the dealer," he ground out. He spun on his heels and stalked back to his desk, sinking heavily into the leather chair.

Santos wiped his hand discreetly over his chest. Vargas threatened and blustered, but he would never strike Santos. Even *El Vaquero* knew which lines not to cross with his bodyguard. Santos tried again to persuade his pig-headed boss. "Such reactionary steps are not necessary, *El Jefe,* and they may bring more attention to the situation that we wish."

135

"No cuido! I don't care. Get rid of the dealer." He passed over a folded note. "Here is the address. Do it yourself. I do not wish to have loose ends." He swiveled his chair towards the window and ignored Santos while he quietly left the office.

Ay, some day Diego would go too far. Wounds had been festering within Santos for over twenty years and the pus of their infection was a grievous lesion on his body. One day he must lance the abscess and cut out the pustule to cleanse it. He did not look forward to that day – Santos was a man to avoid overt trouble – but neither did he fear it.

Downstairs in the parking lot, he pulled the sepia photo from his jacket. The pickup and delivery of the girl in the picture had been the first assignment he had completed for Diego Vargas many years ago. Santos had been a young man then, eager to make his mark, hungry for far more than food to fill his belly.

New to this country, he nevertheless had many years of practice at thuggery in Mexico. Huge and strong like an ox even as a young man in his late teens, he had honed his skills in the fires of Mexico's slums.

But he never forgot the young girl's face, those large dark eyes, huge in her frightened face, the slender body and full breasts. Her name was Maria and she was seventeen. Vargas was a fat pig of a man even then and he liked his girls young.

#

A moment passed before Rafe identified the sound that had interrupted them. Cold reality washed over him, and he saw the same mood-breaker in Isabella's wide, chocolate eyes. Reluctantly, he rolled off her and sat on the edge of the sofa, slanting a look her way.

After the fourth ring he flipped open the cell phone and barked into the receiver. "Hashemi."

Slater's voice sounded equally loud over the phone and by the look on Bella's face, Rafe knew she could hear Slater's words. She furiously shook her head.

136

"Trouble here, Mr. Agent-Man," the sheriff said in his deep, slow drawl. "Better get out here pronto."

"Drugs?"

"Yeah, maybe more of the China White."

"Where?"

"Beale's Lake. Get directions from Bella."

Rafe turned to glance at Bella whose look clearly said, how did he know?

"Give me her address," Rafe covered. "I'll pick her up."

"Sure." Slater's voice sounded puzzled, but Rafe couldn't tell if that was real or he was fishing. "But I got the impression she was with you."

"Why the hell would Torres be with me? She can hardly stand me." Rafe wasn't about to let the sheriff know what'd happened between them tonight. Or that he was sitting on her sofa right now. At her house. At this hour.

"No reason," Slater said cryptically and rattled off the address that Rafe already knew.

He closed the phone and put it back in his pocket, not looking at Torres as he put his shirt back on. "There's another drug death." He ran his fingers through his hair in a quick attempt at combing.

When he looked over at her, she'd buttoned up her blouse, tucked her shirt in her slacks, and put her shoes on. Her high color gave her a vibrant, sexy look. Thank God for the interruption. He felt like a man standing at the edge of a precipice who'd barely escaped losing his footing and plunging off.

Fifteen minutes later they left, taking separate cars to the scene at Beale's Lake, Rafe following Torres because he was unfamiliar with the area. When they arrived at the lake, he noted the Lexus parked outside the gate, all four door open wide. The EMTs were working over a dark-haired girl in the back seat. Slater's battered truck and three patrol cars lined the turnabout, and Rafe and Bella had to park some distance from the gate.

Slater met them once they'd crossed over the barrier. He walked ahead of them down towards the lake. "Park ranger found them when he was making his rounds," he said without preamble, gesturing with a nod of his head, "around three o'clock this morning. Down by the sand."

At the edge of the lake the scene had been cordoned off and the coroner hovered over a blanket, examining the bodies. Slater stooped to recover two glassine packets from the blanket. Each was partially filled with a white, powdery substance.

"What do you think?" asked Rafe. "Is it the high-grade shit?"

"I'd bet money on it," Slater answered, examining the packets before he placed them in an evidence bag. "Take a look at the bodies. Looks like overdoses."

"That's right, Sheriff Slater," Dr. McKenzie, a small, precise man, interjected. "My guess is very high quality heroin because most of the drug wasn't ingested and appears to remain in the packets. Only high grade would cause overdose with that small amount."

He shook his white head. "Autopsy will confirm, but see the blue lips and tinged skin?" He pointed to the blonde's mouth. "And the limb contortion indicates convulsion. If they'd gotten the Narcan, they might've made it, but ... " His voice trailed off sadly. "The cause of death undoubtedly will be respiratory failure."

Waylon Harris, Slater's deputy sheriff, pulled a wallet from the dead man's pocket and handed it to Slater who read aloud off the driver's license. "Jeremy Brown, DOB 2-15-80, credit cards, about ... " He counted the money. " ... two hundred in cash."

Another deputy, holding a woman's handbag, hurried from the Lexus. "You'll want to see this, Sheriff." He pulled out a ladies billfold from the purse and handed it over.

Slater opened it without a word and then groaned. "Holy crap hitting the fan."

"What?" Bella asked.

"Joan Anne Welch." Slater sighed as if the weight of the world had just descended on him.

Rafe looked from Bella to Slater and back again. "So?"

"She's State Senator John Welch's little girl," Bella answered, her face pinched with worry. "Damn, Barrington's going to be all over this."

"Patch," Slater called over to the coroner, "can you get that autopsy report to me ASAP?"

"I always do, Sheriff," the coroner muttered with a grim smile. "I like the mommies and daddies to know right away what happened to their babies."

McKenzie was a dapper man whose voice had the stilted formality of a college professor. Slater enjoyed calling him "Patch," and the doctor enjoyed pretending he disliked the nickname.

"Jesus Christ," Rafe muttered. "They're bringing in this shit fast and in volume." He looked at Slater again. "Seven a.m., your office?"

"Yeah, it'll be that long for the autopsy even with a rush. The medics are taking the other girl to the hospital, but when she's stable we can interview her." He looked down at the dead girl. "I'll do the notification myself. Bella, you'd better contact Charlie."

Even though Bella was technically Slater's superior, she didn't mind taking orders from him. She'd never trusted anyone like she did him, even her own brothers. He was smart, cool-headed, and would step in front of a bus for her. And she knew he hated the family notifications.

"I'll go with you," she offered.

Slater nodded once. "We have to know where they got the heroin," he said to Rafe. "What can your sources tell you? Maybe we should move on it tonight."

Rafe shook his head. "We'd better get a couple hours of sleep. It'll take that long for my contacts to find the dealer, and tomorrow's going to be one fucking long day." But he

139

knew he wouldn't sleep tonight, not by a long shot. He looked over at Bella, whose face was pale and drawn. He wouldn't sleep tonight, but he'd bet she wouldn't either. They'd both be remembering what had happened on her sofa, what would've happened if they hadn't been interrupted by a gruesome death, and neither would find sleep for a very long time.

He parked the rental car in front of the unit he occupied. Rafe and Bella hadn't spoken at all when they left the lake, but he'd raised his hand in a farewell gesture as she drove away.

He turned toward the rental unit. Christ, he was tired of fast-food and living out of his suitcase.

Chapter Twenty-two

The call came in on Rafe's cell phone shortly after he'd finally evaded thoughts of Bella and just closed his eyes and drift off into a dreamless sleep. "This had better be important," he muttered, rousing himself.

"Hashemi?"

"Yeah." He didn't recognize the voice and few people contacted him on this line. "Who's this and how the hell did you get this number?"

"Banadoora." Arabic for tomato. That would be McNally, the red-faced Homeland Security agent who crawled up Rafe's ass so far he wanted to fart the bastard out like the giant turd he was. Rafe waited for the password question.

"Ma ismak?" What is your name? McNally loved this cloak and dagger shit.

"Khiyar," Rafe responded, using the Arabic word for cucumber, a little Homeland Security cornball humor. The DHS boys thought that was hilarious because they said Rafe was always as cool as a cucumber. "What do you want, McNally?"

The agent rattled off the name and address of the contact. Homeland Security was already on this. That meant only one thing – they'd already made the connections between the new drug routes and distributions to terrorist activities.

"The China White profits are being funneled right back into Thailand," McNally continued, "and then into an organization called *Mohandis* in the Golden Crescent."

That meant Afghanistan and *Al Qaeda.*

"Winters wants you to run a parallel investigation with the county D.A.'s office. Don't make waves, just get along with that woman ADA until we have the background intel we need. Then we'll assume jurisdiction over the investigation."

So it's begun, Rafe thought, snapping the cell phone shut. From their overseas intelligence, they'd expected this, but hearing the reality of it was like taking an icy bath. Torres would be royally pissed when the takeover happened, and he felt bad about that, but it couldn't be helped; he had no choice. National security trumped local charges, no matter how ugly the bad guys were.

#

The raid on the drug house lasted less than fifteen minutes.

Slater accompanied Rafe and four federal agents. The residential street was very quiet, most people still not awake to begin their workday. The sun had barely begun to peek in the eastern sky, a hazy purplish-pink that indicated a high pollution day.

Slater positioned himself to the rear, a motion Rafe appreciated, so that his team of agents could take the lead, approaching the front and rear entries with weapons drawn. His federal warrant didn't require an announcement and Rafe had no intention of alerting possibly armed drug dealers of their imminent arrest.

With a nod to the agent opposite him, Rafe indicated the man should kick in the door. Then Rafe went in first, low and to the right.

The interior was filled with a complete, eerie silence. No dogs, unusual for a drug house. They crept in stealthily, clearing each room as they went. The three agents who'd taken the back found the animals, two Doberman pinchers and a giant black lab. Gunshot wounds. In a small rear bedroom, they found the home's occupant, a small, dark man, possibly Latino, though it was hard to tell because his face and the upper half of his body were saturated with blood.

Rafe crouched down by the body. "Knife?" he asked Slater.

"My best guess. Any body parts missing?"

"Torres told you, huh?"

"About your informant? Yeah. Sorry, man."

142

"Well, it looks like this scumbag has all his parts," Rafe answered, thinking of how Lupe had suffered while this punk got a quick death.

Slater knelt beside him. "Looks like a swift, single slice to the carotid. That's why all the blood." He looked around the dirty carpet. "And the arterial spray blood spatter."

"Get the crime techs in here," Rafe shouted at the agent standing by the door. "See if you can find any trace of the drugs." He jammed his fist into his pocket. "How the hell did they get to him so soon?"

Slater stood, pulled on latex gloves, and walked around the bedroom, searching but not touching anything. "How good is your intelligence, Hashemi? Are you sure this is the drug dealer?"

"I'm sure," Rafe said shortly. "The guy would be alive otherwise."

Slater stepped close to Rafe and spoke low in his ear. "Looks like you've got a serious leak somewhere, Hashemi."

"Not necessarily." He waved a hand over the dead body. "Mr. Drug Dealer here could've told someone higher up."

Slater just shrugged and meandered around the room, poking around, curious. A good detective, Rafe thought as he punched a number into his cell phone. When the person on the other end of the line answered, he asked the question. "What's the name?" A few minutes later he snapped the phone shut. He looked over at Slater who was lifting up an edge of the mattress and bending to look underneath.

"His name's Enrique Salazar. Ties to the Norteños."

Slater looked up. "Which means Diego Vargas."

Rafe nodded, suddenly tired of the confining room, needing fresh air. He could hear the coroner and crime scene techs arrive. They'd be hours and he and Slater had better things to do than hang around. He knew the sheriff was right about an inside job, and it was what Max Jensen had suggested. But he'd thought it was a C.I., possibly Lupe or another informant. This looked like a serious breach in security at a much higher level.

Christ, this looked like one of their own had betrayed them.

#

Bella had been with the girl ten minutes when Slater and Rafe entered the hospital room. The girl's dark eyes widened to the size of saucers when she saw the two men, one dressed in a dark suit, the other a uniform, both wearing sunglasses, and looking like bad-ass criminal types.

"It's okay, Shelby," Bella said. "These men are here to help. They need to hear your answers to the questions I'm asking."

"I don't know anything," the girl protested.

Rafe crossed the room and sat on the edge of the bed, taking the girl's hand in both his own. "Sometimes you know something and don't even realize it," he said gently. "Don't worry, we'll help you remember."

Shelby nodded dumbly.

The tenderness with which he approached the girl surprised Bella, and she looked at Slater who made a who-knew facial gesture. She cleared her throat and began again. "Let's start again, okay? Can you remember what time you left the Purple Cow?"

Shelby had already told her she'd gone to the trendy bar with Joan Welch and hooked up with a guy whose name she couldn't remember. Probably didn't ever know.

"It was kind of early, I think, because ... well ... " She paused and looked soulfully at Rafe who still retained her hand.

"It's okay, Shelby. We're not so old that we don't remember going to a bar and getting hammered." Rafe's smile was almost bashful, a peer confessing a secret. Damn, he was good, Bella thought. Where did all this charm come from?

"We were pretty wasted," the girl admitted. "That's why we left early, because we didn't want to get carded." She

144

realized what she'd implied and quickly amended. "I'm sure Joanie was sober enough to drive. She wouldn't screw around with her dad's Lexus." Huge, fat tears welled in the girl's eyes, but didn't spill down her blotched cheeks.

"Do you remember any stops between the bar and the lake?" Bella asked.

Shelby frowned, her shapely dark brows knitting as she concentrated. At last she shook her head. "I'm sorry. I think I crawled in the back and passed out because I don't remember anything after leaving the Purple Cow. And I can barely remember that."

"That's okay, don't worry." Rafe patted her hand and ruffled her hair as if she were a child. "If you think of anything else, give me a call." He removed a card from his jacket pocket and put it in her hands. "Take care of yourself, Shelby."

When they stepped outside the door, Bella protested. "That's it? No more questions? She might know something about the drugs."

"Nope." Rafe shook his head. "She's scared shitless, but she doesn't know anything else. Probably never woke up until the EMTs got to her."

"But we won't know unless we ask her more questions." Bella hurried to keep up with Rafe's long-legged strides.

"Besides," Slater said as they walked toward the hospital elevator doors, "we found the dealer."

Irritated, she snapped, "Why didn't you say so?"

Rafe's face was blank as he stared at her. "I thought that was obvious. I didn't want to upset the girl."

Bella felt her face flush at the implication that she cared less than he did about what Shelby had been through. She punched hard at the elevator button. They stepped inside the elevator without a word. Bella pushed down her temper. "How did you find the dealer so soon?"

"My contacts," Rafe answered, "are really good." He paused and then dropped the bomb. "But the dealer's dead."

"Oh my God! How?"

"Looks like a professional hit. Much like Lupe." The mention of his confidential informant brought a distant look to Rafe's eyes and Bella knew he still suffered from guilt over Lupe's death. "Without the torture."

"The house was ransacked," Slater added, "probably making sure the drugs were gone. The techs will look for traces of the heroin, but they may not find anything."

"We can match that up with the quality found with the Welch girl and the actor." Rafe said.

"It'll be the same," Bella said, determination in her voice. "And it'll trace back to Vargas."

"You're probably right," Rafe said. "The drug dealer, Enrique Salazar, had ties to the Nortenos."

When they reached the underground parking area, Bella watched as Rafe and Slater jumped in Slater's Chevy truck and headed back to the precinct. Even though mountains of paperwork were piled up on her desk, she wasn't going to return to the D.A.'s office.

There was something she needed to do first. She knew Hashemi wouldn't go for any kind of plea bargaining. And Barrington was a spineless jerk who wouldn't stand up to the feds no matter what. Bella was going to have to reach out to Santos first, feel him out about making a deal, even though every fiber in her body screamed against it.

She shivered, but not from the cold. Thinking of approaching Santos was like contemplating walking into the jaws of a ferocious beast.

#

Santos pulled the Cadillac CTS up to the gate of Vargas' house and entered the code to open the barriers. He stood on the wide porch landing and rapped on the door. Usually Magdalena answered the door. He always liked seeing *El Vaquero's* wife, gauging by her demeanor if Vargas was in a bad or good mood. Determining how much Vargas had hurt her by the grief or joy in her dark, expressive eyes.

Today the door swung open and Santos dropped his eyes from where he expected to see Magdalena to the slender form of her daughter Corizón. The child's large dark eyes, so like her mother's, looked very serious and a little fearful. Too serious and too fearful for such a little girl.

"*Hóla,* little one, where is your *madre* today?"

Cory shook her head silently as Santos peered around her into the spacious foyer.

"Is she sleeping?"

Cory looked down at her feet, digging the toe of one shoe into the cement. "She's gone."

"Gone? Some shopping?" Santos laughed and gently caressed the girl's head. "*Ay,* mothers are always going shopping!"

She shook her head and glanced over her right shoulder as if she expected someone to reach out and grab her. "Not shopping," she whispered.

Santos crouched down so that his massive size seemed smaller and his eyes did not look down on her from his enormous height. "How long has your mama been gone, *pequena bebé?*"

Large tears welled up in the girl's eyes but she did not allow them to drop. "Since Sunday." She swiped at her nose. "I miss her."

So long? Santos knew that something was very wrong. Magdalena would not be gone so many days from her child if she could help it.

Chapter Twenty-three

At Torres' office on the second floor, the three of them gathered around the ADA's desk speculating about why the drug dealer had been killed. Bella relaxed behind the desk, her feet propped up on one edge, her shoes off. Pretty red-painted toenails peeked from the hem of her slacks. She'd removed her jacket and slung it across the back of the chair, and the firm outline of her breasts showed beneath the sheer white blouse when she locked her fingers behind her head.

"What does it mean?" Torres asked. "Why kill the drug dealer, someone so low in the organization?"

Rafe slouched against a wide bookcase filled with law books and case law journals to the right of the desk. He found it easier on his imagination to think of Bella addressed her by her last name because he figured it bugged her a little. "Someone's worried we're getting too close, Torres," he answered. "That's what it means."

"Or it could be retaliation because of the botched buy," Slater suggested. The sheriff lounged in the other office chair in the room, a comfortable arm chair that he occupied with annoying familiarity.

Torres bit her lower lip. "But he wasn't killed like Lupe."

"Close enough," Slater answered. Rafe had already filled the sheriff in on the details of the hit on his C.I.

"The message they're sending this time was for us, not the other dealers in Vargas' network." Rafe added. "This murder was a cover-up, not retaliation. The dealer's death was efficient, smooth, and quick, and not nearly violent enough."

"Bloody, though," Slater argued.

Torres' phone rang and she reached for it before Slater could comment further. "Torres." A moment later she grimaced and shook her head in disgust. "What can I do for you this morning, Mr. District Attorney?" She made a finger-down-her-throat barfing motion, and Slater smiled and patted her shoulder, mouthing, "Charles Barrington."

Rafe speculated again about the care-free relationship between Slater and Torres. He couldn't figure out if they were an item or had been an item. Maybe they just had a brother-sister relationship, but whatever it was, he felt a surge of jealousy at their easy-going friendship.

"Yeah, okay. Right," she continued, making a yackety-yak motion with the thumb and fingers of her right hand. Suddenly she stopped fooling around and became all business. "When?"

Slater edged forward in his chair, tension in his big body.

Torres grabbed a pencil and pad. "Where?" Pause. "How many?" She slammed down the pencil and said, "I'm on it." She hung up and leaned back in her chair, locking her fingers over her stomach, a grim but smug look on her face.

"What?" Slater asked.

"A deputy sheriff coming back from Reno, off duty, and yes, one of ours, comes across a large delivery van in the breakdown lane headed east on I-80." She leaned forward, elbows on the desk blotter. "Being the Good Samaritan that all Bigler County deputies are, he whips his car around, crosses the freeway divider – illegally of course – and like a good Boy Scout, proceeds to help the two men change a tire."

Slater sat on the edge of Torres' desk and folded his arms, apparently amused at the roundabout way she told the story. Rafe rubbed his hand through his hair and tried not to scream an obscenity. He made a hurry-up motion with his hands and got a frown for his efforts.

"Anyway, also being a good detective, he notices the heavy weight of the freight on the tires, the general shiftiness of the two men in the cab, and the super heavy-duty locks on the back of the van. He grows even more suspicious when the men appear panicky about receiving his help and then hears faint noises from the back of the van."

149

"What kind of noises," Rafe asked.

A wash of anger tinged with fear preceded her answer. "Human."

Rafe had no doubt what was in that truck and precisely where it was headed.

"Probable cause?" Slater asked.

"Likely not enough," Torres answered. "But he bullies them into opening the rear anyway. Guess what he finds?"

"You tell us, Torres," Rafe said although he was sure he knew the answer.

He recognized a brief flash of pain and something like sorrow in Torres' face. When she answered, her voice was barely above a whisper. "Nineteen young girls, half-naked, half-starved, dirty."

"Where were they headed?" Rafe asked.

"Vargas' whore house." Slater's answer showed he understood.

She nodded and her eyes turned flinty. "Young girls, eleven, twelve."

"Christ," Slater said. "Babies."

"Something else," Torres added. "And you'll like this part, Hashemi."

"Yeah? What's that?" he asked.

"Ten kilos of high-grade heroin in the tire wheels."

"Will the search stick in court?" Slater asked.

"Doesn't matter," Rafe answered for Torres. He knew if he pulled in his Homeland Security buddies, he could bypass the courts altogether, although he knew she wouldn't like that.

"Let's go check it out," he said, glancing at Torres' face and noting the tension. He hoped she wouldn't be too emotionally involved to be effective in the case. "We need to be careful how we handle this," he admonished, looking to Slater for backing.

"We can't be sure the truck belongs to Vargas until we investigate further," Slater said.

Torres agreed. "The registration wasn't in his name."

"But you can fucking believe he's involved," Slater snarled.

Santos opened his mouth to ask Corizón another question about her mother when Vargas walked up behind her, placing his meaty hand on her thin shoulder. "You're late," he snapped and motioned for Santos to enter and follow him down the hall.

Vargas rarely invited Santos inside this inner sanctum. He had been to the house many times over the five years Vargas had occupied the mansion, but seldom went beyond the porch and the grounds. He had patrolled the perimeter of the property, guarded the family at the pool area, but had almost no occasion to be inside the house.

Vargas walked to his office with the agitated gait of a man beset with many problems. Was Magdalena one of the problems and had his boss found a way to deal with it?

Santos remained standing while Vargas stood behind his desk, shuffling through a stack of papers. "Where is Magdalena," Santos asked casually.

"Why the fuck do you care where that slut is?" Vargas snarled, looking up from his desk to pierce his bodyguard with those vicious eyes. An air of edginess surrounded him as if he waited for a reason to vent his anger by giving in to violence.

Santos shrugged. "I do not care. I was just making conversation."

"Well, don't," Vargas snapped, returning to his task of sorting papers. A moment later he looked up as if he'd just considered something. "Magdalena's gone on a shopping trip." He laughed falsely. "That woman loves to spend my money, eh?"

"Where?"

"To Mexico. She will be gone a long time." Vargas looked Santos in the eye and he understood what his boss meant. Magdalena was not coming back. Ever.

Santos had been with Vargas long before Cory was born. He had attended every significant event of the child's life, watching her grow from a beautiful baby to a young girl. He knew the answer, but had to ask nonetheless. "Why did the little one not go with her mother?"

Vargas snorted as if something foul had entered his nostrils. "You know Magdalena. She never was much of a mother. She said it would be better for Corizón to stay here ... with me."

A chill like icy fire trailed down Santos' spine. He heard a small sound from behind him and turned to see the girl standing in the doorway. She did not look at him, but stared straight ahead at her father with a look too knowing for such a young girl.

Fucking pig! His own daughter! But somehow Santos knew this day would come. From the moment the little one was born, he'd understood what would happen to her one day. And he knew that Magdalena was not strong enough to fight Vargas.

Vargas' attention zeroed in on Cory hovering at the doorway. "What do you want?" he snapped.

For a brief moment, she glowered back, a look both defiant and cowering. *"Nada, Papa, nada."* She turned and closed the door softly behind her.

Vargas slumped into the desk chair. "But Magdalena's affairs are not what I called you here for."

Santos noticed that this office, like Vargas' downtown office, was devoid of family pictures. Just the portrait of him with Cory and her recent school photo.

"What happened?" Santos asked.

"Something's gone wrong with the Reno shipment."

"What?" Santos asked.

"The truck from Manzanillo was intercepted outside Reno," Vargas answered. "They have the girls." His face twisted in an ugly scowl. *"Campesinos!* Fucking Mexican peasants! Low riders! They popped a tire and pulled off to fix it, but some asshole cop stopped to help."

"What happened?" Santos repeated.

"They freaked out and blew it." Vargas paced back and forth on the expensive Persian carpet in front of his desk. "Made the cop suspicious and he searched the rear of the van."

Santos had known transporting the girls would be trouble. He'd tried to warn Vargas, but the boss wouldn't listen. "The search won't be legal. The evidence will be thrown out in court."

"It doesn't matter! They know about the girls!" Vargas' broad peasant face dripped with sweat. "They'll trace the truck back to me!"

"The courts will suppress everything. You do not need to worry," Santos repeated.

"You must take care of it!" Vargas shouted, spittle edging the corners of his mouth.

Santos made his voice low and deadly. "And how shall I do that, Diego? Kill them all? The girls and the drivers? Is this your solution to everything?"

"Figure it out. I don't care!" Vargas screamed. "Post the bail and get rid of the evidence. I'm not going down because some *campesinos estúpidos* screwed up!"

"Sea tranquilo. Be calm. Panic is dangerous. No se atierre."

Vargas swiped a hand across his brow. "Yes, yes, you are right. But what about the truck?"

"Nothing is in your name, Diego," Santos reminded him.

Vargas leaned heavily on the desk. "This is true. This is true." He bobbed his head up and down, calming himself down. "Contact Shirley. Make sure she takes care of

153

everything. She will know what to do. Leave no traces in case the police come looking for the other ones."

Vargas waved a negligent hand and Santos nodded, recognizing the dismissal. He let himself out of the office, closing the door with a soft click.

In the foyer Santos reached to open the door when Cory peeked her head out of the music room. She looked fearfully toward her father's closed office door and then ran for Santos, grabbing him tightly around his torso. She looked up at him with wide, frightened eyes, brimming with tears. They seemed to say, *Don't leave me alone with him.*

He pried her arms away and knelt beside her, gave her a little squeeze. "Don't worry, little one. Everything will be all right."

"Do you promise, *Tio Gabriel?"*

"Si, pequena bebé. Prometo." I promise, Santos thought, as he walked to the Cadillac. But how could he keep such a serious and burdensome promise?

Chapter Twenty-four

Rafe took two days to track the commercial van back to Vargas. With Slater's connections he accessed Sacramento business licenses, company subsidiaries, and organizations they'd long suspected were a front for Vargas' illegal activities.

As the sheriff's office had learned while investigating the councilman last year, most of his wide business activities could be traced back to his mother. A tangled web of dummy corporations, one a commercial van dealership, led straight back to Vargas through a subsidiary in the name of the elder Mrs. Vargas. Interesting leverage, Rafe mused, something he could use.

#

An interesting bit of information came in from one of the few deputies Slater claimed could be trusted in Sacramento. Magdalena Vargas had been missing for several days. No one had seen or heard from her, but then again, no one seemed to be looking for Vargas' wife. Slater explained that she'd contacted him last year about domestic violence, but then withdrawn her complaint.

The story about her disappearance was that she'd made an extended trip to Mexico. Had Vargas been worried his wife knew too much about his illegal activities? Rafe seriously doubted that Magdalena had privy to her husband's wide and varied nefarious affairs.

Torres had set Rafe up with a miniature office down the hall from hers. He swore if he turned around, he'd bump his shoulder on the opposite wall. The space was cluttered with several empty file cabinets and shelves ran along one wall. Rafe was pretty sure the so-called office had been a utility closet and wondered if Torres was punishing him for his many transgressions against her.

In a perverse way, he liked to see her get her dander up. She was magnificent when her eyes snapped with an internal fire, her breasts heaved, her jaw set. Oh yeah, better not go down that road, his head warned, even though his traitorous body had other ideas.

Rafe's cell phone chimed at the precise moment that Torres poked her head into the office where he sat at a desk so small it must have belonged to a midget. He didn't need to check caller ID. He knew by the ring tone that the caller was Max Jensen, but he let it go to voice mail.

"Aren't you going to get that?" Torres asked, leaning against the door frame, her arms crossed against her chest. Today she wore a gray skirt with a slit up the left side that reached above her knee and exposed a tantalizing stretch of thigh. Her legs were bare and she wore very high-heeled shoes, gray striped with the toe cut out. Red nails peeked through the ends.

"Nah," he answered looking her up and down. "I'd rather talk to you."

She raised her eyebrows as if she'd learned not to believe any of his bullshit, but he grinned in what he hoped was an engaging manner. "What? You don't believe me?"

"About as far as I can throw you."

"Have a seat, Torres." He waved an arm around the room. "Oh, sorry, the place isn't big enough for another chair."

She laughed and perched precariously on the edge of the tiny desk, bringing her amazing legs too close for comfort. "You are so full of it, Hashemi." She looked around the small space. "We need to talk. You want to go to my office? I believe it's a bit larger."

"Hell, no, let's talk over lunch," he answered, standing and grabbing his jacket where it lay on the file cabinet.

Torres glanced at her watch and frowned. "Breakfast's barely over."

Rafe's cell rang again and he flipped it open to look at the caller ID. Damn! Homeland Security, Agent McNally, the

156

bastard, probably going to horn in on his case. "I have to take this," he said. "I'll come down to your office in a few minutes."

Torres simply raised those lovely dark brows and flashed an enigmatic smile. "Sure, but I'll expect a full report on that call." She nodded toward the phone he clutched in his hand. "No holding back, Hashemi. Remember our agreement."

She exited the room gracefully, her slender hips swaying beneath the gray skirt. *Moeder van God Mother of God.!* Rafe's Dutch was pretty damn good too.

"Agent McNally, no secret-agent codes today?"

"Stuff it, Hashemi," McNally barked. "What's new on the case?"

Rafe was pretty sure DHS already knew about the interception of the girls outside Reno, the human trafficking angle to the case, but he knew McNally wouldn't be as interested in poor Mexican girls as the kilos of smack they'd found in the van.

"You heard about the girls?" he asked.

"Yeah, yeah, so what?" McNally's attitude confirmed Rafe's suspicions. "That doesn't fund terrorists. Drug money does. What'd you find?"

Slater had kept the information on the girls as tight as possible so apparently McNally didn't know about the drugs yet. "Just the girls," he lied. "Were you expecting something else?"

Silence wafted through the phone like a deadly virus. "No, just wondered," McNally said, his voice sounding like someone who'd swallowed a fish bone. "Doesn't matter anyway."

"Why's that?"

"Because there was a hit on the girls. They're dead."

Rafe didn't care much for McNally or his bulldog tactics, but the shock in his voice was genuine. "Jesus Christ! All of them? What about the drivers?"

"Yeah, all of them." After a long moment, McNally rallied. "Thought you were Muslim, Hashemi."

"Humph, that's why DHS shouldn't do their own thinking," Rafe said quietly, snapping the phone shut.

Shit! How could Vargas possibly have gotten the intelligence in time to make a hit on girls and two fucking Mexican drivers? And how was he going to break the news to Isabella?

#

Bella paused outside Hashemi's office, not at all ashamed that she wasn't above eavesdropping. When she heard the click of his phone, she hurried back to her office. Hashemi was playing footsies with Homeland Security and something had happened. The reference to the drivers meant a snafu in the system.

At her desk she reached for her phone. "Slater, have you heard anything new on the girls?"

She knew something was wrong by the prolonged silence on the other end of the line.

"I'll be right up," he said. "Wait for me."

"Slater, what the ... ?" The line went dead. What was going on? And how did the Department of Homeland Security learn something before the D.A.'s office did? Damn, she should be the first contact person on any new development, but she knew DHS had their sneaky little spies everywhere. Slater had better have a good reason for keeping information from her.

By the look on his face a few minutes later, Bella knew he did. He shut the office door behind him, but remained standing, his arms dangling at his side. He looked tired, spent, and worried. A worried Slater was not something Bella was accustomed to seeing.

"What?" she said, rising from her chair, leaning her fingertips on the desk blotter. "What's going on?" She heard the rising panic in her voice, felt a strange buzzing in her ears as her fingers and toes went deathly cold.

"Sit down, Bella."

"Damn you, Slater! I'm not some fragile doll that breaks under the pressure of bad news."

Slater sank into the arm chair opposite her. "Nevada County assisted in arresting the van drivers and taking the girls into protective custody." That he avoided her eyes was a bad sign. "During the transport from the hospital to the jail this morning, a van forced the two transporting vehicles off the road. There were six of them armed with semi-automatics. Very quick, very professional."

Bella dropped into her chair and buried her face in her hands. My god, how could such a thing happen? After a moment, she raised her head. "How did they know? How could they possibly get to them so fast?"

Slater shook his head and rounded the desk to put his large hands on her shoulders. He dropped a kiss on the top of her head. "It's not your fault, Bella. Hell, no one's to blame."

At that moment Hashemi strode into the room, his face a grim reflection of Slater's. "You heard?" He threw himself into the chair Slater had just vacated and scruffed his hands down his face. "Christ, it was a bloodbath."

Bella winced and felt her shoulders start to shake.

"A little fucking tact, Hashemi, all right?" Slater's voice was angry and threatening from behind her.

Rafe's eyes met hers across the desk. "Sorry, I wasn't thinking."

He shifted restlessly in the chair, his elbows on his knees, hands clasped. "At least there's a little bit of good news. God knows how, but one of the girls escaped the attack. One of my agents has her under guard at a local hospital. I didn't get that from DHS. They think everyone's dead. My agents have her under guard at a local hospital." He paused meaningfully. "And no one knows about the heroin."

"You don't trust anyone," Slater confirmed. "The department, DEA, DHS, anyone could be dirty."

Rafe nodded.

"How is she?" Bella asked.

"Stable, and she'll survive," Rafe answered. "When she's well enough, we'll transport her to a safe house in Placer Hills, probably tomorrow."

"She'll need round the clock protection," Slater said. "I'll put Harris on it. He can be trusted."

Hashemi nodded. "If Vargas can get to the van like that and take out potential witnesses so fast ... hell, he can get to anyone."

"Not to Harris." Slater turned to look out Bella's window behind her, his shoulders set and his face pensive. "You've got a major leak, Hashemi. You need to plug it up before more people get killed."

"Don't you think I know that?" Rafe's face turned dark and an angry blush crept up from his white collar. "God, I want Vargas so bad I can taste it."

Bella rose and walked around the desk, leaning against the edge. "Vargas is a maniac, an insane madman. We'll get him on any charge we can make stick." They all realized it was a kind of truce.

Slater moved across the room and paused at the door. "I've got county business looming ahead of me," he said with a wry smile, "but I'll personally oversee the transport of the girl."

Bella nodded. "She's our only witness. We can't let anything happen to her."

"It won't." Slater walked down the hall, his shoes clicking loudly on the linoleum flooring.

Bella and Rafe were silent for long minutes after he'd left. The weight of this latest discovery lay between them like a fog of grief and disappointment.

"Come on, Torres," he finally said. "Let's have that late breakfast."

"I'm not hungry," she murmured.

"Early lunch, then," he wisecracked, but she could see his heart wasn't in it.

Last night Bella had started putting together a proposal for using Santos as a wedge against Vargas. Dangerous business, but she was convinced Vargas' only weakness lay with Santos. She'd seen something in those flat, dark eyes that'd spoken to her in some crazy way. She wanted to approach the lawyer alone.

Without his boss around.

#

Santos did not mind the intrusion of the attractive Latina ADA into his personal life. He had not completely forgotten how to admire a pretty, young woman. What he minded very much, however, was the uncanny resemblance the woman had to the dead girl whose picture he carried with him always.

She approached him at his home, a sacrosanct habitat which seemed a violation. The persistent ringing of the doorbell interrupted his dinner. He ignored the annoying sound for a while, but when it appeared the intruder would not leave, he wiped his hands on a kitchen towel and looked through the peephole before opening the door.

The woman occupied the small landing to his condominium like an avenging angel, holy retribution surrounding her like a refiner's fire. *Ay, madre del Dios!* This one was a starving dog with a scrap of bone. She would not go away.

"Assistant District Attorney Torres." He barred his teeth and look down his nose at her. "To what do I owe this pleasure?"

The strap of her purse hung over her shoulder and even in her high heels she barely reached his chest. She planted both fists on slender hips. "We need to talk."

"We have nothing to say to each other."

"I think we do, Mr. Santos."

He grinned then, amused that such a little one could be such a fierce warrior. "Why should I talk to the district attorney's office? To do so would only disadvantage me."

161

He moved to shut the door on her, but she inserted her foot into the doorway. He glanced down at her foot, back up to her face, and flashed a warning. "That is a dangerous move, Ms. Torres. Perhaps you should reconsider invading my home in such a bellicose manner."

"Bellicose?" The woman smiled mockingly. "You have a fancy repertoire of language, Santos." He noticed she'd dropped the courteous salutation. "Perhaps you should consider how much trouble you and your boss are in."

"And why should you concern yourself with our troubles?"

"Let me in and I'll explain."

He assaulted her with his eyes, hoping to intimidate her. "As I explained, there is no advantage to me in giving you access to my home."

"How will you know if you don't hear what I have to say?" When he hesitated, she pressed her advantage. "Five minutes. If you don't like what I say, I'll leave."

What was it about this one that caused him to open his door to her, to gesture her into the entry and then into the small kitchen where he prepared tamales and a giant salad? He could only conclude that she had piqued his curiosity. Why else would he made such an incautious move?

ADA Torres could only offer him a great deal of trouble. He thought of the picture stashed in his bedside drawer. *Ay, this little avenger was a world of trouble.

Sí, un mundo del apuro.

Chapter Twenty-five

"I am preparing dinner," Santos said with a courteous nod and a wave behind him. "Come in."

Gabriel Santos possessed the old-world courtliness of Diego Vargas, but unlike his boss, carried it like a natural mantle. Vargas wore a thin veneer of civility, but beneath the fancy façade beat the heart of a thug and a barbarian.

Bella had no overt evidence of the difference between the two men; both, after all, were nasty criminals, but on some gut level she believed for all his viciousness, Santos would consider it rude to renege on a promise. If she convinced him to agree to a deal, he would keep his promise.

He reminded her of a fully-grown Arctic male wolf she'd once seen in a documentary, a beautiful, graceful creature with small, flat ears and a thick white pelt.

But one she wouldn't turn her back on.

Bella hesitated a bare second before deciding she'd gain nothing unless she took a gamble. "Thank you." She dropped her purse on a bar stool in the kitchen area and observed Santos as he finished tossing a salad. The rational part of her brain wondered what the hell she was doing entering the camp of the enemy. She knew for a fact that Santos had killed men. Still, he acted so ... normal, relaxing in his own kitchen, preparing dinner for a guest.

Santos was a cold-blooded killer who dealt in drugs and death, she reminded herself, as she folded her hands on the granite countertop. "Let's talk business."

He pierced her with a strange look before answering. *"Prisa, prisa!* Always hurry. That is not the Mexican way. Slow down. Eat."

Was he serious? Have dinner with a known criminal as if they were best friends?

He must have read the expression on her face. *"Ay,* Ms. Torres, you are not afraid of me, are you?" A hint of humor played around his mouth, cruelly bisected by a giant scar.

She bristled. "Of course not." A moment later she sniffed the air. "What's cooking?"

"Tamales. And my tamales are *muy deliciosos.* The recipe was handed down from by *abuela."*

If dinner was what it took to get Santos to make a deal with her, then dinner it was. "Sure, why not?" She glanced at her wristwatch. "I have a few minutes before I have to meet Sheriff Slater." A blatant lie, but at least Santos would think she was expected somewhere.

They ate in silence at a small bistro table and chairs arranged on the patio which looked down on Sacramento's Tower Bridge. The view of the bridge over the Sacramento River at sunset was gorgeous. "This is very good," she said at last, dabbing her lips with the cloth napkin he'd provided.

"Gracias."

Santos poured coffee for both of them and tilted his chair back, balancing a ridiculously small cup in his large palm. He appeared relaxed and comfortable as he studied her for a few moments. "So what business deal do you offer me, Assistant District Attorney Torres?"

He flashed a shark's smile as if he knew things she couldn't understand. "What proposition is so attractive that I would forsake who I am? Compromise my honor?"

"Honor?" Bella heard the incredulity in her voice.

Santos slammed down the legs of his chair and nearly shattered the cup as he banged it on the table. *"Sí, honor!* Are you foolish enough to imagine that a man such as I has no *código del honor?"*

She would have to tread carefully. "Aren't you the same kind of man as Diego Vargas?" she countered, her voice low.

"Is that what you think?"

She shrugged and spread her hands as if the answer were obvious, but remained silent this time.

164

"Madre del Dios!" Santos leapt from his chair, it teetered to the concrete flooring, and he gathered up the used plates. He marched into the kitchen and began rinsing the plates and stacking them in the dishwasher.

Bella trailed him, leaned against the counter, and watched his swift, economic movements a few minutes. "If I thought you were exactly like Vargas, I wouldn't be here."

Those flat, black eyes in the scarred face studied her intently, as if analyzing the sincerity of her words. "Let us sit," he said, indicating a comfortable white leather sofa in a living room off the kitchen.

"What is your proposition, Ms. Torres?"

She turned sideways beside him on the smooth leather. "I'd like you to testify against Vargas."

The look on Santos' face was comic. "Surely you jest."

"I'm deadly serious, Mr. Santos." She refused to look away from him although she felt the wild pulsing of the vein at her throat.

"And for this testimony ... what do I get in return?"

"Some kind of ... immunity."

"Complete immunity?"

"That depends on how damaging the testimony is."

Santos crossed his legs at his knee, a gesture that would have seemed effeminate in a less commanding man. His left arm rested on the sofa back, his fingers drumming idly on the pristine leather. He jabbed her with those sharp, emotionless eyes until Bella began to feel uncomfortable and considered terminating the conversation immediately.

Without knowing she would do it, she stood suddenly, ventured toward the bar stool where her purse still lay, and retrieved her cell phone. She punched Slater's number on speed dial.

"Why do you wish so badly to catch Diego Vargas?" He spoke at her ear.

She ended the connection. "What?"

165

His gruff voice softened and took on the tone of a priest or therapist. "What sin has *el jefe* committed to make your fight with him so personal?"

She dropped the phone back in her purse, feeling like a young girl caught in a misdeed. "There's nothing personal," she retorted. "I'm just doing my job, the task of putting scumbags like your boss away for a very long time."

Santos' laugh was a booming eruption from his barrel chest. "You should not use such fiery words when you are trying to persuade me of something, *pequeno guerrero.*"

Little warrior! The reference to her small stature irritated her and she scowled at him.

Santos read the precise moment when the decision reflected in the little warrior's face. She took on a conciliatory look, as if she had come to a momentous conclusion. He marked how she struggled between resignation and determination. He admired her strength and hardiness. She sat on the barstool, clutching her handbag on her lap, while he walked around the counter to stand opposite her.

"I don't care about the drugs," she confessed, staring out the patio window to the dark night of the city.

"Oh? What do you care about, Isabella?" He called her by her first name, turning the power balance back to himself. She was too intelligent not to realize what he was doing, but she responded anyway.

"The girls," she whispered, "I care what happens to the babies."

"They are hardly babies," he countered, although he knew in his heart that this was not true. They were all *bebés* in much the same way as Magdalena's Córizon was an infant. Certainly all of them were innocent. Although they did not remain innocent long.

"Why should you care so much for poor Mexican girls you do not even know." Santos forced mockery into his voice so that he would not sympathize with her.

166

She hunched her shoulders and slid off the bar stool. "I lost someone. A long time ago."

He strained to hear her voice.

"I know what it means to lose someone you love."

Santos knew the emotion raging in her face was genuine. She could not be such a good actress as to fool him. *Imposible.* "What do you propose, Ms. ADA?"

"Full immunity in exchange for Vargas."

He roared with laughter. "*Un qué idiota usted debe pensarme!* What an idiot – "

"I understand Spanish," she snapped. "And I don't think you're an idiot, Mr. Santos."

"To betray the man for whom I have worked nearly twenty years. What could possibly induce me to commit such folly?"

"Complete immunity from prosecution," she repeated, standing taller.

"Ah," he smiled and spread his hands as if at the antics of a very young child, "that is what I have now."

Isabella turned fierce again, the combatant preparing the attack. "We will catch Vargas," she spat, her nostrils flaring, "and when we do, you will go down with him. Hard. Your hands are very bloody and you have to pay a price for that."

Santos sat on the bar stool she'd just vacated, his knees nearly bumping her leg. "Let me tell you a story, Ms. Torres. When I was a young boy, my father was arrested by the *federales.* Starved. Beaten. Tortured."

She slumped against the counter, staring at him, her face ashen, her body trembling.

"My father would not tell them what they wished to know." He shrugged. "Finally, they brought my mother and my sister into the village square. 'We will rape and murder them in front of you,' they said, 'if you do not give us the information we need.' He confessed, of course."

Santos smiled without joy. "You see, *él creyó sus promesas.*

"He believed their promises," Isabella repeated.

"Si, but they cut off his penis and stuffed it in his mouth anyway. He bled to death.

Isabella shuddered and Santos knew that his story had made its point. "What happened to your mother and sister?"

"I do not need to tell you that, do I?"

She remained silent, her dark eyes wide and incredibly beautiful.

"So, I ask again, how do I know I can trust you to keep your word?"

She acted as though she would not answer. After a moment she slung her bag over her shoulder and walked to the foyer, composing herself, he believed. There she turned and stared at him across the room. A steely look had returned to her face.

"Look into my eyes and tell me you don't believe me," she said. "I don't lie."

"All attorneys lie," he smiled. "I know this better than anyone."

He sighed heavily and stretched his big body as if he were bored with the whole conversation. "But I will take your proposal into consideration."

"Don't take too long," she warned. "I may regret my sudden generous impulse. The deal won't be on the table very long." She slammed the door behind her after she left.

Santos gazed at the shut door for a very long time after she left. "Touché," he said to no one. Eventually he cleared away the remains of the dinner and sat out on the patio to disassemble his weapons. After he had cleaned them, he stored them in the cutaway behind the kitchen sink. These tasks were merely ploys to avoid looking at the picture, but he would not let his curiosity rule him.

Finally, he prepared for sleep. He sat on the edge of the bed, retrieved the snapshot from his nightstand, and lay down to examine the worn photo. Every detail of what Vargas had done to the girl for a period of five years flashed

168

through his memory, and with them, a rage so unfamiliar that he could not breathe stormed in his chest. He rarely allowed himself the luxury of anger, a futile and dangerous emotion.

A vague glimmer of an idea stirred within him, but he thrust it aside. *Es imposible!*

Nonetheless, tomorrow he would search the public records. He would find out who Isabella Torres once loved so much and lost long ago.

#

When Bella pulled into the driveway of her small bungalow, she recognized the rental car parked at the curb. She punched the remote control to raise the garage door and eased her compact car into the tiny space. Through her rearview mirror, she watched as Rafe climbed out of his car and stalked toward her. His body looked tight and angry.

"Where the hell have you been?" he shouted as she swung her legs from underneath the steering wheel.

She grabbed her briefcase, stood up, and slammed the car door before answering. "Good evening, Agent Hashemi. Wasn't lunch enough of a visit for you? And since when have you begun monitoring my comings and goings?"

They'd lunched earlier, an uncomfortable situation where all she could think of was how handsome he looked despite the scruffiness of his five-o'clock shadow and his mussed-up hair. He'd constantly run his fingers through the dark curls, while she'd tortured herself with the memory of the crisp feel of thickness beneath her fingers.

"Smart-ass," he retorted, blocking her way. "Answer the question. Where have you been?"

"If you must know, working the case."

At lunch she hadn't even hinted at what she planned to do – meet Santos on his own turf. Hashemi would've quashed that idea without consideration. They'd talked a little about the case, more about each other, light inconsequential chatter that said little. But the tension beneath the banter spoke volumes.

Her words now seemed to calm him down. "Oh, that's good. What part of the case?"

She shifted from one foot to the other, wanting to get rid of him and soak in a hot bath. "Look, it's late, I'm tired. Let's talk about this tomorrow."

"No," he insisted, taking her keys from her fingers before she could protest. He walked to the back door, keyed the lock, and punched the remote to close the garage.

He looked back at her. "Are you coming?" Without waiting for an answer, he opened the door and disappeared into her laundry room. What an insufferable, bossy ass! Fuming, but resigned, she followed him into the house.

Chapter Twenty-six

By the time Bella had walked through the laundry room into the kitchen, Rafe had already sprawled comfortably on her living room sofa, removed his jacket, and flung it over a wing chair. She toed off her shoes and hung her jacket in the entry closet. Placed her briefcase on the tiled floor.

"How about something to drink?" he asked from his place on the sofa.

"You're not going to be here that long," she snapped.

"Maybe not, but I'm not leaving until I know where you've been and what you've done."

She blew a strand of hair out of her face. "Now you're starting to sound like *mis hermanos, my brothers.* And maybe I was working on the case at the office."

"Nope. You don't have to translate Spanish for me. And maybe I already checked the office."

"Look, Hashemi, you have no right to make demands about how I spend my time."

"I'm the lead on the case. I have every right."

"I'm the ADA on the case."

"We've had this conversation already." He rose to meet her, stood inches within her personal space, and put his large hands on her shoulders. She shivered and pushed him away a second too late to be effective. Damn pheromones!

"Okay, truce," she said, lifting her hand in surrender. "I'll tell you what I've done – but you don't get angry."

He looked suspicious, but nodded.

"And remember, I don't *have* to give you an explanation at all."

"We'll talk about that after I hear what you did today."

Looking into the refrigerator, she asked, "Beer or wine?"

Settled with a glass of fine Rosé, Rafe propped his feet on Bella's coffee table while she tucked hers beneath her. This position was beginning to look both familiar and dangerous, but she didn't ask him to leave again. She wanted him to stay. They spoke around the case for nearly an hour before she decided to come clean about her proposed deal with Santos.

"We've talked the case to death," he said placing his wine glass on a coaster. "What about tonight?"

She cleared her throat and sighed before answering. "I went to see Gabriel Santos." She looked at him from beneath her lashes, waiting for the explosion, but to his credit, he controlled his temper. However, his jaw worked and his eyes blinked as he made every effort to refrain from yelling at her.

His words confirmed her suspicion. "I'd like to throttle you," he said tightly, "or turn you over my knee and spank the daylights out of you. Or – "

"Okay, I get the idea." She stood and took both their glasses into the kitchen. "Do you want to hear the rest, or just pummel me?"

"I want to do both," he grumbled, following her into the kitchen. "You're the one who insisted Santos was very dangerous. What happened?"

"Nothing. I offered him a deal and he said he'd think about it."

Rafe scoffed. "A deal? You can't offer him a deal. He's going to get federal charges and do federal time, no plea bargaining, nothing."

"Right now, he's in my jurisdiction and if I say plead him out, that's what will happen." She tried to remain calm, but really, the man was such a bully.

He crossed his arms and leaned against the counter, a thoughtful look on his face. "What did you offer him?"

"Full immunity."

"Jesus Christ, Bella!" All she heard was that he'd used her nickname for the first time. "You can't give a monster like Santos full immunity!"

"I can and I will." She bristled with indignation and stubbornness.

"What do you imagine he can give you for this full immunity?

"Diego Vargas."

"What part of Vargas?"

"Everything," she answered smugly, "the drugs, the trafficking, and the girls, enough to put him away for life, or give him the needle if we can prove special circumstances."

"And who do you think is going to take over Vargas' business?"

"No one. The organization will be over, finished, destroyed."

"It doesn't matter," Rafe said dismissively. "Santos will never betray Vargas."

"I think he will."

"Don't be so naïve, Torres. It doesn't become you."

Somehow his disappointment in her hurt more than his anger.

He snatched his jacket off the wing chair in the living room and headed for the front door. "I'll see you in the morning."

He'd turned the knob and begun to open the door when she spoke. "Don't go," she whispered, blinking furiously so he wouldn't see the tears threatening to spill down her cheeks. And why was she crying anyway?

He waited for long moments before he answered her, and when he did, his back faced her almost if he didn't want to look at her. "If I stay, it won't end like last time, Isabella," he warned softly.

God, the sound of her name on his lips made her tremble. "I don't want it to be like last time."

"The case—"

She stepped in front of him and wound her fingers around his neck, running them through the thick, soft hair at his nape. "I don't want to talk about the case." She felt hot and cold at the same time, lethargy and urgency warring within

173

her. Her heart thundered in her chest, her breath caught in her throat, and fire raced through her veins.

She longed for the slow, exquisite pleasure-pain of arousal, but her arms, legs, and body had a mind of their own. She ground her hips against the thrusting bulge in his slacks and pressed her breasts against his chest, her nipples hard and peaked through her thin blouse and filmy bra.

"Oh, God," he spoke against her mouth. "You have no idea how sweet you taste." He trailed a line of soft, moist kisses down her neck. "How incredibly soft your skin is."

When his lips met hers, she opened her mouth beneath them and met his tongue with her own. His breath smelled of the faint tanginess of the wine and a clean sweetness. She felt the sharp nip of his teeth against her bottom lip as he drew it into his mouth. She ran both hands through his hair, loving the way the dense strands curled around her fingers. He reached behind her to undo her hair clasp, and her unruly mane of hair tumbled around her shoulders.

"So beautiful," he said, running the hair through his long fingers, rubbing the ends with his thumb and forefinger as if he were assessing an expensively-textured fabric. Undoing the first three buttons on her blouse, he shoved the edges aside, exposed the lacy top of her white brassiere. He trailed his fingers down her throat and scraped his knuckles over the tops of her breasts.

She shivered again, an uncontrollable spasm like the start of an orgasm, threw back her head, and invited him to devour her neck. He followed his hands with his lips, gently pressing kisses along her breasts, pulling down the bra and exposing her nipple to the cool air. She gasped as he took one peak into his mouth and gently licked it, swirling his tongue around the hardened button. Then he sucked, softly at first, but harder as she pressed the back of his head against her chest and moaned quietly.

A wet gush of sex flowed between her legs and suddenly she couldn't bear the gentle teasing. She wanted hard, pounding passion. As if he'd read her mind, he returned to her mouth and deepened his kisses until the assault left her lips swollen and bruised. Lips locked with his, she scrambled to unbutton his shirt and drag the tail from his slacks. He labored to help her, loosened his slacks, and dropped them to the floor.

"Bedroom," he gasped against her open mouth. "Where's the bedroom?"

She gestured with her head down the hall behind her as he stepped out of his pants, picked her up, and gripped her buttocks as she wrapped her legs around his waist. He continued to assault her face and neck as he stumbled down the hall. Reaching behind her to open the bedroom door, Bella almost tumbled out of his arms, but between laughing and panting, they made it to the edge of the bed. Rafe fell clumsily, twisting to keep his weight from crushing her. Holding himself off her by propping up on his elbows, he framed her face with his large hands.

"We can stop this now, Isabella." He pushed her hair back from her face and trailed his fingers over her cheeks. "We don't have to finish. We don't have to do this."

"You're kidding, right?" she panted. "There's no way we're going to stop now."

She twisted her body to flip him over, knowing he let her because her weight was too slight to accomplish the twist without his help. She couldn't have moved his bulk if he hadn't wanted her to. Straddling him, she finished opening his shirt and spread her hands over the fine, springy hair on his chest. His erection pushed aggressively through her slacks, the thick head seeking her wet, hot center.

"I can't wait any longer," she whispered as he watched her climb off the bed and unfasten her slacks. She stood in her bikini panties and disheveled bra, arms akimbo, as his eyes raked hungrily over her.

He clutched his hand over his heart. "Jesus, you're killing me."

She smiled, heady with sexual power, and reached around to unclasp her brassiere, letting it dangle from one hand before she dropped it to the floor. He sat up and pulled her close so that she stood between his knees. Licking each nipple in turn, he began sucking on them again. Oh, God, she felt as though she would come before he even entered her.

Trailing his mouth under her breasts and down to her stomach, he kissed her navel and dipped his fingers unto her panty waistband to slide the garment slowly down her body. He gently spread her legs and touched her between them, probing the wetness there.

"You're amazing," he said, sliding a finger inside her and flicking his thumb on the taut button of her sex. She felt her climax build and wriggled her hips against his hand.

"Now," she said, "I want you inside me now."

He pulled her down to the bed, shoved his shorts off and covered her body with his heavy weight and her lips with his mouth. "Is this what you want, Isabella?" Her name on his lips was an aphrodisiac as she thrust her hips upward to meet the hard, moist tip of him at her entrance.

"Yes," she moaned. "Yes!"

His voice sounded as if he were in control but his heart raced on top of her, a filmy sheen of sweat broke out on his forehead, and he strained to hold himself back. "Say it, sweetheart, say you want me."

"I want you. Oh, God, I want you. Now!" she fairly screamed and at that moment, he thrust into her hard and fast, filling her until she knew she'd come without any movement on his part. But he held himself still, held himself back, and held her quietly, willing the sweet release of climax to subside. He lay on top of her, breathing heavily until he began a slow, sexy thrusting in and out of her. She felt the pressure building again to an exquisite pleasure that exploded through her body like a dam bursting. She bit her lip and tried to hold the sounds back but they erupted in tiny, helpless gasps and moans.

Rafe pounded into her long moments as she rode the length of her climax out and he spilled himself into her. After their hearts had slowed down and he'd slicked back her hair from her forehead, he kissed her softly and rolled off her, tucking her backside tightly against him.

Bella must've drifted off to sleep, or at least thought she'd dozed because when she awoke, the room was chilly and Rafe was gone. She stretched and looked at the bedside clock. One o'clock. She slipped from the bed and pulled a robe over her naked body.

In the kitchen Rafe leaned against the counter, talking quietly on his cell phone. When he saw her in the doorway, he quickly snapped the phone off.

She padded quietly across the cold tile floor. "Who was that?"

"A cop friend in L.A. I think I've mentioned Max Jensen?"

She smiled slowly, still languid from their lovemaking. "I remember Max. I met him at your office."

"Right." He reached over and pulled her against his side, planting a kiss on her cheek. "Hey, you're cold. Let's go back to bed. I'll warm you up again."

She laughed and ran her hands up under his tee shirt, feeling the smooth muscles and sinews beneath the skin. "I'd like that."

In bed she snuggled beneath his arm as he pulled the covers over them. She loved feeling her naked body against his side, the strength in his arms and the power in his thigh nestled between her legs. She rubbed her fingers over his chest. "What did Detective Jensen want?"

"Personal stuff." He paused to cup her breast and nuzzle her neck. "Family trouble."

"Hmmm." His hands slid up and down her hips to distract her completely.

"He's taking a couple weeks off work and coming up here. He'll give me a hand on the Vargas case."

"Oh," she said. And then again, louder this time, as he worked his magic with his clever fingers and hands.

Chapter Twenty-seven

The untraceable cell phone by Santos' bed stand blared out a strident sound, Diego Vargas' tone signal. Santos glanced at the clock before reaching for the phone. Two a.m. *Ay,* did *El Jefe* never sleep?

"Sí?"

"The shipment has arrived."

A shipment of China White through the Port of Wintuan. Why had Vargas called to relay information which would have come to Santos within the hour?

"Venido aquí rápidamente!"

Santos was instantly alert. *"Por qué?* What has happened?"

"There are problems." Vargas coughed out the words.

"What kind of problems?"

"Do not speak over the phone," Vargas growled. He spat out the next words almost as if he'd forgotten the disrespect Santos had shown. "And do not ask why when I tell you to come. Get your fucking ass over here! Now!" He slammed down the phone.

Santos' security men swept Diego's phones and home every week. There was no possibility that he was being bugged, but *El Jefe* had become rabidly paranoid. Such a man made serious mistakes.

Santos arrived less than twenty minutes later. This current shipment was scheduled for distribution north to Reno and south to Bakersfield. If something was wrong, they would have difficulty getting the price they'd asked. Their contacts did not like to wait for their product.

As he approached Vargas' guarded fortress, Santos noted the added security men at the gate and outside the front door. They recognized him, however, and passed him through at once.

179

At the door, he knocked lightly, not wishing to awaken Corizón, and seconds later, Diego swung open the heavy oak door and waved him in. For the first time since Santos had come to work for Vargas at the age of nineteen, Vargas looked haggard – old. He'd been a robust forty-year-old man then and now was nearly sixty, but tonight he bore the lined face and stooped shoulders of a man nearly a decade older.

Perhaps now was the time for Diego Vargas to retire.

"What is the problem with the shipment?" Santos asked, looking around the huge industrial kitchen where Vargas had led him. This room was Magdalena's sanctuary. She loved to cook and the low ceiling dangled with an array of cooking utensils.

Vargas poured himself a Jack Daniels neat, and Santos could tell by the slack mouth that this was not the boss's first drink of the as-yet very early day

Pedro thinks the shipment is light. We must weigh it again." Vargas threw back his drink in one swift gulp. *"Mi Dios,* I do not have time for such problems!"

"How light?"

"He did not say."

"Pedro always worries unnecessarily," Santos said, leaning against the island counter. *"Tomaré el cuidado de problema."*

"You will straighten it out tonight?"

"Sí, right away." Santos turned to leave as the wall phone in the kitchen rang. A flash of panic ran over Vargas' slack features. *"Qué ahora?" What now?* He grabbed the phone off the hook and muttered into the receiver. "Who is this?" Pause. "Yes," he said shortly. Another pause. "Are you certain that it is him?" Pause. "Allow him to pass."

He hung up and turned to Santos. "Another problem. Alejandro is here."

That meant something had gone wrong with the hit.

Alejandro was brought by two armed guards into Santos' office. *El Jefe* sat behind his gaudy, over-sized desk of

180

expensive teak that he'd had specially made several years ago.

Vargas took in Alejandro's appearance. "What happened?" An ugly line of stitches crossed Alejandro's forehead and ran along his right arm. His face was bruised and battered. "You reported that everything went well." Vargas twirled the liquid in his third drink since Santos had arrived.

"Creímos que todo estaba muy bien," Alejandro babbled, *"pero entonces – "*

"English! Speak English!" Santos roared.

"Que?" Vargas asked, his tone like death. "What went wrong?"

The man was too frightened of Santos looming over him to remember his English. *"Uno de la muchacha escapada!"*

Mierde! One of the girls escaped.

"Qué!" Vargas screamed again. "How the fuck could that happen?"

"No sé, El Jefe," the man whispered. *"No sé."*

"Calm down," Santos said. "Here." He thrust a drink into the man's shaking hands. It was hard to believe Alejandro was a hired killer, but his fear of Vargas and Santos ran deep. "Give us the details."

"There was a great deal of confusion. We thought the job was complete, but later, when we counted the bodies, we were short one."

"Which girl?" Santos asked because that was the most important question.

"Tell me she is not one of the older girls," Vargas said. "Or one who speaks English."

An older girl might be more outraged about what had happened to the younger girls. One who spoke English could relate a compelling story. Mexican girls who spoke English often were educated, intelligent, and outspoken. Vargas did not like either older girls or ones who complained.

"I believe it was Esperanza," Alejandro said. "Most of the burned bodies were small."

181

Ay, Esperanza, she could cause serious trouble. "Where is she?" Santos asked.

"Our contact in Nevada told us she's under guard at some hospital near the Tahoe turnoff. I don't know which one. She is under heavy guard."

At the sound of the girl's name, Vargas turned ashen and then angry. He raised his hand to strike the man, but Santos stepped between them.

"Do not blame the messenger, Diego," he cautioned and motioned Alejandro to step outside.

After the man had left, Santos said, "I will find out where the girl is."

"She can destroy me," Vargas said. "She knows too much and she is the only girl who speaks fluent English."

"I will take care of the girl and the shipment," Santos promised. Do not worry."

At that moment, a noise from down the hallway to the left drew Santos' attention. When he turned in that direction, he saw a naked blonde stumbling through the archway into the living room.

"Wass goin' on, honey?" she mumbled. "Come to bed, baby." She held her bare arms out toward Vargas. Her brassy hair glimmered in the pale light and her tanned, toned body looked lean and muscled.

A showgirl, Santos thought sourly.

"Salga de aquí!" Vargas yelled harshly. "Go back to the bedroom, bitch!"

Even around his young daughter, Diego behaved like a pig. At least when Magdalena was here, he did not conduct himself so carelessly. His boss was deteriorating rapidly, Santos thought.

#

"I need a shower," Bella said, climbing off the bed.

"Great!" Rafe smiled, slipping his hands beneath the sheet and running them over her hips. "I enjoy team sports."

She adjusted the shower spray and water temperature, dropped her robe, and jumped in. Suddenly shy, she was grateful the steam blurred the image of her naked body behind the textured glass of the shower. Through the foggy glass she watched Rafe pull off his shorts and open the door. She thought again how magnificent his dark, coppery skin looked, how the muscles rippled beneath the surface of his flesh, and how fine thick hairs covered his chest and legs.

He wrapped his arms around her from behind and cupped her breasts. "You have the most gorgeous breasts. He kneaded them gently and teased the nipples. "They feel like satin, smooth as silk." He nuzzled her neck, moving his mouth over her ear and gently nipping the lobe.

"Your nipples are so small and pink I want to do this." He turned her around and bent his head to take her nipple and breast into his mouth, the rasping of his tongue an erotic and scintillating texture against her sensitive peaks. He reached for the soap and lathered his hands, running his slick palms over the breasts he'd just worshipped with his mouth and his words. His touch lit a fire in her blood as he smoothed her arms, belly, between her legs.

When he finished, she performed the same for him, reveling in the smooth, soapy feel of him beneath her hands. She took his penis and rolled it between her fingers and loved when he groaned. This time he entered her from behind, languidly and slowly, pressing her against the glass shower as he moved within her and touched her in an exquisite rhythm. At last he pounded into her with an almost desperate urgency and she came at the same time as he spilled himself within her.

When her heart had stopped racing and she no longer felt the thunder of his chest against her back, he turned her around and kissed her sweetly on the mouth and cheeks and neck. "That was nice," he whispered, rubbing her wet arms and back. "You are nice."

Nice? she thought, what a ... mild word.

183

Later they toweled off and wrapped their nearly naked bodies in warm quilts. They sat on the sofa in the living room, drinking hot chocolate. Bella stretched her legs across his lap and he rubbed her feet with his free hand. "This is nice," Rafe said, running his hand up her bare thigh.

"What's with the N word?" Bella teased, half disgruntled.

"What?"

"Nice, you keep using that word."

"You don't like it?" he laughed. "I'll find another one."

"It's just so ... pedestrian."

"Pedestrian? Like a jaywalker?"

She punched him lightly on the arm. "Not like a jaywalker, silly, just ... ordinary, average."

"Oh, baby, you're anything but ordinary." He leaned over to kiss her knee, opened the front of the quilt, and gazed at her chest. "And those are ... God, nothing less than spectacular."

She flushed and pulled the blanket around her. "You're embarrassing me," she protested.

He ruffled her still-damp hair and laughed. "But you're so gorgeous when you blush." He winked. "Gorgeous," he repeated, "not at all pedestrian."

She stood, let the quilt fall away from her body, and reached for his mug, wiggling her hips in her skimpy panties as she strutted into the kitchen.

Rafe followed her, reaching for her waist and missing. "Oh, no, baby, not ordinary at all." He caught up to her at the sink and swung her around, bringing his lips down to hers. "I think I'm addicted."

She felt his erection pressing through his shorts into her stomach and laughed. "At least some part of you is."

He lifted her long hair off her neck and pressed a gentle kiss her behind her ear. "Wanna try again?"

She reached inside his shorts. "I'm game."

Then Rafe's cell phone vibrated annoyingly on the counter. "Shit," he mumbled.

"Leave it," she said, working her hand up and down his hard length.

"Ah," he groaned before pulling away with a painful grimace. "I can't." He took a deep breath and flipped open the phone. "Slater," he said, nodding at Bella.

Suddenly embarrassed for no reason she could have explained, other than Slater was on the other end of Rafe's cell phone, she went into the bedroom and slipped on underwear, jeans and a heavy shirt. Rafe remained standing at the counter, naked but no longer at full alert, she noticed. His brow was furrowed in a thunderous disapproval. He reached down and pulled up his shorts, then brushed by her on his way to the bedroom.

She stood in the doorway, watching him put his clothes back on. "What's wrong? What did Slater want at this hour?"

"The girl's ready to talk," he said. "Slater's driving her down here himself. Has a safe house all picked out."

"Good, that means she's well enough to travel."

"Evidently." Anger etched every line of his face and his movements were stiff and hurried. "He wants us to meet him there, but won't identify the place until I'm on what he calls a secure line."

"Why? Doesn't he trust you?"

"He says there's a leak." He paused before scooping his wallet, badge, and change off the dresser. "And he's sure it's not in his department."

"He thinks it's on your end."

185

Slater gave Bella the directions to the safe house, but only after she called him from a pay phone halfway between the courthouse and the unknown location. "Are you sure all this secrecy is necessary, Slater?" Bella complained from the phone kiosk. "It seems like overkill."

His voice sounded tinny over the phone. Poor reception? "After the hit on the van carrying the girls? What do you think?"

"I guess, but ..." She looked over her shoulder at the gasoline pump where Rafe stood beside his car, drumming his fingers on the hood. "Hashemi's pretty angry about it."

Slater laughed shortly. "He'll get over it."

"Still, he's in charge of the case."

"All the more reason for him to plug the security leak he's got. Pass the message on," Slater ordered before hanging up on her. So much for her being able to handle Ben Slater. She settled into the passenger seat and waited for Rafe to buckle up and start the engine before passing on the directions to the safe house.

Rafe glanced over at her. "What took so long?" When she remained silent, he mumbled, "Slater was giving you grief about the leak, wasn't he?"

"He's got a point. Vargas' people found out about the girls long before they could possibly have using normal intelligence venues."

He rapped the heel of his hand on the steering wheel. "I know, but I don't see where they could've gotten the information from. Every damn member of my team has been security cleared dozens of times – background searches, known affiliates, tax returns, family members – very deep checks."

"You should probably have them all investigated again, just to be sure," she suggested.

Rafe took his eyes off the road to gaze at her, a thoughtful expression on his face. "Maybe you're right. There's a breach somewhere, but it looks deeply buried."

After a thirty-minute, silent drive northeast, they arrived at the safe house location, an unoccupied summer home at a higher elevation in Bigler County. Rafe pulled the car onto a gravel driveway behind Slater's truck and a squad car.

By the way he clicked off the ignition and turned to face her, Bella knew he'd been planning what to say the whole trip up into the foothills. He blew heavily through his mouth and scraped his hands over his heavy beard. Then he reached for her, placing his forefinger over her lips, his eyes dark with an emotion she couldn't read.

"We should talk about last night." He brushed a strand of hair off her cheek, trailing his fingers along her jaw line.

She nodded.

"We can't ... we shouldn't let this ... thing between us get in the way of the case," he murmured.

She leaned her cheek against his hand and closed her eyes. "Maybe last night was a bad idea."

He drew back as if she'd slapped him, then gripped the wheel and stared straight ahead as the front door to the house swung open and Slater's large frame filled the frame.

"Hell, yes, it was a bad idea," he finally said, sounding impatient, his jaw working furiously. "But we can't take it back."

"Are you sorry?" she asked.

Rafe opened his mouth to answer, but by that time Slater was tapping on the driver's window and the moment had passed. God, Bella thought bitterly, was last night just a fling for him? Having a one-night stand – how pathetic was that?

She swung out of the car and walked around the back bumper to join Slater. "Where's the girl?"

Slater looked from her to Rafe and back again, as if he were sizing up the situation, aware that something was amiss. "She's inside. Fell asleep on the way down here and I didn't have the heart to wake her up."

He peered into Bella's face again, and she wondered what he could see written on it. Slater was too astute to miss the emotions playing there, and she was too unschooled to hide them. "Are you okay?" he asked, placing a large hand on her shoulder.

She shrugged him off and fled up the small flight of wooden steps into the house. Snow would cover the grounds this high up in the winter so the houses were built up off the ground on wooden frames. From the entry Bella moved into a single, spacious room which contained a kitchen at one end and a living area at the other.

Waylon Harris and Deputies McKidd and Ruiz from the Bigler County Sheriff's Office sat at the kitchen end of the room, surrounding a table where they sipped coffee from mugs. Harris, a tree trunk of a man with skin like polished ebony, jumped up from his chair to greet her. Bella suspected that he had a bit of a crush on her because he seemed to fall all over himself whenever she was around.

Deputy Ruiz was a new recruit, a hefty Hispanic man with a brush of moustache above his lip and eyes that danced with humor. Slater would've assigned Ruiz to this case because of his Spanish background even though Bella herself spoke the language fluently. Slater liked covering all his bases.

McKidd, a tall, bony redhead with large freckles in a ridiculously young face, seemed all arms and legs as he sprawled on the tiny kitchen chair. He'd just popped a powdered doughnut in his mouth and white dust sprinkled across his sparse, reddish soul patch.

Rafe and Slater trailed in from the car. After Slater made introductions all around, everyone poured a first or second cup of coffee. Rafe, Bella, and Slater took the chairs at the kitchen table, while Ruiz, Harris, and McKidd returned to their posts guarding the two entrances to the house.

Rafe checked out the front of the house, noting the wide window that opened onto the gravel drive. The back door led to a deck from which a long stretch of stairs wound downward to a dirt embankment and a copse of slender pines. The entire back wall consisted of floor to ceiling glass windows and the view through the glassed wall was spectacular, but he wasn't interested in that.

"What's the girl's name and how old is she?" Isabella asked as she added sugar and cream to her coffee.

"Esperanza. Says she's thirteen, speaks English very well," Slater answered. "She's exhausted."

"Was she injured in the fracas?" Rafe asked from his position by the window.

"Took a bullet to the upper shoulder and she's sore, but it's not serious," Slater replied.

"What's going to happen to her?" Isabella asked. "When this is all over, I mean."

"After we get the information, she'll go back to Mexico," Rafe answered, not meeting her eyes, knowing she'd go back where she came from, but there'd be no happy ending for her. "Hopefully, she has a family still waiting for her."

"Hopefully, she wasn't sold into slavery and prostitution by that same family," Isabella snapped.

Rafe ignored the anger in her eyes and directed his question to Slater. "Has she said anything yet?"

Slater nodded towards the behemoth Deputy Harris and tapped his own chest. "The four of us – you can see we're not such dainty men. I was waiting for Bella. I think a woman will work better with the girl."

Rafe wondered how Slater had managed to find such a good safe house on such short notice. Good location, isolated, gravel to alert vehicle approach, and only a few trees to hide someone coming up on foot. "Whose place is this?"

"Friend of a friend of a friend, who's vacationing in Italy. This is their second home, completely untraceable."

"Good," Rafe grunted. "The girl's in there?" He gestured towards the hall to his left where he could see several closed doors.

"Second door on the right," Slater answered, glancing at his watch. "She should be awake soon."

As if on cue, the door swung open and a young girl, hardly twelve or thirteen, barefoot and sleepy-eyed, wandered to the end of the hall. She was skinny and dirty, but Rafe could tell she'd be a beauty when she was older, wide round eyes surrounded by long, sooty ashes, skin the color of sun-kissed copper, and a look of sadness on her face that would break a man's heart.

Isabella approached Esperanza, introduced herself, and asked if she'd mind talking to her. The girl glanced at the two men first and, drawing her brows together, finally nodded before turning around to go back into the bedroom. Isabella followed.

An uncomfortable silence descended on the two men as Rafe joined Slater at the table. Rafe could see Harris positioned by the patio door and assumed the other two deputies were posted at the front.

"I guess it could be Nevada County," Slater said, apropos of nothing, after a few minutes of silence.

Rafe looked over in surprise. "The leak? You think?"

Slater shrugged. "Not really.

"But part of it could be," Rafe speculated. "The Nevada hit was awfully fast."

"That's what I was thinking."

Rafe raised his eyebrows. "Shared responsibility?"

"Something like that."

"So the Nevada hit was a Nevada leak," Rafe concluded. That sounded right to him. "Law enforcement?"

"How could it be anything else?"

"And Lupe?"

190

"Your confidential informant in L.A.?" Slater asked. "That one had to be a DEA leak, don't you think?"

Rafe hated the idea, sure no one in L.A. could've tied Lupe to him. They'd been rigidly cautious. Still ... "Shit. It looks like it."

"We can't take any chances with Esperanza's life," Slater warned.

Rafe glanced down the hall to the closed door behind which Isabella was getting details on the hit from the girl. "No, no risks."

Another few minutes passed while Rafe alternated between looking out the large glass window that filled the entire southeastern wall and the closed bedroom door down the hall.

Suddenly another comment, completely out of the blue, came from Slater. This one floored Rafe. "Are you sleeping with her?"

"What the fuck?" Rafe choked on his coffee.

He guessed that Slater hadn't missed the careful avoidance Rafe and Isabella had maintained – the tension between them, not touching, eyes sliding off the other's – so he wasn't as completely surprised by the question as he should've been. Shit! They'd really complicated the case by what they'd done last night. "None of your goddamn business!" he growled in warning.

"Oh, but it is," Slater said in a matter-of-fact voice, "my business, that is. See, Bella's like a little sister to me. I don't want to see her hurt."

At least that cleared up the relationship between the two of them. "Are you so certain I'll hurt her?"

Slater leveled him a hard look. "Maybe, maybe not. I'm here to make sure you don't."

"Shit, all she needs is another brother."

"Yeah," Slater laughed. "And it's not like Bella can't handle herself."

"She's pretty tough." Rafe smiled in memory, mopping up the spilled coffee with a paper towel.

"Still ... she's not so tough in her heart."

Slater was referring to Isabella's lost and probably dead sister. Maria.

"Yeah," he conceded.

#

The microfiche records were surprisingly easy to access in the state archives. Twenty years ago the story caused quite a media blitz. Young Mexican immigrant family. The father a migrant worker, the mother domestic help, but they managed to educate their seven children. The girl Maria was her class valedictorian, a Rhodes Scholar, and the first family member to go to college.

Then she'd disappeared on a graduation trip to Mexico with three of her best friends. The three remaining girls were no help in providing the police with details about how Maria has vanished. But Santos was fairly certain he knew exactly where the girl had gone. After a few months the newspaper coverage waned and eventually dwindled to nothing. By the time the girl was really dead, there wasn't even an anniversary article in the local paper.

Five years.

Maria Anna Torres had lasted five years at the cruel hands of Diego Vargas.

Santos pulled the worn photograph out of his jacket pocket and held it up beside the grainy newspaper photograph on the microfiche screen. The resemblance was unremarkable, although both girls had long, dark hair and wide black eyes. Both were Latina, but the girl in the newspaper photo wore a white graduation cap and gown. In Santos' picture, she was thinner, bare shouldered, and heavily made up.

But he had no doubt the two pictures revealed the same girl. The resemblance to Isabella Torres was uncanny, and the details of the disappearance and presumed kidnapping of

Maria Torres matched what Santos remembered from twenty years ago.

He shut off the machine and placed the photo back in his pocket. Every moment of the transport of the cargo was etched in his memory more vividly than the long, slow death of his own father in the town square in *Real de Cantorce.*

Santos was not a man to indulge in regrets. A man must do whatever is required to survive – and to thrive. But, by God, he wished he had slit the girl's throat instead of handing her over to Diego Vargas. He told himself that if he had known what would happen to her, how the few nights would become months and the months become five long years, he would never had brought her to Reno.

Never left her in the hands of such a man.

But Santos was a young man then, voraciously hungry for the many things that Diego Vargas could offer him.

Chapter Twenty-nine

Bella sat in a corner in a wicker chair while the girl Esperanza crouched on the bed, her slender legs drawn up to her chest, her arms folded around them. Bella had never seen anyone look so hopeless in her life, and her heart wrenched with sympathy at the thought of what she'd gone through.

Bella was careful not to touch Esperanza and lowered her voice into soft, soothing tones. "Can you tell me what happened, Esperanza?"

The girl hunched her shoulders and stared at her feet.

"Sheriff Slater tells me you speak English. *Puede usted hablar inglés? Can you speak English?*

"Sí," the girl mumbled.

"Bueno." Bella smiled reassuringly. "Can you tell me how you came to be in the van with the other girls?"

"Son todas muertas," Esperanza whispered instead of answering the question. *They're all dead.*

"Lo siento mucho. I'm very sorry." Bella scooted her chair closer to the bed. "Where are you from?"

"Toluca." So far south in Mexico. How did she end up here in northern California, Bella wondered?

"Were you kidnapped?"

The girl wet her dry lips. *"Sí,* some men came to my village near *Toluca* and took four of us. Several girls were already in the van. When we arrived in *Tijuana,* the rest of the girls were there."

"How did you get across the border?"

"No sé." She shrugged and picked at the threads on the bedspread. "But it was night and the roads were very bumpy, like dirt roads. Perhaps the *ladrones* found a place that was not patrolled carefully."

"Did you see the faces of any of the men who took you?"

She shook her head and looked embarrassed that she couldn't give better information. *"Solamente los conductores."* Only the drivers.

"What about at the two stops. Did you see anyone else?"

Esperanza scrunched her face and concentrated. "In *Tijuana,* there were two other men. *Muy grandes.* They spoke English some of the time."

Bella pulled a photo six-pack from her briefcase and spread the pictures on the bed. "Do you recognize any of these men?"

"Mí Dios, sí! I will never forget his face." She pointed to the picture of Diego Vargas. "He was in *Tijuana.* He forced the girls into the van."

Bella felt a shiver of excitement run through her. She'd made a clear identification of Vargas. "What else can you tell me about him?"

"He is a very bad man."

"What happened?"

"Once we had crossed into the United States, we stopped somewhere, I do not know where. One of the girls was very young, perhaps ten or younger." Esperanza began crying and swiping at the tears with her dirty fingers, leaving long smudges on her smooth cheeks. "He took her away for a very long time."

Bella felt a chill begin at the bottom of her spine and travel upwards to her neck.

"When they brought her back," Esperanza whispered, "she was bleeding very badly. She died shortly after."

Bella tapped the photo of Gabriel Santos. "What about this man? Do you recognize him?"

Esperanza took the picture and held it close to her face. "No, I have never seen this man."

Bella clenched her fists and tried to command her rational mind to control her emotions, but she couldn't stop thinking about Diego Vargas and his unspeakable brutality. This girl's testimony would be enough to put the monster away for a very long time. And Bella intended to see that happen.

#

Santos made the flight from Sacramento International Airport to LAX in a little over an hour. Two Nortenos picked him up at the airport and left him with a Ford Explorer rental.

Forty minutes later he waited impatiently for the inside man to make the prearranged appointment on the Terminal Island side of the Vincent Thomas Bridge. Santos remained in the Explorer even when he saw the contact pull up to the parking area in an unmarked squad car, and he remained there until the man slipped into the passenger seat of the Explorer.

Santos looked at the tip of his cigarillo as he blew the smoke slowly out his nostrils. "You are late," he said after a few moments.

"Couldn't be helped." The man kept his wraparound sunglasses fixed on his face so his eyes could not be seen, but Santos recognized the edginess, the restless legs, and the wandering hands – all signs of discomfort. What did the man have to be nervous about?

"El Árabe thinks there is a leak from the Los Angeles area," Santos said.

"Don't call him that," the man snapped. "He's as American as me. More than you, my south-of-the-border friend."

Santos let the offense slip by. After all, he did not intend for this American to be around very much longer. When his usefulness ended, he would disappear. Already the man's value to Vargas' organization was questionable.

"So why the all-fired hurry for a meet?" the contact asked.

"El jefe is not happy that the information you have been sending us is tardy."

"Like I give a fuck how Vargas feels."

"Caution, *mi amigo impetuoso,* you should take great care about what Diego thinks."

196

The man cracked his neck, twisting it one way, then the other. "Tell him I've got it covered."

"He will want to know the details."

"I'm going up north to Bigler County."

Santos raised both eyebrows. "Oh?"

"Yeah, I've got a connection there."

"Bueno." Santos placed a large paw on the man's shoulder. "Diego will be very happy, and when the boss is pleased, he rewards handsomely."

#

The attack on the safe house occurred shortly after two o'clock in the morning.

Rafe had driven north to investigate the possible leak in the Nevada County Sheriff's Department, make some confidential calls regarding his own department, and Bella had gone to her office to prepare her case against Vargas.

For the first shift Slater assigned Ruiz to the front door, McKidd and Harris to the back, while he stretched out on a cot in the hall by Esperanza's bedroom door. He could hear the girl moving around in the room, the squeaking of the bed springs and then the flushing of the toilet.

He imagined she wasn't going to sleep very well tonight. He'd have to make long-range plans to protect her. Moving her around seemed the best security until the trial ended. And with Vargas' long reach, who knew how long that could take?

Slater must've dosed off because a foreign sound, the dull clank of metal on wood flickered through his subconscious and brought him springing to full alert. He reached for his handgun lying on the floor, and slipped it out of the holster as he sat up and swung his legs over the edge of the cot. As he stood, he quietly turned the knob on the girl's bedroom.

She lay quietly under a pile of blankets, black strands of hair the only thing he could see from his angle. He eased the door shut and, clinging to the wall, traced his steps back through the great room to the patio window. He saw Harris' broad frame backlit against the pale glow of the moon, but McKidd wasn't in sight.

Suddenly Harris hunched over, weapon in hand. Slater still couldn't see anything, but obviously something had drawn the deputy's attention. He strained to see what had alerted Harris, holding his breath, tightening his grip on his weapon. *Where the hell was McKidd?*

Focused on the scene in the back entry, Slater didn't hear the front door open until a floorboard suddenly creaked behind him. He swung around, raised his weapon to fire, and aimed at a large, dark shadow lurching toward him. But he wasn't fast enough and all hell broke loose.

Slater took the first bullet high in the chest, the pain of it searing through his muscle and shattering his clavicle. He got a round off before he was spun around from the impact, but it went astray. The second bullet caught him low in the back and he wondered briefly if it would paralyze him. The third one sank deep into his thigh.

At the sound of the first report, Harris flew through the back patio door, crouching low, aiming his weapon, and firing like a madman. The first intruder went down with a shot to the head and one to the chest, but the second one managed to hit Harris in his upper thigh, close to the groin. He went crashing down like a felled buffalo, his handgun skittering across the floor.

A third hitter entered from the front landing and ran down the hallway.

No, Slater screamed silently, feeling his blood drain steadily onto the hardwood floor, knowing he was helpless to keep the attacker from getting to the girl. Shivers started to rack his body, his skin felt clammy, and his mouth was parched. He recognized his body going into shock.

As the second shooter advanced on the defenseless Harris, Slater panted shallowly and tried to scrabble out of the way, reaching for his backup weapon at his ankle. But he was too weak and his arm flopped uselessly.

198

He clamped his chattering teeth together and made a last-ditch effort. He hardly felt the weapon leave its holster, but suddenly the grip was warm against his damp palm.

The second hitter loomed over Harris and lifted his gun for the head shot when Slater's bullet took out the back of the man's skull. Harris lay sprawled on his back, bleeding profusely from his leg. A hit artery, Slater thought wildly, knowing there was nothing he could do, trying to crawl towards his deputy anyway.

Then Slater heard the girl's screaming above the roar in his head. She raced out of the bedroom into the hall and ran smack into the third hitter. Slater saw Harris' fingers jerked faintly in an attempt to reach his discarded weapon.

At that moment, another figure entered through the glass patio door behind Harris. Slater opened his mouth in warning, but no sound came out. A hard blow to the back of Harris' head with the butt of a semi-automatic rifle and all movement stopped. God, Slater thought, they were all going to die here. Now. Right before he passed out, he glimpsed the round sweating face of Manuel Ruiz as it twisted into something vicious with satisfaction while he loomed over the fallen, and surely dead, Harris.

Eyes fluttering shut, from a distance Slater heard faint jumbled words: *"No! Qué – haciendo?"* and a muffled response *"El jefe dice –,"* followed by a final blast of gunfire.

His last thought was, *Thank God Bella wasn't here.*

#

"Slater, Slater, can you hear me?

Bella's pretty face, worried and damp with tears, floated in front of Slater's eyes as he fluttered them open.

"Esperanza?" he moaned. "Is she alive?" His voice petered off into the creaky sound of an old man and he tried again. "Did they get her?"

Bella shook her head. "Let's just worry about you right now."

Slater felt the motion of the gurney beneath him as she placed her hand on his forehead. "What happened? Christ, is everyone dead?"

"They're taking you into surgery." She gripped his hand. "Don't worry. Rafe and I will handle everything." He saw the sheen of tears in her eyes and felt the soft press of her lips on his before his lids became so heavy he couldn't hold them open.

He heard Hashemi's voice at his feet. "You'll be okay, man. They'll fix you up."

That must mean the girl was dead, Slater thought, as a ton of grief and guilt pressed on his chest. And he must be dying because Bella would never kiss him on the mouth, and Hashemi hated his guts after the little talk they'd had about her at the safe house.

Suddenly, the memory of the slaughter that'd happened there panicked him and he struggled to sit up. "Ruiz," he muttered weakly. "He's – "

Heavy hands held him down. Hashemi's, he thought. "Take it easy, man. Calm down."

A moment later a mask descended over his mouth and he floated off to a blessed, undulating oblivion.

#

Santos knew the text message that came through as he boarded a plane from LAX to Sacramento was meant for Vargas and had somehow been sent to his by mistake: *Se acaba. It is done. What next?*

Santos settled back into his first-class seat and fumbled with the seat belt before responding. Hasty action was not his style and he hadn't ordered any moves against the witness or anyone else. After all, many things could happen between arrest, arraignment and trial that could extricate Vargas from the charges ADA Torres brought against him. Santos was a cautious man, but rushing in headlong without thinking about the consequences was exactly the kind of action that Diego Vargas would take.

Quién? Who? He texted back.

A few moments later the answer in English: *prime + 3.*

That meant the girl plus two others were dead. *Mierda!* Santos swiped a hand over his face as the auditory warning that all cell phones were to be turned off came over the speaker phone from the flight attendant. *Theirs?* he asked.

Sí. 2 + M.R. ours.

Fuck! M.R. stood for Manual Ruiz, their informant in Bigler County. The girl was surely dead, along with three deputies or agents, whoever had been guarding her, probably the sheriff included. Ruiz had become a casualty,too, either accidentally killed during the attack or eliminated by the assassination team under Vargas' direction.

Santos wondered if the lovely ADA Isabella Torres was one of the casualties and felt a brief unfamiliar wave of regret. More likely the sheriff and deputies.

And, if they were fortunate, *el árabe,* the DEA agent.

But, Mother of God, how was he to clean up this mess? And who had survived the slaughter?

Chapter Thirty

"That bastard!" Anger and sorrow warred for a place in Isabella's expression. She dashed at the tears that spilled down her golden cheeks.

Rafe wrapped an arm around her shoulder and walked her toward the hospital exit doors. "There's nothing we can do about Slater now. He's in good hands."

She shrugged out of his hold and turned away as he reached for her again. "I'm not leaving him."

He stared at her back, thinking Isabella could easily have been at the safe house when the hit occurred. She could've been talking to the girl, and right now lying in the operating room, fighting for her life or sprawled on the safe house floor riddled with bullets. He clenched his fists at his sides.

Goddamn it! He should've protected her better, protected them all. But he was too tunnel-visioned to see the rat scurrying around in his own house. And he still had little more than an inkling who that rat was.

Five feet away from him, Isabella hunched over, her arms holding herself as if a terrible pain gripped her. He ached for her, for Esperanza's death, and for the possible loss of a good man like Ben Slater, but he fell back on rationale to reassure her.

"The surgeon said it would be hours before Slater came out of the operating room," he said logically, turning her around to face him. "Be reasonable. You need to get some rest."

He glanced at the black and white wall clock which hung unattractively over the nurses' station – six-thirty in the morning. "You won't do Slater any good here."

"What if he ..." Fresh tears started down her face and her nose ran.

He wanted to kiss her red cheeks and puffy eyes, but he handed her a handkerchief instead. "He won't. The man's too fucking stubborn to croak on us."

Isabella laughed, a sad little attempt that sounded like a dying songbird. "Yeah, Slater's obstinate as hell."

He tried to coax a smile from her. "Must be where you learned it from."

Twice within a few minutes he'd heard her swear, something she rarely did, and he knew she was under a lot more strain than she admitted. "He's going to be okay, Isabella."

She nodded solemnly and touched his upper arm. "Yeah, sure."

He sighed heavily and tried to reason with her again. "If you don't want to leave the hospital, let's go to the cafeteria and get some coffee."

When they reached the lower level, the cafeteria's security gates were down over the kitchen area, and they settled for vending machine coffee and stale breakfast rolls. They chose a small table near the back exit doors of the nearly empty room. Several nursing staff sat across from them and a custodian mopped at a corner area to their left.

Isabella ignored her coffee and stared through the glass windows into the dark night, the security lights dotted across the walks and parking lot. "I told her she'd be safe," she finally whispered. "I told Esperanza everything was going to be all right."

"You couldn't have known."

"No, no, you're wrong. I know what kind of monster Vargas is. I should've anticipated this move." She ran her fingers through her dark hair, loosening the knot at her neck until it fell messily around her shoulders. She looked young and vulnerable with her hair down and her face free of makeup.

"Slater's the expert," Rafe contradicted, blowing on his coffee although it was barely lukewarm. "He thought she was protected. Hell, I thought she had enough protection too."

"Poor Esperanza," she murmured. She looked exhausted, shadows under her eyes and lines around the sides of her mouth. "One minute she was a young schoolgirl, probably on her way to the market place, and the next minute her life was a living nightmare."

She covered her face with her hands and let the sobs take over.

"Ah, Bella, don't ... please don't cry." He jerked his chair as close to hers as it would go and pulled her into his arms. "I hate it when you cry."

The nurses across the way gave them a strange look, but Rafe supposed they were used to displays of grief in a hospital. Bella sobbed until her tears soaked the front of his shirt and then pulled back to look at him. "I keep thinking of Maria," she whispered."

"Ah, baby, don't do this to yourself."

"I can't help it. Maria left home just like Esperanza did. She kissed us and said goodbye, took a flight to San Diego and a bus across the border with a group of her friends." She wiped her nose with the heel of her hand. "And that's the last we heard of her, the last we saw her." She clutched at his shirt. "Just like Esperanza."

"What did the police do to find Maria?" Rafe asked, knowing they wouldn't have done much, couldn't have done much except make official contact with the Mexican police. And a young Mexican-American girl like Maria – she would've been easy to kidnap, easy to hide down there. The family didn't have a chance in hell of finding what happened to Bella's sister.

She shrugged. "They made a lot of noise, but in the end we knew that her being a Latina was a disadvantage. No one was going to look for a poor immigrant man's daughter." She smiled bitterly. "Maria wasn't even born in this country. They weren't going to search for her too hard."

"I'm sorry." Rafe rubbed her shoulders through her thin shirt.

She straightened up, a determined look on her face. His arm fell away. "Vargas had something to do with Maria's disappearance."

"Bella, be reasonable. You can't know that for sure."

She clenched her fist against her breasts. "I know it here," she insisted.

"Even so, even if you're right, Vargas would never admit it. And he wouldn't remember one girl twenty years ago."

She sighed deeply and slumped against him again. "You're right, but this thing just ... sometimes it consumes me."

"You can't let what happened to your sister get in the way of nailing Vargas for what we know he's guilty of," Rafe reminded her.

She'd thrown on jeans and a long-sleeved shirt when they'd left her house, but she now shivered, whether from the cold room or the topic Rafe couldn't tell. He draped his jacket over her shoulders, picked up their empty coffee containers, and threw them in the trash receptacle across the room.

When he walked back to their table, he sat down and searched her face intently. She seemed calmer now. "We have to talk about what this attack at the safe house means."

Nodding, she clasped her fingers together on the table top and leaned forward, all business. "The hit was a bloody assassination. They meant to kill everyone, including Harris and Slater, the other deputies, along with the girl."

She nodded solemnly.

"Let's start with who had access to the safe house, hell who even knew about it."

She ticked them off on her fingers. "You, me, Slater, and the three deputies assigned to guard Esperanza. Six people," she said bitterly. "Harris is Slater's right-hand man; McKidd and Ruiz I don't know."

"What about the Nevada police?"

"They knew she was being transported, that Slater signed her out, but they couldn't have known where they went." She bit her bottom lip and clutched his hand. "Rafe, we didn't even know until an hour before we arrived at the safe house."

"They could've been followed from Nevada."

But she began shaking her head before he'd finished. "Not with Harris and Slater riding shotgun. No one gets by Ben. He's too good."

Rafe remembered the bullets that Waylon took. "How is Harris recovering?"

"One bullet nicked an artery and the other was a through and through. He was very lucky, lots of blood loss."

"The killers must've thought he was dead, Slater too. McKidd and Ruiz were killed at the scene."

"Harris is out of surgery and stable now."

"We should talk to him again."

But an hour later, when they made their way up to the third floor, Harris was under heavy sedation, a unit of the blood he'd lost pumping in through an IV tube. They decided to let him rest. Slater was still in the operating room, a team of doctors working feverishly over him, but a surgical resident came out and told them he was holding his own.

"You go," Bella told Rafe, standing close to him. "You've got work to do on the case. I'll wait here and call you when there's something to report."

Rafe nodded. He hated to leave her alone like this, but he needed to get to the morgue, see if they'd identified the dead bodies of the two intruders, and then contact his DHS contact. Find out how the hell Vargas' team got to the safe house so fast, where they got their information.

He pulled her tighter and she didn't resist him when he lifted her chin, tracing his thumb along her lower lip. "You going to be okay?"

Her mouth quivered but she nodded bravely.

"That's my girl." He touched his lips to her mouth briefly and hugged her, liking the warm, full softness of her against him. "We'll get this son of a bitch, Isabella," he whispered in her ear, the hair at her temple soft against his cheek. "I swear to God we'll get him."

#

Rafe's cell phone rang as he was climbing into his car.

"Hashish, old man, where are you?"

"Max? What the hell?" He inserted the key in the ignition and fastened his seat belt with his free hand. "Where am I supposed to be?"

"Uh, at the airport? Picking me up?" Max Jensen laughed. "Dude, you forgot about me, didn't you?"

"Ah, Christ, Max, all hell's broken loose here." He backed the car out of the parking space and headed toward Douglas Boulevard. "Yeah, I forgot. Okay, I'm about an hour away. Hang out till I get there, okay?"

"Nah, I'll get a taxi. Just give me your motel and room number and I'll meet you there."

"You sure, man?"

"Hell, yes. Don't worry about me, Hashish. I'm a big boy. I know how to make my way around."

Rafe stopped by the courthouse to pick up the coroner's report and a stack of documents. When he reached his motel over an hour later, Max was waiting inside the room.

He'd flashed his police badge and finagled the desk clerk into letting him in. Now he sat on the worn floral occasional chair, his feet propped up on a coffee table, a bottle of Jack Daniels in one hand and a glass in the other.

"How long you been here?" Rafe asked, surprised the detective had gotten there first, considering the distance from the airport.

"Just walked in." Max took a deep swallow and refilled his glass. Judging by the near-empty bottle, Rafe knew it wasn't his first drink. Even though he was close to being wasted, he didn't slur his words. Rafe remembered that in college, Max

207

could drink his frat brothers under the table and still ace an early-morning exam the next day.

"So, what's the big disaster here in Podunk, California?" Max asked.

"Our sole witness in the Vargas case was murdered this morning," Rafe said, suddenly bone-weary and wanting to sleep more than anything else.

"No shit!" Max exclaimed. "What happened?"

Max already knew about the hit on the transportation van and the deaths of the other eight girls and the drivers. Because the two men had California drivers' licenses, Rafe had asked Max to run their names through the L.A. databases. No hits, but Rafe had figured the licenses were fakes anyway.

"Long, sad story," Rafe answered, loosening his tie and slipping off his shoes. He sat on the edge of the bed and stared at his linked fingers. "Christ, Max, I'm so tired of this crap. Vargas and his organization have destroyed so many lives." He thought of Isabella and her sister Maria, of the drug overdoses and the girls sold into prostitution. "If I don't nail this fucking son-of-a-bitch soon, I'll go nuts."

"You will, old man, you will."

Rafe shrugged and flipped open his cell phone. "God, I hope so." He punched in the speed dial number for Agent McNally at the Department of Homeland Security.

"Excuse me just a minute." Rafe stepped into the bathroom, lowered the toilet seat, and sat down. When McNally answered on the other end of the line, Rafe went through the security code protocol even though he felt like a fool. Through the crack in the bathroom door, he could see Max laughing and made a circle with his forefinger at his temple.

"Did you find anything on the prints?" Rafe asked when McNally paused long enough for him to get a word in. He'd called DHS to run the prints on the Mexican van drivers when Max hadn't come up with anything.

"Zip."

"What about the girl Esperanza?"

"The Mexican police don't have anything on her, not even a missing person's report."

"Shit." Rafe rubbed at the growing pain in his right temple.

"You've got a fucking leak on your end, Agent Hashemi, and you'd better plug it quick."

"Or what, McNally? Or you'll take over the case? Don't be an ass. And don't be so sure the leak isn't on your end." He snapped the phone shut, wondering just how long it'd be before his superiors pulled him off the Vargas case.

"Trouble?" Max asked when Slater left the bathroom.

"A shit storm," Rafe growled. "There's a leak from somewhere and I'm afraid it's in my own department."

"Anyone in mind?" Max asked casually.

Rafe took three aspirin, downed them with a swig from the liquor bottle. "Not a single idea."

Chapter Thirty-one

When Slater was wheeled from recovery to his room in the intensive care unit, the nurse warned Bella to limit her visit to the allotted five minutes. "He's stable, but critical," the horse-faced woman in her starched white uniform ordered, "so don't tire him out."

Bella stared at him as he lay there with his eyes shut, face swollen and bruised. Tubes and IV lines, along with an oxygen hookup and other machinery made him look like a kind of recovering Frankenstein. He was naked from the waist up and his chest bandaged in criss-crossed sections.

Earlier she had insisted that she be allowed to read the medical report. The purple and red flesh of his left shoulder contrasted starkly against the white bandage that covered the spot where the first bullet had been removed. A second bullet had struck a rib from the back, but fortunately missed the lung and the spine. Another bandage wrapped around his right thigh where the third bullet penetrated the skin and barely missed the femoral artery.

"Slater," Bella whispered, touching his arm gently.

His eyes fluttered open. "Hey, Torres." He smiled briefly and closed his eyes, but opened them a moment later. "Glad you're here." He struggled to sit up.

"Oh, no, big fellow. The nurse will skin me alive." Bella carefully pressed him back on the slightly-elevated bed. "And where else would I be but here at a time like this?"

He groaned. "Whoa, I'm weak as a kitten. World's spinning a little."

"You've been through major surgery." She fiddled with the covers and plumped up the pillow. "But the doctor says you'll be fine. Eventually."

He sighed and glanced at the tubes and machines surrounding him. "A hell of a thing."

She pulled up a chair beside the bed and sat down. "I was worried about you." She patted his arm, almost afraid to stop touching him. "Your mom called. She'll be here tomorrow."

"And Kate?"

"She's flying back from D.C." Slater's girlfriend Kate Myers was on special assignment in Washington.

"I don't want them to worry about me."

"Can you recall any details of what happened?"

Slater's jaw tightened under the pallor of his skin. "I've been remembering them since my mind crawled out of the damn anesthesia. That fucking Ruiz. He was the leak. In my own house, dammit." His fist tightened on top of the covers. He killed Harris."

"No, no, Harris is okay, recovering, probably faster than you. You saved his life."

Slater breathed a heavy sigh of relief. "Good God, I knew the second shooter went down from my bullet, but I was sure Ruiz had killed Harris."

"Ruiz?" Bella gasped. "The new deputy? Are you sure, Slater?"

"Hell yes, I saw his face. He was definitely after me and Harris, probably killed McKidd."

"I can't believe it," she said. "He seemed so ... friendly."

"Shit, how could I have made a mistake like that? I vetted him personally."

"He must've been deep," she said, covering his hand.

He shook his head, throwing off the words of comfort. "I trained him myself. I totally bought that young Hispanic pulling himself up by his bootstraps crap!"

"Nothing popped on him?"

Nothing. No priors, no gang affiliations. Zip."

"That's all you could've done," Bella said, "but it makes you wonder why something didn't flag on him. You don't go from a clean record to an assassin with multiple kills."

Slater was silent a moment, thinking. "Only one way he could've gotten by my screening."

Bella shook her head and frowned, not understanding.

"Deep cover, like you said, but with an assist from someone with deep pockets," he said with grim satisfaction. "Vargas must have recruited Ruiz, kept him clean for years, and placed him in my house."

"To be used like this," Bella finished, understanding at last. "When he needed him inside a police department."

"To silence a witness," Slater ground out. "And kill one of my deputies."

"And try to kill you and Harris."

"Son of a bitch!"

Bella watched the head nurse stroll by and peer through the glass doors of the ICU room. Checking up on her, she supposed. "We'd better be careful. The East German nurse just slipped by, spying on us."

Slater tried to laugh, but clutched his side. "Tell Harris to visit me before he leaves."

But at that moment Harris popped into the hospital room, glancing guiltily behind him and hopping in on a crutch. When his eyes fell on Slater, stretched out like a mummy on the narrow bed, wires all over the place, his face turned dusty. "Ah, hell, Sheriff, are you as bad off as you look?"

"I always liked your tact, Waylon."

"Sorry, sir."

"Looks like you're healing up nice."

Harris tapped his thigh, wrapped in a waterproof cast liner. "Yeah, I was pretty lucky the first bullet caused a slow bleed, cracked the bone. Otherwise I'd be dead." He hovered over Slater's bedside and looked seriously into the sheriff's face. "And, 'course, a slug to the head woulda been the end of me." Harris looked solemn as gratitude molded his dark face. "Thanks."

"What are you talking about?" Bella asked, feeling panic rise in her throat. "What bullet to the head?"

"Slater managed to deflect a bullet meant to kill me. Damn Ruiz – excuse me, ma'am – he tried to take me out. *Me, his partner."* Anger and indignation glistened on his brow like a slick sheen of sweat.

"Well, Ruiz is gone now," Slater said with deadly pleasure. Bella had never heard him so satisfied over someone's death. "One of the assassins shot him."

"Why?" Bella asked, but she knew the answer already. Vargas didn't want anyone alive to testify against him.

"What about you?" Harris asked. "How long before they let you go home?"

"A week, maybe," Slater answered, but Bella was certain it'd be longer. Dark shadowy smudges lay beneath his eyes, he'd lost weight, and he looked bone-tired.

The nurse entered, eyeing both Bella and Harris. "What's going on here?" she demanded in a strident and voice. "I thought I made it clear – one patient at a time, five minutes, no more."

Properly chastened, Bella kissed Slater on the cheek. "I was just leaving," she murmured, heading for the door.

But Harris simply glowered at the nurse, and under the weight of his large frame, she retreated with a loud humph and a noisy stomp. Bella waited quietly at the door.

"Better get back to your bed, Harris," Slater advised, catching Bella's eye, "or the East German nurse will have your ass."

Harris laughed his deep belly chuckle and then turned solemn. He gripped Slater's hand, the one without the IV catheter, and squeezed hard.

"Ben," he choked out, "I ... I can't ..."

"I know, Waylon. Me too," he said gruffly. "Go on, deputy, get out of here."

#

All Bella could think of as she left the hospital was coming up with a proposal to entice Santos into turning on Diego Vargas. She had a twinge of guilt at keeping the plan from Slater, but one voice of opposition – and Rafe's was loud and clear – was as much as she could handle.

213

How on earth had Vargas managed to maintain such deep cover in Bigler County? A rabidly vicious man, nonetheless, he wasn't particularly clever. He tended to react rather than act. She didn't think he could have kept such wide-range and tight control of his organization without a lot of help from men far smarter than him.

Santos, for one. And a whole slew of traitor cops – Sacramento, Nevada, even in Bigler County where Slater was so scrupulous about investigating his new candidates. The hierarchy and organizational structure had to have been in effect for years, decades even.

The enormity of it boggled her mind.

Ruiz was only one of the infiltrators, but there were sure to be others they'd have to uncover. First, they had to get their own rat inside Vargas' organization.

And if she had her way, that rat was going to be Santos.

Whatever she had to do to get the bodyguard-lawyer to agree to testify against Vargas – that's what she'd do. When she put her mind to something she was indefatigable as hell and stubborn as a mule to boot. She wondered briefly about Rafe's department. Slater had suggested that someone inside Rafe's realm of contacts was leaking information to Vargas. Was that possible? She had a hard time believing Rafe wouldn't be as scrupulous as Slater, but even Ruiz has slipped by Ben's cautious vetting.

By the time she reached her office at the courthouse, it was late afternoon and there were dozens of messages to deal with, phone calls to return, and briefs to prepare for her other court cases. She'd been working for an hour when Charles Barrington barged into her office without knocking on the closed door. "Mr. District Attorney," she said in surprise, "what can I do for you?"

Barrington hardly ever made him way across the street to the old courthouse, preferring to enjoy the comforts and lushness of the brand new structure where he'd set up his own offices. She knew immediately this wasn't a social call.

214

The D.A.'s round pink face was screwed up like a baby getting ready throw a temper tantrum.

"What going on with the Vargas case?" he demanded.

"We lost our witness," Bella said as Barrington strode into the room and threw himself in the chair opposite her desk, slouching like a petulant teenager. "Along with a deputy. Waylon Harris is being released today and Slater's out of surgery and stable. Thanks for asking," she added, the sarcasm barely controlled.

"What did you do?" Charles accused.

Bella could feel her face coloring with anger. "Why do you assume I'm the one who screwed up?"

"You're in charge," he retorted.

"Oh, really? I thought the feds were in charge. The DEA specifically." She didn't want to cast blame on Hashemi for the debacle at the safe house, but Barrington couldn't play it both ways. He's the one who insisted they turn the case over to the feds.

He waved his hand over his head as if her remarks were unimportant, or worse, ridiculous. "Don't get territorial, Isabella. And whatever you do, don't get on the wrong side of this Hashemi guy. I want this case closed as soon as possible. It looks bad that you're dragging your feet. I want someone charged and convicted. Soon." With that he stomped from the office, slamming the door behind him.

#

The first step Santos intended to take was to contact the Latina assistant district attorney and acquiesce to her no-doubt inadequate plea bargain. He imagined the agreement she offered would not give him the terms he required, but he did not worry about renegotiating to get more lenient consequences for himself.

The greater advantage would be acquired by having her approach him, but time was of the essence and he could not wait longer for her to contact him. *El Jefe* was becoming as

215

dangerous as a trapped animal, and his next movements would be unpredictable.

Santos looked up from his desk where he was examining the books when Jesús Navarro knocked quietly on the office door. *"Sí?"* he barked. He did not like his employees to disturb him when he engaged in the important task of analyzing Diego Vargas' private records.

"Excúsame, por favor, jefe." The man held his hat in his hands and twirled it between work-worn hands.

"Que?"

"Tenemos un problema grande. No sé qué hacer. Ayúdeme, por favor," the man began babbling, the words falling over one another as if he would strangle on them.

"Inglés!" Santos commanded. "Speak English." Spineless man, he thought. Why was Diego so unwise in his choice of men to carry out his most delicate assignments?

Navarro took a deep breath and began again. "We have a serious problem. I do not know what to do, *jefe."*

Santos threw down his pen and rubbed at the pain that began to radiate from between his eyes. "What is the problem?"

"Ruiz is dead."

"Mierda! Mala suerte de mierda!" Santos ranted, forgetting his own junction about using English. "God dammit!"

"But the girl, she is dead, as *El Vaquero* ordered."

Santos' brows pulled downward as he felt a great white rage build within himself. *Pinche cabron!* Vargas was a fucking pig with no sense of caution or finesse. He rampaged through a delicate situation like a bull gone mad with the lust of blood.

"At the sheriff's safe house, *sí?"*

"Sí, in the foothills to the north."

"What other casualties?"

"Ruiz and the other deputy, but not *el hombre negro." The black deputy.*

"And Sheriff Slater?"

"Él está condiciones criticas, pero sobrivivrá."

"English!" Santos roared as he felt a strange relief that the sheriff would survive.

Chapter Thirty-two

Several hours after Charles Barrington stalked out of her office, Bella closed up her files, grabbed her briefcase and drove home to her bungalow in Placer Hills. Rafe waiting for her on the front porch, sitting on the cement landing, his fingers linked and dangling between his legs.

A warm thrill of pleasure ran through her when she saw him. She almost felt like she was coming home to ... to someone who cared. Ridiculous, but the feeling made her irrationally happy. She smiled and waved as she pulled her car into the garage and then met him at the front door. But when they entered the small house the mood changed without warning. The reality of their trying to forge a relationship in the midst of a major investigation struck Bella as foolish. They both paused in the tiled entry, a sudden awkwardness festering between them as they warily eyed one another.

Rafe saw the hesitation he'd been feeling reflected in Isabella's eyes. "What now?" he asked, his eyes caressing her smooth face, his hands skimming down her sleeved arms. He knew they were both too tired for any romantic shenanigans, but he'd wanted to see her – for just a moment or two. The debacle of failing to secure his young witness was an overwhelming defeat. If Isabella rejected him now, he'd feel the sting of remorse even more. It was tempting to blame Slater since Ruiz was clearly the one who'd informed to Vargas, but Rafe had grown steadily more uneasy since the death of his confidential informant in L.A. He was becoming more certain that another leak coming from DHS or is own department accounting for the multiple blown covers and direct hits since he'd taken over the Vargas case.

"Do you want to stay?" Isabella's large brown eyes flashed in the dimly lighted foyer. A tiny frown marred the perfect

218

skin between her brows as she chewed on her bottom lip with her teeth.

A wave of relief washed over him as he thought about catching that lip with his mouth. "Of course I want to stay. I wouldn't leave you alone after the hell of a day we've had."

"Is that it, then? You want to protect me?" She sounded defensive and searched his face as if looking for the answer to some unfathomable mystery. But he was just a man and today, of all days, he didn't have solutions to much of anything.

He placed his hands on her shoulders, noting how his dark flesh contrasted against the lighter creamier skin of her long, slender neck. He smiled at the intensity of her words and her confronting stare. "I want to keep you safe."

She turned away, pulled off her jacket, and hung it carefully in the closet, then turned to reach for his. He followed her into the kitchen where she turned on the coffee maker and began to prepare the brew.

"What's wrong, Isabella?" He enjoyed the feeling of her name rolling off his tongue.

She gave a tiny shake of her head instead of answering him.

"No, I'm not going to let you get away with that." He placed his hands on her shoulders and leaned his body into her back, marveling at the slender bones of her shoulders and arms. "Something's bothering you besides the attack. What's wrong?"

She reached for the mugs on a high shelf and his hands dropped to her waist. "What are we doing, Rafe?" she asked on a sigh.

He allowed his hands to drop further so that they rested on her hipbones. "God, I don't know. I just want to be with you. I can't seem to control that."

Briefly she leaned back into him, her bottom soft and firm at the same time in the way that women were. His arousal was immediate. A tiny moan escaped her as she rested the back of her head on his chest, the mugs clattering to the countertop with a jarring sound. Rafe ran his hands up her sides from her hips to her midriff, playing with the soft silkiness of her blouse. His cock thrust demandingly at her bottom, an appendage with a rogue mind of its own.

Tracing the undersides of her bra, he trailed his fingers back and forth beneath the lacy garment until he reached the spot where her nipples swelled through the layers of fabric. He felt them harden beneath his thumbs, tight round nubs that he had a mindless urge to kiss and lick. He imagined his tongue swirling around their hardened peaks, and he ground his hips into her rear, as if seeking entry.

Nuzzling her neck, he placed tiny, wet kisses on the line of tender flesh from the juncture of her neck to her ear lobe and back again. Her labored breathing increased steadily with every touch of his lips on her skin. He inhaled the heady, mixed scent of her cologne and her damp body, and thought he'd like nothing more than running his tongue along the flesh of her inner thighs, of seeking out and then breathing in thescent of her arousal.

"What are you doing to me?" she moaned, turning in his arms and wrapping her hands around his neck, pulling his head down to kiss him hard and demandingly on the lips. He thrust his tongue to meet hers and tasted the sweetness of her breath and the wet softness of the inside of her mouth. Her fingers fumbled with the buttons of his shirt, her hands trembling.

He laughed as his own breath came short and quick. "Here, let me."

"Okay," she breathed on a shudder and busied herself tugging at his shirt tails until they loosed from his trousers. Then she ran her hands up and down his bare back and around to the hair on his chest. "I love this part of your body," she whispered as she dipped her fingers down to the funnel of hair below his navel. She unbuttoned his pants, trailed the zipper down, and reached around him to the flesh of his ass.

"Whoa, slow down," he panted, wanting to savor the moment but prolong it at the same time. Quickly, he wriggled his pants over his hips, stepped out of them, and toed off his loafers. He kicked trousers and shoes aside and stood in front of her in his shorts. Looking down, he saw the outline of his erection rigid as a two by four against the white of his underwear, straining to poke through the opening. Bella pulled the shirt off his shoulders and that piece of clothing dropped to the floor.

"Now you," he said, unsnapping her skirt and letting it puddle around her ankles. Underneath it, she wore only skimpy black panties. As he ran his hands around her hips, he fingered the bikini cut and the lacy softness of the material against her belly and thighs. He trailed his hand between her legs and tested her dampness through the underwear.

"You're wet for me," he marveled, a surge of possessiveness humming through his blood.

"Yes," she gasped as he slipped his thumb beneath the panties. "I want you badly. Now. Inside me. I don't think I can wait."

He laughed again, although his own heart was racing like a engine and his cock threatened to jerk off on its own journey. "I won't make you wait," he promised. He pulled her blouse off her shoulders, unfastened her bra in haste, noting the trembling of his hands as he worshipped her flesh with them, and contrasted the sleek paleness of her against his dark fingers. She stepped out of her shoes as he scooped her up in his arms and hurried down the hall to the bedroom.

They tumbled onto the sheets and somehow she landed on top of him, her lush breasts pressing into his chest with a soft silkiness that drove him mad. She attacked his mouth with fierceness and opened her legs around his hips. "Oh, Rafe," she cried when she came up for breath.

221

Feeling her at the edge of her climax, he pulled back, both hands holding her head, thumbs running across her high cheekbones. "Wait, let me catch my breath. I want you to come first."

"Oh, I can't wait ... I'll explode," she groaned.

He flipped her over, ripped her panties off her, and opened her legs. He thumbed the thin line of hair on her pubis, dipping down until her felt the moist peak of her clitoris. He bent his mouth to the core of her flesh and suckled, gently at first and then with increasing intensity as she bucked against his mouth, her fingers tangled in his hair, her hands urging him against her. He entered her with his tongue, all the while rubbing the swollen nub of her clitoris until he felt the first tightening surge of her muscles. He thrust harder, using his finger in simulation and roiled his tongue around her. A wash of her juices emptied onto his fingers, but he kept working her until the last spasm of her orgasm subsided and she no longer clenched his head between her thighs.

She sighed a long, releasing breath of pleasure and with a final passionate kiss between her thighs, he inched up beside her. His cock, hard and hot, lay against the moist coolness of her belly, and he gently kissed her nipples, working his way up to her mouth.

"Hmm, I can taste myself on you," she said.

"Good," he answered. "I like the taste of you."

A flush of color crept up her neck to her cheeks. "I've never ... no one's ever done that to me before."

"Good," he repeated, pleased for some foolish reason to think he was the first to pleasure her like this.

"I liked it."

He raised an eyebrow as he traced lazy circles around her nipples and under her breasts. "Liked it?"

A broad smile lightened her face, her teeth flashing white in the dim light. "I loved it," she corrected. "I loved what you did with your tongue." She kissed him hard. "And with your

222

fingers." She pushed her tongue into his mouth, scraping over his teeth and probing the inside. "And your mouth."

"You little tease," he growled as he covered her body with his own."

"Now it's your turn," she smiled and spread herself wide to accommodate him. He growled, a throaty sound that came from deep in his chest, and pulled her close. "Come here, you." He buried his face in her hair and inhaled deeply as if he were breathing in her very soul. "You smell good."

Hours later, sated and relaxed, Bella prepared a light supper and afterward they lounged on the couch, the television tuned to a sitcom rerun, the volume turned low. Rafe took her legs and stretched them across his lap, gently rubbing her feet. She felt languid and drowsy.

"You still look beat," he said, brushing his hands over her calves.

"Emotional tiredness," she said. "All that carnage ... I can't stop thinking about it. I alternate between feeling helpless and being furious."

Rafe nodded and ran his hands over her thighs, the gentle kneading relaxing and arousing at the same time.

"I promised that girl ... promised Esperanza that she'd be okay. I feel like I failed her."

"No one could've anticipated what happened. We did all we could," he soothed.

"What do we do now?" she asked.

"We use your plan," he answered, squeezing her calf. "We get Santos to turn," Rafe answered

"But you said – "

"I know," Rafe interrupted, "but now everything's different. If we have to get in bed with a killer to catch a bigger killer, then that's what we'll do."

"Who do you think it is?"

"Besides Ruiz? The inside man?"

She nodded.

"I don't know yet. But I'll find out and when I do ... "

She sat up and reached for his face, tracing her fingers down the stubble on his cheeks, running them across his lips. He sighed heavily and splayed his fingers through the hair at her nape and lowered his lips to hers. A delighted thrill ran through her, tired as she was, and she opened her mouth to him. The steady pounding of his heart rumbled through her hand on his chest, and suddenly she wanted him again, close to her, no clothes between them, his large, warm hands sliding down her body. She tugged at the tee shirt he'd slipped back on. His bare flesh beneath her fingers was warm and smooth and he smelled of the mingled scents of their sex.

He groaned as she reached his chest and played with his flat, hard nipples. "God, Bella, what you do to me." He shoved her lightly backwards onto the wide sofa and covered her body with his, pulled her robe off her shoulders and bared her breasts. He lowered his mouth and –

Isabella's portable phone jangled alarmingly on the end table right by their heads.

"Let it go," Rafe murmured, busy with her breasts and his clever tongue.

Her breath shaky, she whispered, "I can't. It might be important ... about the case." She reached over her head to grab the receiver off the set and answered quietly. "Torres." No sound came out and she cleared her throat. "Torres," she repeated.

"What the fuck are you doing with the case?" Only Barrington was rude enough to call her at home at this hour of the night.

Bella pushed the speaker phone button and placed the receiver back on the handset.

"Have you worked something out with Hashemi?" Barrington demanded.

"Uh," Bella said, staring at Rafe's narrowed, dark eyes, heavy with desire. "I'm working on something with him right now."

224

"Good. I don't need to remind you that he's got powerful friends in high places."

"Well, maybe I should sleep with the guy then," Bella quipped, her mouth inches from Rafe's, his breath hotly sucking the air out of her. "Maybe then he'll let me in on the action."

"Do whatever you have to do," Charles said coldly. "Just don't screw this up again." He paused before he slammed down the phone. "And don't let them take all the credit, either."

"Well, you heard him," she moaned as Rafe tongued her nipple and moved lower to her navel, tracing lazy circles down her body. "I ... have to do ... whatever ... you want."

"Hmmm," Rafe said, sliding downward and pushing aside her panties to reach the wet, hot core of her. "It's never wise to ignore your superior's orders."

Chapter Thirty-three

"I'm going to be there with you when you make the deal."
Rafe braced himself against the bathroom door, his fingers
gripping the top of the door jamb.

"No, I have to do this alone," Bella answered, her face
warm with insistence as she leaned against the counter and
wrapped her arms around her chest. "And besides, he won't
go for the deal if you're there."

"He won't go for it anyway," Rafe argued, "and if I'm there
at least I can add some pressure."

"No," she repeated, turning back to the mirror.

Shirtless, the pair of shorts revealing his long legs, Rafe
glared at her. The flesh of his chest was burnished copper
with dark tendrils of hair curling around the middle and
funneling downward to disappear beneath his waistband.
"He's got to know the feds give him a better deal."

"Santos won't go out of state, and you could send him
anywhere in the country. Besides, it's my deal to make," she
insisted stubbornly.

"That's stupid, Isabella." Rafe's dark brows slashed in the
middle of his forehead like sharp swords. "A man like Santos
is too dangerous for you to confront alone. Don't even
consider it."

His bossy tone rankled her and she took a breath to lash out
when Rafe's cell phone buzzed on the dresser top. He held
up a finger to show her they weren't finished with the
conversation, a signal that forced her to control an eye roll.

He barked into the phone, eying her through the bathroom
door. "What?" After a moment, he continued in a more
controlled tone. "Ah, Max, shit, man, I forgot you were
staying in my hotel room." He ran his fingers through his
hair and the edges stood up wildly. "Sure, yeah, whatever

226

you say." He nodded, listened a moment, and then repeated an address. "Fine, I'll see you there."

He turned back to Bella. "Max," he said unnecessarily.

"Your cop friend from L.A.?"

"Yeah, he's split from his wife and came up to get his mind off the situation."

"Why here?"

"He was raised in northern California. I think his family still has property up here." He laughed shortly. "And he probably wants a distraction from his personal problems. Thinks getting involved in my case will help."

Admittedly, Bella had little contact with Max Jensen, but knew he and Rafe had some history. "You must be good friends."

"We are," he said shortly. "Look, Bella, let me go with you when you bargain with Santos."

She shook her head, but kept her voice even. "I'll be fine." She smiled gamely. "The wild beast likes me, remember?"

"That's what I'm afraid of," Rafe muttered. "He likes you too much."

"I'm counting on that to get what I want from him."

"It' a dangerous game you're playing." He reached for her as she wrapped her arms around his middle. He smoothed her hair back from her forehead. "Santos is like an alligator. He strikes with cunning unpredictability when you least expect it. You can't know what he's going to do from one minute to the next."

"I know what I'm doing." Bella allowed the smallest note of exasperation to creep into her voice. "You have to trust me on this."

Rafe glowered at her as she twisted out of his arms and ran a brush through her hair. She half expected him to argue further, or at least haul her over his shoulder and carry her off, cave-man style to some imagined safety. She braced herself for more discussion, but he simply stared at her, a calculating expression on his face. As he spun around to leave the bathroom and make his way through the bedroom where they'd begun the discussion, she wondered what plan he was concocting.

Slipping on a robe, she caught up with him in the small kitchen where he'd just poured himself a cup of coffee. She stood beside him at the counter, reached across his large body and pulled down a mug for herself. They stood silently side by side, his back leaning against the countertop, her facing the coffee maker percolating the brew.

Rafe sighed. "All right. I won't force you to let me in on the meet with Santos."

She smiled. "Good."

"Even though I could."

She merely lifted an eyebrow by way of challenge.

"I could take over the entire investigation. Make my own federal deal with Santos. Get to him ahead of you."

She dropped her jaw. "You wouldn't."

Suddenly serious, he spun her around to face him. "Yes, Isabella, I would. If I thought it would do any good, if you wouldn't go off half-cocked and do something reckless out of sheer stubbornness. But for now I'll settle for you acting responsible around this thug."

The tone of his voice, worried and sympathetic at the same time, warmed her. She leaned into his] body, drawing a little comfort for the task ahead. She had to cut a deal with a monster in order to catch in her net what was undoubtedly a larger monster.

Gabriel Santos was the devil incarnate. Of that she had no doubt. He'd been responsible for the death and destruction of countless victims in his role as enforcer for Diego Vargas' drug cartel. But she had a personal stake in seeing that Vargas went away for the rest of his natural life. She believed he had a hand in her sister Maria's disappearance twenty years ago, even though she had absolutely no proof.

"What are you going to offer him?" Rafe asked at last.

"I'll take the death penalty off the table," she answered promptly, even knowing Santos wasn't the kind of man who'd submit to life in prison.

Rafe shook his head. "He'll never go for it."

Bella shrugged.

"What do you expect from *him?*"

"As much as I can get. Vargas and his connections for sure, more if I can get it."

"For life without parole? Santos is a wild animal. He won't let himself be caged like that."

She knew Rafe was right. She read the worry written on his face, concern for her safety.

"I'll be okay," she said, edging away. "Don't worry."

Rafe captured her face in his hands, the long brown fingers rubbing across her cheeks, the thumbs trailing sensually over her lower lip. She caught his thumb between her teeth as she rested in the cradle of his thighs.

"I'll be careful," she promised again. "I won't let him trick me. I just need to get everything from him that I possibly can."

"Don't let him hurt you, Isabella," Rafe whispered into her ear, his breath warm at her temple. "I'll have to kill him if he hurts you."

#

Rafe had just left the hospital where he'd checked up on Slater, whose condition was much improved. Slater had told him everything he remembered about the attack at the safe house. Who else, Rafe wondered, had Vargas gotten his hooks into early on and set him up as an informant for the cartel? He hooked up his seat belt, started the ignition, and swung his car onto the freeway, heading toward the courthouse where he knew Isabella was cementing her deal with Gabriel Santos.

Max Jensen called again as Rafe stopped at a gas station to purchase a northern California map. He slipped on his sunglasses as he merged with the traffic on Interstate 80.

229

"Hashish, old man." Max's voice held an undertone of forced conviviality.

The strain of his marriage must be getting to him, Rafe thought. "Are you okay, buddy?"

"Nah, Hash, I'm a fucking mess."

Rafe tried to laugh. "Just like my case, huh?

"Sounds like I came just in time to rescue your ass." Max's tone didn't quite measure up to the words.

Since Isabella didn't want him at the courthouse anyway, Rafe thought, why not drop by and cheer up Max? "I'll be there in thirty," he said, flipping the cell phone closed.

He followed the directions Max had given him to the house in South Highlands. Max greeted him at the door of a ramshackle stucco house whose lawn needed mowing and whose wood trim needed painting. "So, the Vargas case is a mess, huh? Good thing I'm here to solve everything for you."

"Yeah, man, I could use a fresh set of eyes." Rafe looked around the porch landing at the general air of neglect and lifted his eyebrows in inquiry. He knew Max was a neat freak.

"Uh, listen, this is my grandma's place. She's in a nursing home, but her only son, my Uncle Brett, hasn't gotten around to selling it yet. He's letting me bunk here for a while."

"Sounds great. I'm in a lousy extended-stay motel."

"Hey, Hashish, why don't you grab your stuff and stay here with me? It'll be great, just like old times at Stanford."

Rafe hesitated, wanting to stay at Isabella's, wondering if they'd complicated matters by moving their relationship up a notch. On the other hand, maybe distance would help them remain objective on the case. And he wasn't sure he was ready to share his personal relationship with Isabella just yet. Even with his best friend. And at the far back of his mind, a little warning jiggled that he couldn't quite figure out.

"Hell, why not?" he finally answered.

#

The first meet with Santos took place in an isolated area off the American River Parkway near Discovery Park. Bella left her car in the designated parking lot and walked the short distance to the park alone.

A deputy and an agent waited by the car, armed and looking fierce. Rafe had battled her over the location, the time of day, and the lack of protection, but she'd made it clear that Santos wouldn't talk to her unless he was certain he couldn't be overheard. Or recorded. She carried her cell phone ready to speed-dial for help, but although she didn't feel completely safe, she wasn't really concerned that Santos would harm her. Killing an ADA was a stupid move, and Santos was too crafty to let emotion rule him. She was counting on that. In fact, she suspected that it'd been Santos who'd kept Diego Vargas in check these last few years. Anyway, *El Diablo,* as she'd heard Santos called, had made the initial contact.

At this hour of the day, the area was lively with bikers and dog walkers, and Bella waited at the place Santos had designated. She heard him before she saw his bulk looming through the shadows of the trees, even though he trod carefully. She guessed he didn't want to startle her.

As he approached her, he searched the area around them with those fathomless black pits. He reminded her of the *gigantes y cabezudos* of the Spanish festivals of her childhood. His face had the same wooden features of the paper-maché figures.

"I have decided to tell you what you want to know," he began without preliminary.

Her surprise must have shown on her features. "Why? What caused you to change your mind?"

She thought at first that he might not answer her.

"I have been with Diego Vargas since I was a young man," he explained, "over twenty years."

At the word twenty, she jerked involuntarily, not believing the time element could mean anything, but coincidence.

Nevertheless, hoping for proof of a connection to her lost sister.

"I have a picture," he said apropos of nothing after a long silence. "You look very like her."

Bella trembled and covered her mouth to keep from crying out. She didn't pretend not to understand and was furious about the possibility that a man like Santos had a picture of her beloved sister. Silently she held out her hand, and he reached inside his pocket and placed a snapshot carefully in the center of her palm, closing her fingers over the worn edges.

She peered at the photo, not really able to make out the features. Perhaps it was a picture of Maria. Or it could be her mind playing tricks on her. "How did you get this?" she demanded.

"I will tell you that later," he said, "after our agreement is complete. I can tell you what happened to her. I imagine that information would be very valuable to you."

"I can't bargain with you for personal reasons," she answered even as her fingernails dug into her palms and the beginning of a plan scurried through her mind.

"But you can bargain with me to get *El Jefe.* Consider the information about Maria a bonus. And perhaps you will feel generous enough to give me a bonus in return during your negotiations."

She knew he spoke the truth when he mentioned her sister's name. "You bastard," she whispered as he took the photo from her lifeless fingers.

"Yes," he said, "that is true for my father never married my mother. Think about what I can give you. Not only Diego Vargas but ... He spread his hands in an old-world gesture and smiled with those beautiful white teeth, but the look in his eyes reminded her of a snake ready to strike.

#

"Uncle Santos?" The voice over the cell phone was small, quiet, and sounded very, very young and frightened. He was

232

shocked to hear Cory's voice on his cell number because only Vargas and a few close advisors contacted him by this means. *"Ay, Cory, mi pequena muchacha querida! Cómo está?*

"Okay, I guess." She sniffled. She had been weeping.

"How did you get this number, little one?"

"I have Papa's phone," she whispered. He could imagine the small girl, slender and dark like her mother, hunched over the phone in the dark, fighting back tears she could not quite control.

"Where is your papa?"

"He's sleeping. He snores real loud." She paused and then rushed on in a tumble of words. "Uncle Santos, he's been drinking ... a lot."

"Where is he, Cory?" he repeated.

"He ... he's in my bed," she sobbed, "and I can't go to sleep because he's so loud."

A rage wholly unfamiliar to Santos gripped his body. Rage mixed with a helplessness also alien to his nature. *Pinche cabrón,* he ranted silently as he had many times before about his boss.

But this time, he vowed silently, the pig will be stopped.

Chapter Thirty-four

The second meet with Santos took place in Bella's office the next morning at the courthouse. Saunders had taken temporary command of the sheriff's office since Harris hadn't recovered sufficiently to reassume his duties and. Saunders arranged for extra guards to be assigned at the courthouse entry.

Santos had been patted down and carefully searched for weapons before being admitted past the metal detectors in the foyer to the stairs leading to Bella's office on the second floor. Two armed guards stood at attention outside her office door along with Saunders. His ebony face reflected his disapproval of Santos' presence in his precinct and his bald head gleamed wetly from the overhead lights.

After the formalities, the two attorneys measured one another across the expanse of Bella's desk. Then she retrieved a sheet of paper from a military green file folder on her desk and slid it carefully across the desk. Santos relaxed in the comfortable arm chair, for all the world as if he hadn't a care in the world. He narrowed his eyes and reached for the paper, never looking down, but piercing her with a sharp, cunning appraisal.

"What is this?" he asked.

"The terms of your plea bargain agreement." Bella leaned back in her desk chair, her elbows on the arm rests, her fingertips bouncing slightly against one another. She had taken the death penalty off the table.

Like last night, she was oddly lacking in fear around Santos, even though a general air of malevolence hung around him like a carnivorous bird of prey. She'd recovered from last night's shock and today she felt in control. She recognized the last rolling momentum of the case against Diego Vargas and knew it would lead to a triumphant end.

Santos would not refuse the deal. She didn't know why she was so certain of this. Perhaps it was the pallor that showed beneath his dark skin or the erratic drumming of his huge fingers on the desk that made her sure. Something had tipped the scales in her favor and Santos was ready to cut a deal. He had made the first overture. He had shown her the photo.

When she'd called him this morning, she had detected an unfamiliar air of resignation in his voice.

"ADA Torres." His gravelly, formal voice had wafted over the phone line. *"Verdad.* I had just intended to call you."

"Really?" Bella forced coolness into her voice, desperately wanting to maintain control. "I'm glad to have saved you the trouble, Mr. Santos."

His deep rumble over the phone line sent chills down her spine and reminded her of Rafe's warning that she was dealing with a dangerous animal. To her surprise, considering last night's guarded meeting, Santos had readily acquiesced to joining her here, on her home ground, instead of within his own familiar territory. She wondered briefly what story he'd spun for Diego Vargas, or if he'd kept the clandestine appointment a secret from everyone who knew him.

"He thinks I am conferring with some of our associates," Santos said as if he had read her mind. "Import associates."

She didn't pretend not to understand the tacit admission of drug dealing. Or that he kept secrets from Diego Vargas. "That was judicious of you."

Santos barked out a sound that was a cross between mirth and menace. *"Ay,* I am a wise man."

She nodded and waited for him to pick up the paper lying on the desk in front of him. When he did, he read the document with what seemed deliberate languor.

"And since I am a wise man," he continued, "not given to foolish bargains, tell me, Ms. Torres, why should I consider this offer?" He dropped the paper and waved a negligent hand over it, conveying the paltry insignificance of her carefully- constructed plea bargain agreement.

Bella tightened her lips. "It's a good deal. You should consider it."

Plea bargaining on felony charges was a tricky negotiation at best, much like bartering in an Egyptian bazaar. She made an offer, he countered, and they parried and thrust until they came to mutual agreement.

He surprised her with his next words. "A good deal, but not an excellent one."

She allowed a modicum of impatience to show in her expression. "Mr. Santos, if my office brings charges against you, they will likely be multiple counts of murder, conspiracy, and drug trafficking, not to mention kidnapping and human trafficking."

"Charges you cannot prove," he countered.

"Maybe, maybe not." She waffled the fingers of her right hand in a so-so gesture. "But I think you want something more than exoneration from the charges." She leaned forward across the desk and lowered her voice, navigating solely on instinct. "I think Diego Vargas is out of control and you'd like to rein him back into the parameters of sanity."

"Bueno, for one so young, you are very sure of yourself, but Diego is *El Jefe.* I am merely his lieutenant."

"I doubt you have ever been *merely* anything."

He nodded in acknowledgement of the veiled compliment.

Bella pushed back from the desk and swung her legs around to the side before rising. She turned her back to Santos and gazed out the wide expanse of her office window to the courthouse lawn below. She would not be the first to mention the picture, she vowed ."What would you consider an *excellent* deal?" she asked reflectively.

"Complete immunity," Santos replied without hesitation.

She spun around, ready to register scorn on her face and in her voice and bumped into the wide, iron behemoth of his body where he'd approached her unawares. "You're joking," she said breathily as she retreated a step and crossed her arms in front of her body.

His scarred face remained impassive. "I never jest about money or prison time."

"There's no way I can grant you complete immunity," she protested.

"Naturalmente. But of course you can."

"What are you offering?" But she knew that he was offering something so much more important to her than convicting Vargas. And the thought of it nearly made her weep.

Santos turned silently to glance at Saunders still leaning against the wall, his hand resting on his revolver. He jerked his head toward the deputy, a clear indication that he wouldn't speak further with someone else in the room.

Within seconds of Saunders leaving the office, Bella's desk phone rang. She stared stupidly at it for several moments, hating to break her rhythm by answering it.

Santos nodded toward the jarring sound. "You should answer the telephone, counselor." He rose and patted his jacket pockets. "I will step outside to have a cigarillo and give you privacy."

Bella grabbed the receiver. "No smoking in public buildings," she said automatically to his retreating back.

Santos smiled, his large white teeth flashing in his scarred face. "But of course. I would not want to be charged with such a *significant* misdemeanor." He stepped quietly into the hall and closed the door softly behind him.

"Hello, hello," Rafe's voice sounded faintly over the line before Bella lifted the receiver to her ear.

"Hi," she breathed into the phone, happy to hear his voice, grateful to get a break from the oppressive weight of Santos standing inches within her personal space.

"You sound flustered. Is everything okay?" Rafe asked

"Yeah, well, sort of."

"Is Santos still there?"

"He stepped out for a minute." She hesitated and then plunged on. "He's going to be a hard nut to crack." She hadn't told him about Santos and the photo of Maria and wondered why she'd kept this significant piece of information from him.

"I'll come right over." His voice was decisive and she knew he'd rush right in and fracture the fragile progress she was making with Santos.

"No, no, it'll be fine."

A heavy pause hung weightily, dead space over the line.

Rafe cleared his throat. "Okay, then. Well, I called to let you know I'm going to stay with Max for a while."

"Max Jensen?"

"Yeah, his grandmother's house has been empty for a while. He's staying there."

"Oh." She felt an unexplainable chill. "How convenient."

"Are you sure you're okay?"

"Of course. Look, I've got to finish this meeting, seal the deal."

Bella stared at the phone long moments after she'd hung up. Max Jensen had relatives in the area. A house to stay in. Why did that situation seem strange to her? Why did she suddenly remember the knowing look on his face when she'd encountered him in Rafe's L.A. office waiting room? What had sparked that sense of unease then, so brief she'd nearly forgotten it?

Deputy Saunders escorted Santos into the room, and when the lawyer had sat, the deputy took up watch again, this time outside the door.

Santos and Isabella Torres measured each other across the counselor's desk like two warriors lined up for battle. He could tell by the set of her pretty jaw that she had no intention of letting him win. She believed she had right and the law on her side. Santos had long ago put such foolish ideas aside, but the ADA was young enough to believe in them still. Nevertheless, he regretted being the one to burst the bubble of her idealism.

Her dark eyes serious, her lips lushly red, she very much looked like the woman whose picture he kept in his inside jacket pocket. A new picture today, a more focused image, one that Isabella would have no trouble identifying.

"Tell me about Diego Vargas," she demanded with the fierce aura of an avenging angel about her.

He examined his hands and thought how to measure the impact of his words. "First, let me tell you a story, Isabella."

"Ms. Torres," she corrected him, narrowing her eyes. *Ay,* she would do serious battle with him. But he believed her need for vengeance would win. It was the way of the human condition.

"I'm not interested in fairy tales, Mr. Santos. I deal in the truth, nonfiction if you will. What's the truth about Councilman Vargas?"

"I will give you the complete truth, but only for full immunity."

"You know I can't do that, even for ... "

Santos laughed softly, enjoying the righteous indignation on Isabella's face. She held so much power in those small hands, that slight body. "Ah, but of course you can."

She looked at a spot over his left shoulder, her face smooth and completely devoid of the turmoil that must rage within her. To capture a man such as Diego Vargas was a great professional coup. And a personal victory. But she would not want to let Santos himself go without punishment. To free him would rankle her to no end.

When she remained silent, looking for all the world as if the answer to her dilemma lay on the wall behind him, he decided to make the situation more complex. He reached inside his jacket pocket and pulled out the second photograph, the vivid colors speaking louder than any of his words. Turning it face down on the desk, he pushed it carefully across the smooth wood until it touched her splayed fingers.

He noted the tremor in one hand as she tapped the edge of the picture. She knew. At some primitive level, she understood the significance of the photo. "I've already seen this," she said, easing one corner toward her.

"Not this one. It will change your mind," he said simply, not bothering to keep the sorrow out of his voice. He received no pleasure from telling her about the picture. From showing it to her.

Slowly she turned over the photo, confusion furrowing her brows, a look of puzzlement in her dark eyes. He recognized the exact moment when the truth dawned on her. Her eyes widened in disbelief and then closed in agony. "It's Maria!" Her fingers covered her mouth as if she'd vomit the grief out of her body.

"*Sí,* your sister."

She swiveled around in her chair, presenting her back to him. He barely heard the muffled sounds of her grief. *Ay,* such a strong woman! She had immediately recognized the significance of the bright dress and garish makeup on the face of the young woman in the photo. Santos waited for the emotion to pass, for Isabella to assimilate the agony of seeing the photograph, to ask for the details of her sister's life.

"Is she alive?" The question came from a neutral voice, as though she had cemented her sorrow behind a stone wall.

"Do we have an agreement?" he countered.

"Be specific."

Santos made his voice the roar of Moses coming down from Sinai. "There must be no misunderstanding in this plea bargain. Full immunity for particulars about your sister's death." He knew if she gave her word, she would see that the agreement held. She would not renege on anything, but her pause was longer than he had expected.

240

Did the little lawyer desire his incarceration so badly that she would forego information about her beloved sister? Had he misread her? But finally she nodded, bobbing her head up and down as though she could not stop the action once it was in motion.

"Is she alive?" she repeated, her voice an immeasurable sea of pain.

"No."

He thought he heard a small sigh. "When did she die?"

"Within a year after she disappeared."

Anger whipped her around, and the wet splotches on her face glinted like sun on steel. "She was taken, kidnapped. She did not *disappear.*"

He inclined his head in acknowledgment. *"Sí,* she was kidnapped. *Secuestrado."*

"And you had something to do with it."

"Sí, along with Diego Vargas."

She flinched at the name. "I knew it."

"I can give you specific details," Santos offered, locking eyes with her, "of your sister's last months."

Chapter Thirty-five

Santos waited patiently while Isabella Torres paced the interior of her office, pausing occasionally to stare at him as if the sun rose or set tomorrow based on her imminent decision. After several long minutes, he repeated his offer. "I can tell you every single detail – name, places, dates – but I do not think you will wish to know them all."

Indeed Santos wished *he* did not know about the last years of the girl's life, the final moments of her agony.

He'd come upon Maria several months after she'd been delivered to La Casa de Mujeras. Sheer accident caused him to be in the hall at that moment on that particular night. She still had some fight remaining in her then, a defiance and will not yet broken that he admired.

Ay, she was so very beautiful and as a young man he was half in love with her at the moment he first looked at her. When she saw him, she recognized him and threw her slender body into his arms, clutched his waist, and begged him to return her to her home.

But Santos knew there was no going back for the lovely Latina. She could not return from the difficult road she had walked. He wanted to explain this to her, but at that moment, Diego stepped from the room he usually occupied when he stayed at the whore house. Without a word, he jerked the girl from Santos' arms and cuffed her with the back of his hand. When she landed on the carpeted hall, he kicked her with the toe of his boot, but not too hard because damaged merchandise was not valuable.

Isabella Torres turned toward the window, wrapping her arms around her waist as if to keep the core of herself – heart, lungs – from spilling out.

While he waited for the attorney to make her decision, Santos remembered the night Maria had died, five years after she'd been among the very first vanload of girls that came over the border from Mexico.

Diego was in a foul mood that matched the nasty fog that settled in over Modesto, California, during the winter. As his driver, Santos kept one eye on the dangerous, fog-slicked road and one on the rearview mirror where Diego sat with the dull-eyed and lackluster girl. She had aged ten years since Santos had last seen her, track marks on her arms indicated the drugs used to subdue her, and she no longer spoke to anyone, let alone appealed to the boss's body guard.

When Diego began to paw at the girl's clothing, she simply lay back on the leather upholstery and spread her legs. Santos knew she would not last long. Already she was past the age of girls that held Diego's interest. In truth, Santos did not know why the boss had kept her so long. If she did not die of a drug overdose, she would surely perish at the hands of Vargas' insatiable violence.

When Isabella turned back to him, Santos saw the steel in her jaw and the determination in her eyes. "Yes, I want the details," she said. "I want to know every single moment of her life after she was taken from us."

"Pero, por supuesto. But, of course. Ask the questions and I will answer."

"Did she suffer?"

Santos shrugged. "How does one measure the suffering of another person?"

"Don't play games with me," she snapped. "You are getting – what did you call it? – an *excellent* deal." She sat down, leaned forward across the desk, her hands bracing her tight body. "Did. She. Suffer?"

"Solamente un poco. Only a little. She was not passed from man to man as the other girls were, but stayed with one protector the entire time." A lie, but perhaps a small consolation, although, in truth, Santos did not know why he bothered with it.

"Vargas?"

"Sí."

"You expect me to believe a man like Vargas treated her well?" Her face had lost all color, but her voice dripped with scorn.

"Believe what you wish, but Diego Vargas was a younger man then and he seemed fond of her in his own way. Perhaps his later ... proclivities were not fully developed."

She nodded slowly. He realized with surprise that she believed him and took some comfort in the false knowledge.

"How did she die?"

Santos had driven the girl and Vargas to a very upscale motel. The fog was a deadly blanket that made further driving northeast to Sacramento impossible. He booked two adjoining rooms, one for himself and one for the girl and his boss. Why Diego had taken the girl with him on this particular trip Santos did not know at the time, but later the truth of his boss's actions became clear. He had another, younger girl waiting for him in Nevada.

"She perished in a car accident. She and Diego were going from Los Angeles to Sacramento by automobile. Passing through Modesto, we hit a severe fog bank. That is when the accident occurred." So easy to sequester a lie within the truth, he thought.

"You were driving?"

"Sí. The car rolled and Diego and I were trapped in the vehicle, but she was thrown from it."

The noises had come through the thin walls separating the two motel rooms several hours after Santos had fallen asleep. The sounds woke him up and he lay in the darkened room, listening for signs that he was needed. Another loud thump.

He knocked on the adjoining door. "El Jefe, is everything all right?"

No sound, but the dull thud of pounding and then Diego's heavy breathing, a guttural nastiness that Santos knew well.

"Diego, qué usted?"

"Nada!" the man growled through the door while the steady, sick thumping of flesh on flesh continued.

Santos shouldered the door open and took in the scene at a glance.

"Did she die quickly?" Isabella asked.

"Yes. Instantly. She did not suffer. I tried to perform emergency medical aid at the scene." He spread his hands in a sign of futility. "But she was dead before the ambulance arrived. Very quickly."

Great glimmering tears pooled in Isabella's dark eyes, but she did not allow them to fall.

"Diego Vargas is a man with many faults, many sins," he reassured her, "but Maria's death is not one of them. He treated her with care. He may have been a bit in love with her." Santos looked at the unlit tip of his cigarillo and realized he was not speaking of *El Jefe* but himself.

The room had been a bloody mess, and the girl ceased to breathe long after Diego continued to pummel her broken body with his fists and feet. Santos had no time to administer futile first aid. He checked the pulse at her neck and closed the once-luminous eyes.

"Get this fucking piece of shit out of here," Santos roared, sweat dripping down his face onto his already fat body, his cock still hard and jutting from the thrill of beating the girl to death. Santos did not try to revive her, and he was a long time cleaning up the mess.

"Is there evidence that I can use to tie her death to Diego Vargas?"

Santos shook his head, sadness and relief warring within him. "The evidence disappeared long ago."

"Then I will hang him with what you tell me."

"Verdad."

Three hours later, he had given the assistant district attorney all that she needed, and she had agreed to grant him full immunity in exchange for his testimony against Diego Vargas in a court of law.

245

"I'll need to run this by the district attorney," she said, weary lines etched around her mouth and between her eyes. "But I don't anticipate any objections."

In fact, Santos knew that Charles Barrington would be delighted that the ADA had resolved the case without further media criticism. And he would likely garner the credit for himself instead of giving the credit to her.

"You can sign your official statement after it's processed," she said. "If Vargas finds out that you've informed on him, you won't survive long enough for the trial."

Santos thought Isabella would not mind his death so much as losing him as a witness. He smiled and stretched his hand across the desk. Surprisingly, she extended hers and his large bear's paw engulfed her small hand like the mating of a giant and a dwarf. But her grip was firm and when she squeezed his hand, he knew that she was a survivor.

He was glad that he had not told her the truth about her sister.

Ay, ella era un ángel que se vengaba. The little lawyer was an avenging angel.

As soon as Santos left, Bella contacted Rafe on his cell phone. "It's done."

"Great. He gave you everything?"

"Yes."

"Names, dates, places?"

"All of it."

"That's great. Son of a bitch. How did you manage that?"

"I'll tell you later." She paused, the stress of the last few days rushing in like a storm to rip the strength out of her. "Can I see you?" she whispered. "I need to be with you."

She hated that her voice sounded small and pleading, but she didn't want to return to her small, empty house. She didn't want to images of Maria death to choke her mind like a poisonous vine. She wanted someone to help her forget.

"Of course, sure. Why don't you come here, the grandmother's house? Relax a little. You've had a hard time."

246

She agreed although she didn't really want to spend time around his friend Max Jensen. She wanted to cuddle, pour her heart out, cry for her lost sister, say her last goodbye. Rafe gave her directions before he hung up. Maybe later they'd go back to her house. He could read the transcripted interview of the information Santos had given her. This was Rafe's case, too, and he should be in on the close of it. He wouldn't be happy about Santos getting off scot-free, but in the end he'd understand that the plea bargaining was all part of the prosecution chain. Vargas was the big fish.

Before going to South Highland Heights, Bella stopped by the hospital to look in on Slater. It was early enough that no visitors had arrived yet, and she was happy to get him alone. After catching him up on the Vargas case, she waited for his comment, sure he'd be furious that she'd cut such a deal with a man like Santos, but he remained silent. "Are you going to say anything," she finally asked.

"You did what you had to do, Bella. No shame in that." Slater looked much better today and she now suspected his stay in the hospital would be shorter than she'd expected.

"You know how I hate these plea bargains."

Slater knew only the bare bones of her sister's disappearance. She didn't want to tell him about the new photo and the story Santos had spun about her sister. She wanted to believe the tale of a car accident taking her sister's life. It was so much cleaner than the nightmares she'd had since she was old enough to know what stealing a teenaged girl meant. She kept telling herself that Santos would have no reason to lie to her. He'd gain nothing from that.

"Just be careful, Bella. Sometimes these things have a way of blowing up in your face."

She looked at him sharply. "Do you think someone will get to Santos before he can testify?"

Slater shrugged and swiped his big hand over his scruffy beard. "Who knows? There's gotta be another leak besides Manuel Ruiz."

"No one knows about the plea bargain but you, me, Santos, and Rafe. Even Saunders doesn't know what went on inside my office," she argued.

"What about the meet last night? Did you have backup?"

"Just a deputy and one of Rafe's agents and they both were cleared.

"Anyone else?"

"No, no one ... but ... " Her mind went to the phone calls she'd made to Rafe and the company he kept when he answered them. Her mind flipped to Max Jensen. Had Max known about the meet last night? Had he overheard details about the plea bargaining?

"What, Bella?" Slater looked alarmed and the last thing she needed was him getting his blood pressure up when he was still recovering."

"Nothing, nothing at all. Rafe's checked everyone out, so it's fine." She arranged the covers around him and plumped his pillows. "You take care of yourself, okay?"

He grabbed her hand and pressed it against his chest. "Keep Rafe close to you," he warned. "He'll protect you."

"How do you know?" she laughed, kissing his cheek.

"Because I can see it in his eyes."

"What do you see?"

"He's half in love with you, Bella. He'll keep you safe."

She smiled, but wondered if it were true because she certainly thought she might be half in love with Rafe.

Chapter Thirty-six

Less than an hour later, Bella pulled into the circular, gravel driveway in front of the house where Rafe had given her directions. The house was in a marginal neighborhood in South Highland Heights. Row upon row of cookie cutter houses that were new forty or fifty years ago lined streets with grass growing between the cracks in the sidewalk and broken out street lights. Apparently idle teenagers hung around in front of run-down houses with unkempt lawns.

The house to which Rafe had directed her – 1300 Morene Way – was a little less dilapidated than the others. A white house with green trim, it sat further back from the street and boasted a large oak tree in the scanty lawn of the front yard.

Bella rang the doorbell, but not hearing a corresponding sound, rapped sharply on the door. Rafe answered, looking casual in jeans, a black tee shirt and sandals. He held a large spatula and wore a draped cloth around his waist.

"Barbecue," he said, kissing her quickly on the cheek. "Are you hungry?"

She still wore the black suit and sheer white blouse she'd put on for the Santos interview and looked down self-consciously.

"Never mind that," Rafe said, gesturing through the living area toward a patio door that looked out on a small, neglected back yard.

Max Jensen was setting out a platter of produce alongside several bottles of condiments on a high, but narrow, serving table. He waved through the glass door.

Bella looked around the living area which opened up onto a small kitchen to the right where one lonely bar stool was pushed up against the bar counter. The living room itself held only a small television teetering on a wooden box by a fireplace and a single recliner. A folding tray held several pieces of mail, an empty beer, and a magazine.

She ducked her head back into the foyer which opened up to another nearly empty room on the left. Not only did the house have a general air of deterioration, but it was practically devoid of furnishings. How odd. "Where is all the furniture?".

Rafe shrugged as Max made his way into the kitchen.

"The burgers are ready to flip, buddy," he said to Rafe. Bella felt Max's light blue eyes sweep from her head to her feet. "Hi, Bella. It's good to see you again."

She nodded, feeling awkward and uncomfortable. Something didn't sit right with her about Max and the house, but she put on a bright smile and tried to shake off the uneasy feeling. After all, she barely knew the man and he'd been a friend of Max for a long time.

"My grandmother just got out of the hospital and went into long-term care at a nursing home in Sacramento," Max explained. "My uncle Brian is kind of a lazy dude, hasn't gotten around to getting the house ready to sell." He took a deep pull on his beer. "He's sold most of the furniture, but actually, this works out well for me."

"I'm glad you have a place to stay," Bella murmured politely.

"Yeah, well, staying with my wife in L.A. wasn't an option." He grimaced. "And I thought I could keep busy doing repairs around here while I get my head straight."

Bella heard the bitterness in his voice and mentally chastised her silent criticism of him. After all, the man's wife was leaving him. She flashed a sympathetic look towards Rafe.

"You'll work it out," Rafe said, clamping his hand on his friend's shoulder. "Just give Shirley time."

Dinner passed quickly and Bella enjoyed the time spent more than she'd thought. Max had an easy, affable nature.

For dessert he cut up slices of fresh fruit which they all ate on the back patio.

"So, how's the case going?" Max asked Bella, juice dripping down his chin.

"Good." She wasn't going to elaborate about the deal she'd made with Santos. Not around a man she hardly knew.

"Max was helping me down in L.A. Knows all about Vargas and Santos," Rafe said.

Bella remained silent, sending a warning message with her eyes. It wasn't so much that she didn't trust the police officer. She'd just learned her lessons well from Slater. Play your cards very close to your chest and only reveal what you absolutely had to, especially to someone who was an unknown factor.

"Isabella's got someone to turn on Vargas," Rafe said casually.

Why was he ignoring her subtle message, Bella wondered, wanting to kick him under the table.

"Really? That's great. Who?" Max stared directly at Bella.

Amazed at the man's audacity, she mumbled, "Still too early in the deal. I'd rather not say." She smiled to soften the rejection. "Don't want to jinx anything." She caught Rafe's sharp look out of the corner of her eye.

Apparently Max let it go because he changed the subject. "Did Rafe tell you how me and him came to know each other?"

"College, wasn't it?" Bella answered, wondering where he was headed.

"Max and I were college roommates, freshman year," Rafe explained, a puzzled look on his face as if he were trying to figure the answer to a math problem.

"But we'd known each other since fifth grade," Max corrected, "when you were a skinny little dude that all the kids razzed because of your dark skin and tight hair."

Rafe looked thoughtfully across the rim of his beer bottle as if analyzing the years that lay between then and now. "I

251

was ten years old, my mom had just dragged me from the oppressive heat of the Middle East, and my language still had the stiltedness of my Arabic."

The Middle East? Rafe had never told her anything about his ethnicity, his family, or his homeland. A shock of alarm trailed down her back. How could she know this man so intimately and yet not learn anything concrete about him? She felt her face flush as Rafe examined her, reading the subtleties there.

"Yeah, dude, you got your ass kicked nearly every day on the playground."

"Until you starting standing up for me." Rafe swung his eyes from Bella to Max and their strange green color sparkled against his dark skin.

"I can't even count the number of times I rescued you," Max chortled.

"Until I shot up like a giant during seventh grade."

"There was that."

"And then I didn't need you to save me."

Bella swiveled her head from one to the other of the two men. A volume of history lay between them, but she couldn't decipher the subtext of their words. Something was off between them, but what?

Rafe rose with a groan and took his plate inside to the kitchen, Max and Bella following close behind. "I'm going to take Isabella home now," he said to Max. "I'll come back tomorrow night. You can drive my car to the precinct tomorrow."

Max looked nonplussed for a moment, but quickly recovered. "Sure. Thanks for the loan of the car."

Rafe tossed the rental car keys and Max caught them left-handed. "Maybe you two will let me sit in on the plea bargain interview." As Bella and Rafe exchanged a quick look, he added, "Help take my mind off the wife."

When Bella hesitated further, he said, "Or not. Whatever." He flashed an easy grin.

They hardly spoke on the drive back to Isabella's house, but when they pulled into the driveway, Rafe turned to her and put a hand on her shoulder. "What's up with you and Max?"

"Why?"

"You acted like he'd taken your toys away." He laughed, fingering the soft curls at her nape.

"Why is he helping you on the Vargas case," she countered

He shrugged a little too casually. "Max is an old friend."

"Have you told him about Santos?"

"He knows there's a leak, knows you have someone who's going to testify against Vargas."

"But he doesn't have a name."

"No," he said shortly, angry with himself more than Isabella because he knew better than anyone that in the vault meant in – the – vault. No one got to know anything. He stepped out of the car and followed her through the garage and laundry room into the kitchen. "Look, Max ... I've known him since fifth grade, like he said. He's not the leak."

Her eyes looked sad as if she pitied him. "Are you sure?"

"Hell, yes!" He raked his fingers through his hair. "Maybe." He thought of the discrepancies over the last few years, of how Max had been privy to everything – Lupe's identity, the deliveries and pickups of the drugs – God dammit, everything! "Ah, Jesus Christ!"

Instead of berating him as he deserved, she wrapped her arms around him and pressed her body into his. "We don't know what's true yet."

"Shit, Bella, it's my business to know!" He hugged her tightly. "But Max ... God, he'd have to be in some kind of deep shit."

"We can't do anything about it tonight," she whispered in his ear, teasing his lobes. "Santos knows how to take care of himself. And tomorrow I'll get him in protective custody."

He looked askance at her. "You think he'll go?"

"Not gently," she laughed, "but he'll go. He wants Vargas as much as I do."

"Really? Why?"

She shrugged and shook her head. "Don't know. Don't care," she spoke into his mouth, "but after Santos is secured, you can approach Max, discover the truth." She blew into his ear. "Right now I just want to put the whole Vargas case behind us. Just for tonight." She deepened the kiss and he let himself sink into the soft warmth of her face, her body and returned the kiss until she was breathless.

They'd shed their clothes by the time they reached the bedroom. As she leaned backwards onto the bed, he pulled her upright. "No, I just want to look at you a minute."

He ran his hands over her breasts, reveling in the soft peaks that hardened a moment later beneath his thumbs. His hands traced the length of her waist and hips and traveled down her thighs nudging them apart with his hands. He knelt in front of her and traced his tongue around her navel and dipped lower to the edge of her pubis. "God, you are so beautiful."

"Wait," she said. "I'm so grubby. Let's shower first."

"I like that idea."

He stepped into the shower and adjusted the temperature and spray, then pulled her in after him. He took the brunt of the pulsating water so her hair wouldn't get wet.

She wrapped her legs around his hips and leaned her back against the shower wall. "I can't wait," she breathed. "I want you. Now!"

"Huh uh," he panted, "I want to go down on you. God, I want to bury my face between your legs and suck you until you scream and come in my mouth."

"Oh, God, don't talk like that. I'll explode."

"Then we won't wait." He thrust hard into her and felt her core already tightening and pulsing around him, and a few moments later he climaxed hard into her wet, slick body. The throbbing seemed endless and he felt the resounding clutching of her inner muscles around him for a long time.

Afterward they washed each other slowly and languidly and by the time they'd dried off, he was ready for her again. She turned the overhead fan on to cool their still-hot bodies and they tumbled naked on the bed. He slid down her body and lifted her knees around his shoulders, sank his mouth into her sweet, hot center and kissed and teased until she cried out in pleasure-pain. "God, Rafe!"

He rode her climax with his mouth and his tongue as she gripped his hair and lifted her hips toward his face for greater access. She came for a long time and he felt a possessive pride in giving her such pleasure. He slid back up her body, turned her hips to his quickly hardening cock and sank his face into her neck. Her hair formed a dark curtain around him as he breathed in the scent of her soap and shampoo and sex.

One hand teased the now-sensitive nub of her clitoris and the other played with her nipples. The hard, hot length of his cock pushed hard against her soft hips, a fierce warrior demanding access to the castle. Jesus, he wanted to mount her again like a stud horse after the filly in heat.

"Are you a filly?" he whispered, nuzzling her neck.

"What?" Her voice was heavy with the drowsiness of a body sated with sex.

"Are you up for another one?"

She must have felt the hard length of him against her ass – how could she miss it? She giggled and turned around, draping one leg over him and finally straddling his body. His cock lay pointing straight up for all the world like a dangerous weapon.

"Shall I disarm your weapon?" she teased, grabbing him with her small hand and beginning a rhythm before bending over to wrap her mouth around the tip of him.

He groaned and gave himself over to her ministrations, which banished every thought of Max Jensen's possible treachery from his mind.

Chapter Thirty-seven

The two men were shouting at each other, their voices loud and vicious, certain to wake up Corazon who was asleep in the other room. Santos clenched his jaw and tightened his fists until they became great sides of ham, weapons to kill with a single blow.

When he stepped into Vargas' office, the noises ceased abruptly. Diego planted his feet on the rug in front of his desk, his florid face even ruddier than usual, a white dress shirt pulled tight across his gut, and a patterned blue tie choking him off at the neck.

In front of him stood Max Jensen.

"All I'm sayin' is you've got a traitor in your organization." He punched his bony forefinger into Diego's chest. "And I'm not fuckin' going down because you can't control your cartel."

Santos stepped between the two men and nudged the policeman aside. He took Vargas by the arm and led him to his great leather swivel chair, then brought him a glass of water. "What's wrong," he asked, turning back to Jensen.

"Someone's going to name names," he grumbled. "Dates, times, places – Christ, God! – everything!"

Santos knew the little ADA would not have released his name to anyone she was not positive she could trust. Who then? "How do you know this?"

"Never mind how I fucking know! Vargas' whole operation is crumbling around him, and I'm not gonna be destroyed in the process!"

Santos took one step forward and not-so-gently shoved the man into an armchair. He loomed over him, planting both arms on either side of the chair. "How?" he asked again without raising his voice.

Jensen licked his lips as if he were thirsty. Santos knew he was buying time and did not want to give his source. He sighed heavily "What does it matter now?" He struggled to rise, but Santos' arms kept him bound to the chair as if they were steel ropes. /

"Cómo?" Santos' voice was a deadly whisper.

"Hashemi, the agent, told me. Rafe Hashemi."

"Ah!"

Jensen peered around Santos' arm to catch Diego's eye. "We've been friends since we were kids."

Santos took a calculated risk. "So tell us, Detective Jensen, who is this great traitor who has infiltrated *El Jefe's* organization? Who is the man with the *cojones* to attack a man like the councilman?"

"I – I don't know," Max muttered.

Santos turned back to Vargas, spread his hands, and shrugged elaborately. *"No puedo luchar al enemigo que no conozco."*

Vargas' small pig eyes, flat and emotionless, stared back at him for several moments. Then he swung them back to Jensen.

"What'd he say?" Jensen demanded.

"'He cannot fight an enemy he doesn't know,'" Vargas answered, bouncing his eyes back and forth between the two men as if he could not determine who to trust. *"Verdad,* it is true. When you hand me an enemy I can see, touch, whose blood I can taste ... " The words spewed like venom from his mouth. "Then come back to me."

"I'm telling you – "

"Get out!" Vargas roared.

Santos followed the detective out through the gates to the rental car parked just inside the drive. "When you discover who this ... traitor is, see me personally." He flashed a warning smile. "Do not disturb *El Vaquero's* peace of mind needlessly again."

He thought the detective would protest. Indeed, his fists clenched and his eyes narrowed. "You tell Vargas to be careful," he warned. "Some big shit's gonna hit the fan. I'm not going to get put in a position where the turds land on me." Without another word, he stepped into the car and drove off.

Max Jensen was now a huge problem, Santos thought. One they would have to soon deal with.

When he returned to Diego's library, the man was pouring a large glass of brandy. He devoured the drink in one gulf, swiped at his thick lips with the back of his hand, and threw himself heavily into his chair. "Get rid of that detective. He is more trouble than he's worth and I do not want anyone to trace him back to me."

Santos stared down at Diego from his position by the bar. "Are you certain? He has provided us with excellent information over the years."

"Fuck, yes! And make it so the body is never discovered."

#

Bella ran a finger down Rafe's bare chest, distracting him from unpleasant suspicions. "Do you want to talk?

"About what?"

She lifted one slender shoulder, her face quiet and sympathetic. "Max."

He shook his head.

"Tell me a little about him," she urged.

"Max? God, just like he said. I was a skinny dark-skinned kid whose mother was some kind of hippie reporter in the Middle East." He looked down at her and ran his hands over her back. "My father was a soldier in the Jordanian army. They met, fell in love, made me in a single night of passion, and then he died in the Six Day War."

"With Israel?"

"Yeah."

"Oh, Rafe. I'm so sorry."

"Mom stayed ten years over there. She wanted me to learn the culture of my father, but finally she realized that part of that culture was indoctrinating males in their supreme role as patriarchs over their women and children." He laughed. "She was too much of a feminist to allow that, so she came back to the states."

"And you were a strange fish out of water."

"I was. Could hardly speak English, couldn't adjust to the sea of white faces around me."

"But you inherited your mother's green eyes," she guessed, kissing him at the corner of each one. "Those beautiful, green eyes."

"Freakish." He smiled. "Max was the only person who accepted me back then. After Nine Eleven, even though I was an agent by then, the shit hit the fan on anyone of Arabic descent. Max stuck by me through all of it."

And that was the trouble, he thought, as he fell asleep. The only way to catch Max, if he was dirty, was to lay a trap.

The next morning Rafe realized he'd never asked Isabella about the deal she made with Santos.

"What was the bonus he gave you?" he asked, sitting at the small kitchen table, sipping his coffee.

She'd told him that Santos had given her everything she wanted and added a bonus.

"My sister," she said simply.

"Maria?"

"Yes. Vargas is the one who took her. Santos has known all this time. He had a picture of her."

"Jesus Christ! Are you sure it's her?"

"Yes, I'm positive."

Rafe stood and wrapped his arms around her, tucking her head close to his chest. "Babe, I'm so sorry."

"I'm glad he told me."

"You had to know."

"Santos said she didn't suffer much, that she stayed with Vargas about a year and died in a car accident."

Rafe frowned over the top of her head. A year? Car accident? That didn't sound like the Diego Vargas he'd been hunting these last three years. But why would Santos lie to Isabella? What could he hope to gain? "That's good. It's good she didn't suffer."

"And it's good that we know what happened to her. Now our family can really bury her."

#

Max Jensen appeared to be keeping Rafe under close wraps. He'd hovered around the Placer Hills Courthouse all morning and finally ended up with Bella and Rafe in her office. She'd hoped to talk to Rafe about the details of Santos' official statement, but with Max tagging along, she could hardly discuss something so confidential. So far, Max didn't know the name of their informant. If the detective really was dirty, she didn't want to provide the key information.

Max stood casually by the window behind the desk where Bella swiveled gently back and forth in her chair. Rafe sprawled in her guest chair on the opposite side of her desk. She flashed him a meaningful look which he appeared to understand.

"Uh, Max, buddy, we've got the ... uh, informant coming in so the D.A.'s office can take his official statement."

Max turned around from gazing out the window. "What? Oh, yeah, sure, you want me to skedaddle?"

"Well," Bella began.

"We're not sure if he'll give the statement in the presence of a third party, so to speak," Rafe interrupted.

"Oh, then I'll just shove off." Max headed toward the open office door and turned back around at the door frame, a grin on his face. "Hey, you're not going to tell me who he is, are you?"

Bella smiled, trying to assume a teasing look. "Oh, I don't know, Max. I'm an officer of the court. How can I breach a confidence?"

"Yeah, buddy, Isabella takes her job very seriously," Rafe added.

"Bite me." Max laughed. "I'm too damn curious for my own good."

"Killed the cat, they say," Rafe responded.

"Tell you what. I'll just toss out names and when I land on the right one, you blink twice."

Rafe chuckled, the sound hollow in his own ears. "Get out of here, dude."

Minutes later Max walked out of Bella's office, reached his car in the courthouse parking lot, and waited, a grim smile on his lips and a flush to his cheeks. He'd get the name of the traitor inside Vargas' organization himself.

#

Everything was signed, sealed and delivered, Bella thought with satisfaction as she pulled her car out of the parking lot and headed south on I-80. Rafe had left several hours earlier a few moments after Santos had signed the agreement. Of course, Diego Vargas' bodyguard-lawyer had refused any kind of protective custody with a sly smile that spoke volumes of his own ruthlessness in saving his own neck.

After finishing up the paperwork, Bella waited to hear from Rafe. She believed he intended to confront Max Jensen directly even though he had no proof of the man's duplicity, and his name was not among those Santos had revealed in his recorded statement. Maybe her instincts were wrong. Maybe Max was just what he appeared to be – a good detective and a good friend to Rafe.

She drummed her fingernails on the desk top, trying to form a plan. What trap could they lay to be certain? She jumped up and reached for her jacket. Dammit, if Rafe was going to confront Max, she was going to be there, too.

#

Santos drove away from the courthouse after giving his official statement to Isabella Torres, along with the DEA Agent Hashemi and the incompetent district attorney,

Charles Barrington. Unfinished business loomed ahead of him, business he could no longer put off.

Taking out a police detective was a serious matter, but in this thing, Vargas was correct, if not for the right reasons. Jensen presented a dangerous threat to Santos, who had hoped the detective could remain as his informant long after Vargas was sitting in a federal penitentiary or state prison. Now he realized the timing of the matter was all wrong. Santos would have to create his own network of informants after Vargas was gone, and after all, that was probably the wise thing to do.

The drive to the house where Max Jensen was staying was quicker than he'd thought, but when he arrived at the ramshackle place, he froze at the sight of the automobile parked in front. *Madre del Dios!* He recognized the car as belonging to Isabella Torres.

He drove slowly by the house for a cursory look and then parked some distance away. He walked casually down the street. No children played on the streets. No teenagers loitered on doorsteps. No housewives gardened nor old men walked their dogs. The neighborhood bore the stamp of careless neglect, a community running steadily downhill from middle class to low income.

When he approached the house, he walked stealthily around the side yard, through the unlocked gate, and paused at the corner of the back patio. The door was open and through the screen he could hear voices.

"Why did you fucking lie to me?" Jensen's voice resonated loud and angry, but held an undercurrent of fear.

"I didn't lie to you," Isabella Torres answered. "Where's Rafe?"

"Fuck Rafe!"

"I'm leaving." The sound of scuffling and the crash of something being overturned.

Santos pulled his weapon and edged closer to the screen covering the sliding glass door of the patio.

"Stop it! Let me go!" Isabella shouted, anger tinged with fear in her voice.

A loud smack and a harsh gasp.

Santos was an expert marksman. He had no doubt of his prowess in that area, but when he peered through the open door, he saw Jensen holding Isabella in a death grip, his arms wrapped around her waist and chest from behind, a knife glinting at her throat. Her cheek bore a large red mark where Jensen had slapped her and her blouse was torn. One shoe lay across the room, the heel broken.

"You bitch!" Even as Jensen snarled the words, Santos could hear the slurring that indicated he was under the influence of drugs. His eyes were wildly dilated and his face flushed.

Santos stepped into the room, holding his weapon leisurely at his side. "Detective Jensen," he spoke, his voice a calm contrast to the chaos in the room.

"Santos!" Jensen's eyes bulged out of their sockets and he shook his head as if to clear his vision. "What the fuck are you doing here?"

"You and I – we have unfinished business."

"You ... you, God, you screwed me over, you son-of-a-bitch!"

"Easy, Detective Jensen." Santos turned to Isabella. "Are you all right, Miss Torres?"

She nodded without speaking, but Jensen did not loosen his grip on her.

"Let Miss Torres go, *por favor.*"

"Fuck no!" Jensen screamed.

"I do not like to make requests more than once, but for you I will. Let the assistant district attorney go." Santos heard his own voice, calm and deadly, a sign to those who knew him that his anger was barely controlled, "and I will not cut out your tongue."

What happened next occurred within seconds, but to Bella they seemed unbearably long. She saw Santos raise the gun

263

he'd dangled so carelessly from his fingers at the same moment she felt the sharp prick of the knife at her neck and smelled the coppery odor of her blood trickling from the wound.

Instinctively she collapsed her legs beneath her, shifting her weight so that Max's body was exposed. She heard the loud report of the weapon in the small room and smelled the acrid odor of the gunshot residue. Max toppled to the floor as a red flower blossomed on his chest and the knife clattered from his hands.

Santos stepped forward, kicked the knife away and checked Max's pulse, but Bella knew by the vacant look of his eyes, that he was already dead.

"Are you all right?" Santos asked, helping her to her feet.

As the shock of the near fatality reached her brain, Bella began trembling, her teeth chattering and her knees weak. Santos led her to the single chair and pushed her head between her legs.

"Breathe slowly and deeply," he advised. "In and out. Slow. *Muy bueno.*" His voice was a deep rumble that was oddly comforting.

A moment later she looked up to see him handing her a glass of water. "Thank you," she whispered, wondering at the oddity of the situation. Of Santos being her rescuer. She looked up at him through her lashes. "Max Jensen was the one name you didn't give me," she reprimanded, hearing the petulance in her voice. "You held out on me."

Santos laughed. "I see you are recovered, *poco combatiente,* and ready to do battle with me." His white teeth gleamed in his burnished face.

As she handed back the glass to him, for the first time she noticed his hands. They were lined with white scars slashing through the dark skin, but they were slender, the fingers long and beautiful like an artist's. Suddenly she remembered his first name, which she'd remained ignorant of all the months she'd been working on the Vargas case until she took his statement this morning.

Gabriel. She stared at his hands and imagined the fingers gently tapping out the sweet, haunting notes of a trumpet.

Chapter Thirty-eight

Six Weeks Later

They'd discussed the ramifications, the in's and out's of the case until they were both sick of it, Rafe imagined. Disgusted by the wide ring of human trafficking, the sordid circle of drugs and dealers, the abuse of Magdalena Vargas and her daughter Corazon..

"How long did you suspect Max was the leak?" Isabella asked. She lay on the couch with her feet stretched across Rafe's lap, her pretty toes painted a rich crimson which he found wantonly attractive.

"Since Lupe's death, but I didn't want to face it ... Jesus, he'd been my best friend since ... forever." He closed his eyes against the pain of admitting Max's betrayal.

"I'm sorry."

"Yeah, well, shit happens. I'd been watching him closely since Lupe died, but I didn't have concrete evidence. Just circumstantial stuff, ideas I'd put together here and there. I was checking with a reliable source when you went to find me at the grandmother's house. Fuck, I hated that he was the one, hated arresting him, turning him in."

He leaned over and kissed her knees. "God, when I heard the call come over the police band – "

"I'm okay now."

"Yeah."

He pressed his thumbs into the arch of one foot and listened to her moan softly. The sound conjured up erotic images of other groans and the tiny breathless sounds she made when he was deep inside her, pounding into her willing body. Suddenly the urge for a repeat performance caused a tightening in his groin.

"Why do you think he did it?" Isabella asked. "I mean, why would he care? Why didn't he just walk away?"

Rafe tried to push back his body's response and concentrate on what she was saying. He knew she wasn't speaking of Diego Vargas or Max Jensen. "I think Santos has a kind of thing for you."

She wrinkled her brown in that funny way she had that he found adorable. "You mean you think he *likes* me?"

Rafe shrugged and moved his hands farther up her leg, dipped under the hem of her skirt, and caressed the soft flesh of her inner thigh. "Maybe more than 'like.'"

"He's a cold-blooded killer, a man absolutely without principles or moral parameters."

He enjoyed watching her go into her warrior stance like a female ninja.

"Don't smile like that," she warned. "You know that Santos is going to take over the organization, build it back up again."

Rafe nodded. "But it'll take him years to do that, and when he does, I'll be right on his ass."

"Yeah, but he'll be tougher to catch than Vargas. It's strange but he has some kind of off-kilter internal guide. He'll kill at the drop of a hat, but he wouldn't let Vargas abuse his own daughter."

"He's a practical man and a survivor." Rafe slipped his fingers beneath the lacy edge of her panties. "Like you."

Isabella – Rafe could never think of her as Bella and even in his thoughts he used the name that conjured up the Isabella of the night they'd met in the bar – pushed him aside and leapt off the couch.

Confused, he stared at her. "Isabella, there's nothing wrong with being a survivor."

"I'm not like Santos," she insisted.

"Of course not." He reached for her again. "Look, Santos gave you the information about Maria for no practical reason. You'd have given him full immunity regardless of getting the true story about your sister."

"That's true." She sank back onto the sofa and let him wrap his arms around her. "Learning about Maria was ... a bonus."

"The important thing is that Vargas is locked up, he's not getting out of prison until he's a very old man, if even then, and you have some peace of mind about your sister."

Her face softened as she reached for his, holding it between her two small hands. "And I have you." She smiled and brushed her lips against his.

He laughed as he dipped his mouth to hers. "What more could you ask for?"

"Uh, why don't you show me?" she whispered in his ear, darting her tongue out to tickle and tantalize his lobe. "I might get out of practice."

"No chance of that," he answered, toppling her back onto the sofa and hiking her skirt up to her waist. "I intend to allow you plenty of time to ... refine your skills."

I love hearing from my readers. After all, you're the folks I write for!

If you enjoy "The Traitor," I'd love you to leave a review at http://www.amazon.com. To express my appreciation for your support, I'd enjoy sending you a free download of any one of my other books.

You can contact me at jorobertson44@yahoo.com.

Life-time readers, life-time learners!

Other Books by Jo Robertson

The Watcher
a romantic thriller

The Avenger
a romantic thriller

Frail Blood
an historical thriller

Made in the USA
San Bernardino, CA
25 March 2017